ROYALLY ENTANGLED

HER ROYAL HAREM, BOOK ONE

CATHERINE BANKS

TURBO KITTEN

Turbo Kitten Industries™

P.O. Box 5012

Galt, CA 95632

www.turbokitten.us

Catherine Banks

www.catherinebanks.com

www.turbokitten.us/catherine-banks

CATHERINE BANKS
FANTASTICAL SERIES & OTHER ADVENTURES

CHAPTER 1

I never expected moving into a new apartment would land me in the center of a supernatural harem.

But then, how could I have? I hauled my measly two boxes of possessions up to the second floor, seemingly ordinary apartment. Well-kept. Clean. The manager, Ms. Patty, clearly took pride in her building.

Two thousand dollars a month worth of pride, I reminded myself as I unlocked the door to my new home. It had to be worth it.

When I walked in the door, something felt...wrong. I couldn't pinpoint what, though. Ms. Patty had overseen the furniture delivery the day before, and looking around, I could see everything was placed where I had asked.

Why, then, was unease clenching in my gut? I bit my lip, set my boxes down, locked up behind me, and took a look around the apartment. It didn't seem anyone was here or had messed with anything.

Maybe it was just in my head. After what had happened back in my hometown, it wasn't really any wonder I felt on edge. But as long as Demarcus didn't find out where I was, I should be okay.

I would be okay. Especially, if I kept the necklace my grandmother had given me on. It made me feel safe and always reminded me of my grandmother, who I missed very much.

I wondered what my neighbors would be like. There were nine total apartments, but three of them were vacant currently. When I had asked what the tenants were like, she had just laughed and said, "They're all best friends...for now."

I had no idea what she had meant by that.

Things had been a bit crazy in Jinla with the four main Other clans at war. The mages, dragons, werewolves, and elves had been at war for decades now, but humans like me had no idea why. Jinla was the hub for Others since the four clans had their headquarters based here. Just on my walk from the train station to here, I had seen two elves, a goblin, and two guys I was fairly certain had been werewolves. Grandma thought I would have been afraid of Others, after being attacked by some, but I knew that there were always bad apples in the bunch and I couldn't blame an entire race of Others for one or two bad beings. Plus, I had dated a couple Others and they had been the most loving beings I had ever met.

The four Other clans were ruled with monarchies, unlike the President of our human democracy. A few hundred years ago, we had had a king as well, but now the President worked with the Others' Kings to ensure we kept peace between all races. The Others had huge areas in Jinla for their headquarters, but also a lot of land outside this city. There were entire states owned by one of the Other clans.

After putting my clothes away and popping a frozen pizza in the oven, I turned to my favorite past time, video games. My gaming console was just in sleep mode, so I woke it up and launched my current favorite game, *Ghost 2*. One of my clan members had already created a chat lobby, having been on an hour earlier due to different time zones.

"Yo!" I said in greeting.

"Jo!" several male voices responded.

I didn't have many friends in person, but I had a great group of about ten online friends – my best friends. We talked about everything. Some people didn't understand it, but my virtual friends were the closest people I knew. We had met in person a couple of times, but most of our interactions were through our headsets and in the games.

"Jo, did you see the specs for the new hard raid?" Dragonknight asked. He wasn't really a dragon or a knight, but that was his gamer tag. We created our own gamer tags, or gamer names, when we signed on to the console for the first time. Mine was not creative at all, *Jolie*. Yep, just my first name.

I took my pizza out of the oven and settled onto the couch for the evening.

"Yep, it looks hard, but I'm ready for the challenge," I replied.

Three hours later, I realized that I had in fact, not been ready for the challenge. We said our goodnights and I collapsed onto my bed, waking up with barely enough time to make it to my first day of work without being late.

When I got to work, I rushed into the huge building, and the receptionist pointed at a map off to the right. "Room twenty-one."

There were over ten floors, and I was glad I only had to go to the second floor.

I had landed a writing position with one of the most popular gaming companies. It was a huge honor and a nice pay increase from my last job.

"You must be Jolie," a man in jeans and a *"vampires drool"* t-shirt said.

"I am," I replied and held out my hand.

He shook it and motioned for me to follow him. "Your desk is right over here. Someone will be by in a bit to walk you through the processes we have here."

Once I got started, the work and its processes were simple

enough. The day flew by, and after a full day, I clocked out and headed back towards my new place.

On my walk home, I put in my noise cancelling headphones and sent a message to the group chat with the clan. Without telling them any information that could get me in trouble, I hinted at the awesome games I'd gotten a sneak peek of. Just as I hit send, something slammed into my side and carried me across the intersection. I gasped and looked up to find a man carrying me and a bus barreling past where I had just been walking. He'd saved me from being hit by the bus I had not seen or heard.

How cliché of me to have my nose down and almost get hit by a bus!

He smiled down at me and said something, but I couldn't hear him. I took out my earbuds and asked, "What?"

"I asked if you were okay?" he repeated with a wide smile, setting me on my feet.

He was drop dead gorgeous. Dark brown hair, blue eyes, nice cheekbones and jawline, and muscular, not too buff, but his chest was defined even through his shirt. I mentally checked to make sure there wasn't drool dripping down my chin.

"Yes, thank you."

He set me on my feet and I brushed myself off and smoothed my clothes down.

"I'm glad," he said softly.

"Thank you, again," I said and started to walk away, still in shock.

"Wait," he called and caught up to me.

"Yes?" I asked.

His biceps looked incredible in the shirt he had on. It hugged his shoulders and chest, and was cut in the perfect spot to accent his biceps. Had he lucked out in finding the shirt to fit like that, or did he just make everything he wore look amazing? His dark hair was styled up, his beard and goatee perfectly shaped to his jaw. The clothes he wore were nice, definitely more expensive than the skirt and V-neck t-shirt I currently wore.

"Well, I did save you and I think I deserve a date," he said and stuck his hands in his pockets, thumbs outside of them.

A date? This sexy male wanted to go on a date with me? Hell yes!

"A date, huh? What would this date involve?"

I was glad I came off cool and composed, despite my brain trying really hard to fry itself with the fact I had almost died and this delicious being was talking to me. It had been a few years since I'd had sex, and he was making me think all kinds of dirty things.

"Dinner and dessert."

The way he said dessert made me shiver in delight. I definitely wouldn't mind some dessert that involved him.

"Okay," I agreed, keeping my drool in my mouth.

"Great! This way, milady," he said and bowed.

"May I know the name of my savior?" I asked with a fake accent, staying in line with his "milady" comment.

"Rhys. And you, milady?"

"Jolie."

He stopped and held out his hand.

I looked at it a moment and then asked, "Clan?"

His smile disappeared. "I wouldn't save you just to hurt you."

"It's been a rough few years," I replied stiffly and avoided looking at his eyes. It would take me an hour at least to explain all of the misfortune that I had experienced. And, I really didn't want to go over what had happened last year, the reason my grandmother had given me the necklace.

"Dragon," he whispered.

Thank the Goddess.

I shook his hand and met his eyes. "I'm sorry. I'm not racist. I don't care what you are. It's just—"

He kissed my knuckles and smiled. "I understand."

We resumed walking and I felt his eyes on me as we moved down the sidewalk. Dragons were notoriously observant, so I didn't let it bother me.

"Where would you like to eat?" I asked.

"Me?" he asked, his eyebrows raised. "I don't think a woman has ever asked where I wanted to eat before."

I chuckled. "Well, you saved me, so I owe you dinner."

"What about here?" he asked and indicated the restaurant beside us. It was a nice Italian chain restaurant that served amazing breadsticks. We had one in my hometown.

"Great," I agreed and opened the door for him.

He grinned and walked in.

"Thank you," he said softly to me.

"You're welcome."

The hostess seated us quickly and ordered our food as soon as we sat down. The restaurant was a bit slow, which was good for us.

"So, Jolie. What were you doing when you didn't see the bus racing towards you?" he asked and snapped his breadstick in half before eating it.

Texting my video game clan.

"Texting some friends," I said somewhat truthfully. "I just started a new job today and had promised to message them afterwards."

"Oh, you're new to town?" he asked.

I nodded. "Just moved in last night."

"I wish I had known. I would have taken you on a tour instead of to dinner," he said. His brow furrowed a brief moment and then he smiled. "Maybe I'll stop you from being hit by a car tomorrow and can convince you to go on a second date."

I laughed.

"Let's hope I don't need rescuing again. Once in a lifetime is enough for me."

"You're human, right?" he asked softly and tilted his head. His nostrils flared as he drew in my scent.

"Mostly."

"Mostly?"

"I am, like, a thirty-second Gorgon," I admitted to him. The most famous Gorgon of all, Medusa, was a distant relative of mine. At least, that's what my Grandma had told me. Generally, it wasn't something that I brought up right away, but I wanted to be honest with him right up front. I was hoping it might get me into his bed tonight. *No, stop that, you dirty mind. You are not sleeping with someone you just met.* I'd never had a one-night stand before, not that I was against it, I just hadn't had one before. But, I didn't want to start my life in Jinla with one.

"Interesting," he replied with a smirk.

"What do you do for work?" I asked him, leaning on my elbows on the table to give him a nice view of my cleavage. I didn't flirt often, and I wasn't great at it, but I could get by.

"I'm an architect," he replied.

"That's really interesting," I admitted.

"It can be, yes."

"Do you enjoy it?"

He nodded. "I like creating things."

Our meals came and we ate and chatted. I ordered some wine and before I realized it, I was a bit tipsy. Okay, I was drunk.

"Where to next?" I asked with a warm smile, feeling warm all throughout my body.

"There's a bar right around the corner," he said. "Want to go get some drinks?"

He led the way out of the restaurant and I stumbled when we walked down the sidewalk.

"Easy," he said with a chuckle and put his solid arm around my waist, so his large bicep fit into the curve of my side. I had to resist the urge to explore the muscle with my hands.

"Sorry," I said with a soft laugh. "I guess I had more to drink than I thought."

"Would you prefer to go home?" he asked, stopping and leaning against the side of a building, right next to the alley.

I leaned into him, my breasts pressed against his chest, and whispered, "But I haven't had dessert yet."

His eyes sparked and he leaned down, lightly brushing his lips over mine. "Dessert does sound good right now."

I pulled him down and kissed him deeply, sliding my tongue into his mouth, and wrapped my arms around his neck.

He picked me up and I instinctively wrapped my legs around his waist, our kiss never breaking. He walked down the alley until we were hidden from view, and a distance away from the large trashcan we were using to block us from the sight of passersby. I dropped my legs long enough to let him unzip his pants and put a condom on. He lifted me up again, pushing me against the wall, and slowly entered me, moving my thong to the side to do so. He was big, but not too big. When he was completely buried in me, he moaned and whispered, "You feel amazing."

I moaned and moved my hips with his.

He growled and clamped his mouth over mine, stroking his tongue across mine in sync with the pumping of his hips. My orgasm hit after only a couple of strokes and I squealed into his mouth as we continued to kiss. Stars danced behind my closed eyes as I floated on euphoria that continued as he didn't stop.

I had forgotten how great sex was with dragons. This male was an alpha and the safety and security he made me feel as his arms held me and we became one for a short time, was euphoric in and of itself.

Another wave crashed over me and my fingernails dug into his muscular shoulders.

He nipped my neck gently, my hips bucking against him as he did.

He moved faster and harder, orgasms tearing from me one after the next, but soon he lost his rhythm as he orgasmed.

We broke our kiss, both panting and satisfied.

"Wow," he whispered.

"Mmhm," I replied, euphoria and the alcohol making me beyond happy. This town was starting off wonderful.

We got dressed and I stopped him at the edge of the alley. "Thanks, for tonight."

"Going to pass on drinks?" he asked with a smirk.

"I think dessert satisfied me plenty."

He bowed elegantly and kissed the knuckles on one of my hands. "Then I bid you goodnight, milady." He held out a business card. "And I would love to hear from you again."

I took the card and curtsied. "I shall call upon thee, good sir."

He bent and kissed my cheek. "Seriously, call me. I'd love to take you out again."

"Okay," I said with a nod.

CHAPTER 2

During my morning commute, I hummed along to a song, thinking about my date last night. I would wait at least two days before calling him, if I did at all. He was sexy, but he seemed like he might be super protective, which I didn't particularly like.

That sex had been great, though. Or perhaps that was just because of how drunk I had been and how long it had been since the last time. No, it had been good, and he was damn sexy.

After almost getting hit by a bus, I had done some research and found out there was a great public transit system in town. Now, I was on a bus instead of getting hit by it. The buses were clean and most of the people riding were dressed in business casual clothes. I felt underdressed in my jeans and t-shirt, but this was my preferred attire and work didn't care what we wore since we didn't have visitors. Plus, as a videogame company, we were more about the games and less about impressing suit-wearing corporate types.

My stop was approaching, so I stood up, picking up my backpack from the floor by my feet as I did. The doors opened, and the man next to me snatched my backpack and ran off the bus.

"Hey!" I screamed after him and jumped down and onto the sidewalk

Something blurred as it rushed from behind, whizzing past me, and then knocked the purse snatcher, er, backpack snatcher down. I jogged forward and the blur turned out to be a handsome man with bulging muscles. He turned to look at me, his foot holding the criminal down, and smiled. His eyes were amber, which told me immediately what he was.

Werewolf.

He grabbed the backpack from where the criminal had dropped it and held it out to me. "Here you go," he said with a wide smile.

I took it and smiled. "Thank you, so much."

The werewolf was a few inches over six feet, had a beard and goatee similar to Rhys's, black, slicked back hair, and was obviously of Italian heritage. The leather jacket he had on only added to his masculine appearance, which my inner Jolie was drooling over. This town had a lot of hot guys. I was so glad I had moved here.

Police showed up, but paused when they saw the werewolf with his foot on the guy. "Deryn," they called in greeting. "We've got it from here."

The werewolf raised his foot and stepped back so that he was beside me. "He snatched this woman's bag," he explained. "Lots of witnesses to attest to that."

The police nodded and handcuffed the guy whose eyes were wide as saucers as he stared up at Deryn. Was he scared because he was a werewolf? Or was there another reason? The cops seemed to know him.

"I'm Deryn," he said to me and held out his hand, still smiling wide.

I shook it. "Jolie. Thanks again, Deryn. I don't know what I would have done if he had gotten away with this." I slung my backpack onto my shoulders and pulled my hair out from under the straps. "Do you work near here? I could take you out to lunch as repayment for helping me."

He smirked. "You don't have to repay me for doing what was right. However, I'd love to go out on a date with you."

"I can't go out tonight," I said a bit sadly. I had a raid planned with my clan and I couldn't back out on them. We were determined to beat the hard raid.

"What about making it a lunch date then?" he asked.

I smiled and felt my shoulders rise. "Okay."

He took out a pen, pulled the cap off with his teeth, and held his hand out, palm up. I set my hand in it and he turned it over to write his phone number on my palm. He took the cap out of his mouth and put it back on the pen.

"Text me the time and place and I'll be there," he promised.

I nodded and smiled, glancing down at his number. "Okay."

With a wave, he walked away, head held high, shoulders back, and smiled at everyone he passed by. His butt looked incredible in those jeans and I wasn't the only woman to notice. With one last look, I turned and went to work.

"You're late," Justina said and shook her finger at me. "Lucky for you, everyone is in a meeting, so they won't know." Justina was tall, thin, and gorgeous. She was part Egyptian and part Italian, add in being a dhampir, and she was almost perfect. I had met her when I came to interview over a month ago and we had instantly become friends, texting nonstop since that day.

"Thanks," I said and plopped down into my computer chair. "Some jerk tried to steal my backpack."

"Oh no!" She gasped and rushed to me. "Did he hurt you? Are you alright?"

She grabbed my arms, raised them, and spun me around to search for injuries.

I shooed her worries away and sat back down. "A werewolf was on the bus and stopped him for me. So, I wasn't injured at all."

She smirked, a knowing look on her face. "Oh! Was this a sexy werewolf? Not that they make any other kind!"

I chuckled and nodded as I looked down at my hand with his number on it. "Definitely was. He asked me on a lunch date."

"A lunch date! Damn girl, you move fast! Wasn't it just last night that you were with that dragon?"

I blushed and mumbled. "Yeah." Now, I was really regretting telling her about that. I should keep things like that to myself.

"Hey, no judgments here! I try to get two different men each week, though my options are slim lately, but that may be my high standards. Just make sure you give me more juicy details!" She laughed, throwing her head back as she did.

"Where should we go?" I asked Justina. "I don't really know any of the lunch places here."

"Fifth Street Bistro," she said immediately.

I sent a text to the number he had provided, glad that my hands weren't sweaty, since that happened somedays.

Me: This is Jolie from this morning. Thank you again for getting my bag back. How does noon at Fifth Street Bistro sound?

"You need to get pictures of these guys for me," she said. "Work best friends share everything."

I chuckled. "I'll try." I'd love to have pictures saved

Deryn: Perfect. I'm looking forward to it.

She peered over my shoulder and whistled. "You are so getting laid tonight."

I put my phone away and shook my head. "Stop it."

"I'm jealous," she said and sat down in her chair. "It took me a week to find some good males here."

"I definitely like this town better than my hometown," I said with a smirk and laughed.

The meeting ended and our coworkers came out, chatting and going to their desks, ending our reprieve. Should I feel bad for going on two dates in as many nights? Neither had been premeditated. Neither had been *expected*.

I became engrossed in my work, letting the story take me, and it wasn't until Justina yelled my name that I snapped back into reality.

"What?" I asked, taking my headphones off and looking up at her.

"Lunch!" she yelled at me. Several people turned to look at us, but I ignored them, leapt to my feet, and grabbed my ID and cash out of my backpack.

"Thank you!" I yelled back and ran out of the office, shocked to find it was five minutes until noon already. On the elevator ride down, I typed in the address and used my maps app to find it. Justina saved me by giving me a location only a block away, so I wouldn't be late.

I walked outside, smoothing my clothes, taking deep breaths to calm down. I had dated werewolves before, and they were great at smelling emotions. I did not want him to think that I was nervous about our date, or flustered. I turned the corner and saw the bistro, it was pretty busy already, and standing outside was Deryn.

I took one last deep breath and walked towards him, confident and relaxed, with a wide smile on.

"Hi," I said to get his attention since he was texting or emailing someone on his phone.

He looked up and smiled. "Hi."

"You wait long?" I asked, despite the fact I was exactly on time.

He shook his head and slipped his phone into his pocket. "Nope. How has work been?"

We got into the long line of patrons, and I turned to face him. "Pretty good, actually. I would have been late for lunch if my friend hadn't shown me the time."

"What do you do?" he asked, tilting his head to the side slightly.

"I'm a video game writer," I answered truthfully.

His eyes widened. "You game?"

I nodded, not surprised that he was shocked by that. A lot of males were shocked to discover that I played video games. They were even more shocked when they found out how much I played. "Yes, I do. Do you?"

"Lots!" he said happily. "What's your favorite type of game?"

"RPGs and FPSs."

"Me too! Have you played *Ghost 2* yet?"

"Only every night since it came out," I said with a chuckle.

"Did you beat the hard raid?"

"Not yet. My clan and I tried last night, but got hung up on the last part."

"That's awesome that you game. I haven't met a girl in real life who games before."

"We're out there, just few and far between."

"That's an understatement," he said and chuckled. "So, what's a gorgeous gamer girl like you doing single?"

He thought I was gorgeous? I knew I was attractive, but I would never have described myself as gorgeous. I had long, dark brown hair that was naturally wavy, high cheekbones, thick lips, and an hourglass figure. Even with how much I played video games, I made sure to work out and eat healthy most of the time, so I was in good shape.

"I just moved here from out of state."

"Really? Maybe I can take you for a tour?" he offered. "Show you the best parts of the city?"

"I would like that," I replied and stepped forward, following the line as it moved.

"What do you think of our city so far?"

"I really like it. I like the diversity here and how everyone gets along." I also liked that there didn't seem to be many vampires here. I was hoping to avoid vampires as much as possible. They were not my favorite race of Others.

"Deryn," a deep voice called.

Deryn turned and scowled at the large male behind him. The male had dark sunglasses on and was a brick wall brought to life.

"What?" Deryn asked, irritated by this male's presence. They obviously knew each other, but that didn't explain why he was upset by him just talking to him.

"You're wanted at headquarters," the male said.

"I'm busy," Deryn snarled. "It can wait."

"It's urgent."

Deryn rubbed his temples. "You guys always say that, and when I get there, nothing important is going on."

"I'm just the messenger," the male said and shrugged.

Those around us were slowly moving away from Deryn and the newcomer, their eyes wide, and stances stiff. Why were they scared? Was it because Deryn was a werewolf? I couldn't see people in this city being scared of an Other, since there were so many of them here.

"Fine," Deryn said with a sigh. He turned to me and said, "I'm really sorry about this. It's a family matter."

Pack matter, was what he meant.

I smiled. "No problem."

"Dinner, tonight?" he asked. "I'll make it up to you."

"Okay, if it's early." I could go to dinner with him and then get home and raid with my clan afterwards. I would make it work.

He kissed my cheek and inhaled sharply. "I'll send you details later. Thanks for understanding."

He left and people looked at me questioningly. I realized with a sigh, that I hadn't snapped a picture of him for Justina, but it was too late. She would have to wait until later to get a picture. I ordered a quick bite to eat and took it back to work with me.

I ended up staying late at work to help some coworkers with a project, so I didn't even get to go home before my date with Deryn. Justina had been bummed that I hadn't gotten a picture yet, but I promised her that I would try tonight. That had appeased her enough she loaned me a change of clothes for my date. I asked her why she had the clothes in her desk, and she had simply said, "You never know when you'll need them."

I stood outside of the restaurant Deryn had chosen and rubbed my arms against the chill that was starting to set in. A drink sounded really good right now.

"Waiting long?" he asked as he approached.

I smiled and shook my head. "Nope."

He wore a pair of slacks and a button up shirt that accentuated his strong arms incredibly well. Yes, I had a huge thing for biceps. Well, muscles in general.

I wore a nice blue dress, that hugged all the places men appreciated the most. Thank goodness Justina and I were the same size.

"You look amazing," he whispered and leaned forward to inhale my scent next to my chin.

I inhaled his scent back and practically purred. He smelled like pine. "You look great, too."

He quirked his eyebrow. "You've dated a werewolf before?"

I nodded.

"How long ago?" he asked.

"Two years ago," I informed him. Knowing he would want to be sure that he wasn't overstepping another wolf's grounds, I added, "I'm completely unattached."

He smiled wide and pulled open the door for me. "Just what I wanted to hear."

The restaurant was incredible, reminding me of an opera house, with thick, burgundy drapes and low lighting. The host took us to a table that had been marked reserved, and they immediately brought out champagne and two flute glasses.

Deryn raised his glass of champagne. "To new friends."

I smiled and clicked my glass against his. "New friends." I took a long drink and then looked at the menu. It was extravagant and expensive, I wanted to try it all.

"What do you recommend?" I asked and set my menu down.

"The prime rib is amazing," he replied, still looking at his menu.

"I'll have that then," I said with a nod of my head, glad I had a decision made.

He looked up at me and smiled. "I know you'll love it."

"So, what type of work do you do?" I asked him.

"I make a lot of decisions for the family business," he replied. "My dad is the CEO, but he's training me to take over and decided the best way to train me is just to hand me the reins for ninety percent of the operation."

"That sounds like a lot of work," I said sadly. He wasn't that old, but had a lot of responsibility.

He smiled, joy filling him again. "Yeah, but I get a lot of time off to spend with my friends."

"What do you do for fun, besides play games?" I asked.

"My friends and I usually hang out and drink, or play something together. We're all really busy and have high level jobs, so the time we spend together is strictly relaxation time."

That sounded really nice. Sounded like what I needed.

"And why is a sexy, alpha werewolf like you single?" I asked, resting my chin on my linked hands on the table, raised up on my elbows.

"Haven't found the right one," he said with a shrug.

"Well, I'm flattered to be considered," I whispered huskily.

He smiled and mimicked my position. "I'm glad that I found you early on."

"Oh?"

"I know you'll have plenty of suitors knocking down your door once you've been here a while."

"I doubt that, but I'm glad I met you early as well."

He smiled at me, and it warmed me all the way to my toes.

My phone buzzed, and I looked at it.

Dragonknight: We still raiding?

Shit. I had forgotten to message them.

Me: Be on in an hour or two.

Dragonknight: Okay.

"Everything alright?" Deryn asked.

"Forgot to message my clan that I would be late to raid tonight because of our date."

"Do you need to go?" he asked, completely serious.

He would let me leave our date early to go game? This guy was definitely a keeper!

"No, thank you. I let them know I'd be on in a couple of hours."

"I really wouldn't mind," he said. "I know what it's like when you make plans with your clan. Especially, if you and your clan members don't live near each other."

Was he perfect or was I dead? Had that bus actually hit me and everything after was just a dream?

"I appreciate it, immensely, but they understand that I just moved here and I need to meet people in real life."

"My lucky day," Deryn said with a wide smile.

"Your orders?" a waiter asked.

～

DERYN HELD OPEN THE TAXI DOOR, LOOMING OVER ME AS I STEPPED up to him. "I had a great time tonight," he said softly and brushed some hair behind my shoulder.

"Me too," I said sincerely and stood up on tiptoe to kiss him lightly on the lips. "I'd love to do it again."

He leaned down and kissed me deeply, his tongue sweeping across mine. I leaned into him, as we continued to kiss. He tasted like champagne and strawberries. When we finally separated, I was grinning like a fool.

"Good night, Jolie."

"Good night, Deryn."

The taxi dropped me off, and I took the stairs up to my apartment, needing some exercise. Deryn was a lot of fun and super sexy. I would definitely be calling him to hang out sometime soon. He was really easy to be around.

Rhys was sexy, but I didn't really know much about him. That was something I could fix by going out with him again, on an actual date. But damn, that sex had been great!

After taking a shower, I sat down to turn my game on, but saw my phone blinking.

Deryn: I enjoyed tonight. Maybe Saturday we could get together to game? I've got a lot of old school games, including some karting games.

I smiled and chewed on my nail as I debated what to say.

Me: I enjoyed tonight as well. That prime rib was amazing. Saturday should work. I'll text you Friday night to confirm?

Deryn: Sounds great. Can't wait to see you again. :)

Me: Same XD

My phone chimed again and I expected it to be him, but it wasn't.

Justina: Did you get a picture?

Me: No. Sorry. Xoxox

Justina: Did you get laid?

Me: No! Geez.

Justina: hahaha lmao

Me: We're hanging out Saturday.

Justina: "hanging out" Nice!

Me: Sigh. I'm not a slut...normally.

Justina: You do you, hun.

Me: Going to bed. Bye.

∼

DURING LUNCH, I WENT TO THE PARK AND FOUND A QUIET PLACE to meditate. All morning I had been warring with myself about whether I should feel bad about dating both Rhys and Deryn, or whether it was fine. I took a deep breath and sat on the grass.

Closing my eyes, I tried to make all of the sounds disappear as I relaxed.

Five minutes later, I was groaning and grumbling.

"Meditation works best when you're quiet," a male voice whispered beside me.

My eyes snapped open and I turned to find a male elf sitting right next to me, mimicking my sitting position with his eyes closed. He was handsome, most elves were, and I really wanted to touch the pointed tip on his ear. He was incredibly stocky and looked to be Latino, with warm bronzed skin.

He opened his eyes and smiled at me, warmth filling his eyes and radiating from him. How could one being be so happy, that it infected another person? He held out his hand.

"I'm Foxfire. Everyone calls me Fox though."

I shook his hand and smiled back, my shoulder dropped forward, and my breath released in a content sight. "I'm Jolie."

"It's nice to meet you, Jolie. You must be new to town."

"How'd you know?"

"I visit this park often, and this is the first time I've seen you. I would remember if someone as beautiful as you had come through here before."

My smile widened. "Flirt."

He chuckled, stood up, brushed his butt off, and then held his hand out to help me stand. I accepted, letting him pull me into a standing position before I wiped off my butt to get rid of the grass and dirt.

"I'm sorry I interrupted your meditation session," he told me.

I laughed. "It wasn't much of a session, as you could tell."

"Troubles at home?" he asked, the edge of his smile slipped slightly.

I shook my head. "No. Just started a new job here, and I've only been here a few days, so it's been a bit crazy."

He waved toward the park's main path. "Care to go for a walk?"

His eyebrow ticked up a little when he asked, and my heart fluttered.

"I'd love to," I said, hoping I didn't sound as breathless as I felt.

We continued down the path, side by side, the wind whispering through the canopy of trees. There wasn't another soul in sight, and for that, I was glad.

"Do you work, Fox?" I asked, once I'd worked up the nerve. I could flirt with Rhys like a pro, but something about Fox made me feel childish and inexperienced.

He nodded. "I'm on my lunchbreak right now."

"Me, too."

"Does that mean that I might get a chance to see you again during the week?" he asked.

His eyebrow did that thing again, this time paired with a smirk that made me feel weak in the knees.

"Only if you're very nice," I said, not letting on to my infatuation as I flipped my hair over my shoulder.

"I'm always nice," he replied, and with that, he produced a silver rose out of thin air into his palm. He held it out to me, and I gratefully accepted it.

"Wow," I whispered. "It's beautiful."

"Not nearly as beautiful as you."

So, he was a sweet talker, too! I couldn't contain my smile as I pressed my nose to the flower to smell. It had a muted scent, but it was calming and reassuring, just like his presence.

"Thank you," I said from behind the rose before offering my smile to him directly.

We walked in silence for another five minutes, enjoying the flowers and trees, a small reprieve from the city life that surrounded the park. It smelled clean and fresh here, reminding me of my small hometown and the fields that had surrounded my house.

We didn't get nearly enough time together before he told me he had to get back to work.

He dipped his head forward slightly, then looked up, and asked, "Would you meet me here tomorrow?"

I tucked a strand of hair behind my ear, immediately warm and open to the idea. "I'd like that."

He pulled out a cell phone from his pocket and handed it to me. "If you'll please…"

I entered my phone number and name into his contacts and sent myself a message with his name, so that I wouldn't be surprised if he texted me later.

"All set," I said, handing his phone back with a smile.

He kissed my cheek and waved as he walked away. I twirled the rose as I went back to work and inhaled the slightly sweet smell that it gave off. I might as well have been walking on air as I strode back into the building.

"Who gave you that?" Justina asked.

"None of your business," I whispered, not letting the fact that I had added a third guy already to my phone book bother me. Or the fact that she would definitely have something to say about it.

She rolled her eyes and went back to working.

I sent a message to Rhys, not wanting him to think I had forgotten about him.

Me: Works been crazy. Dinner on Saturday?

Rhys: I was worried that you had forgotten about me.

Me: No way that I could forget about you.

Rhys: Dinner sounds great. 7?

Me: Okay. You pick the place, and message me the address, and I'll meet you there.

Rhys: Can't wait.

I would spend the day with Deryn, and then go out with Rhys for dinner. I was a single woman and I didn't have any attachments to these men. So, there was no reason that I couldn't date a few of them.

After work, I went out to a nearby bar and sipped on a vodka lemonade while I people watched. It was one of the best ways to figure out what the town was really like, and what went on. There were various races in the bar. Among them were were-wolves, elves, dragons, and even some mages. There were way more humans though, our race taking up at least seventy percent of the population of the bar.

"Hello, is this seat taken?" an incredibly deep male voice asked.

I turned and smiled wide. He was hot, incredibly hot. What luck I seemed to be having!

"No, it's not taken."

He sat down and held out his hand. "Hi, I'm Nico."

"Nice to meet you," I said with a smile, but didn't shake his hand, picking my drink up to give me an excuse.

With a flick of his wrist, he produced a playing card. "Would you like to see a trick?"

I turned to face him fully and nodded with a wide smile. "Yes, please."

He snapped his fingers and a red rose appeared, a smile spread, and he set it down on the bar top in front of me. Then, he showed me his hands, front and back. The next instant, he held a full deck of cards and was shuffling them.

I clapped and he chuckled. "I haven't done the trick yet."

"I'm still impressed," I told him.

He showed me the cards, front and back – they looked like normal cards. "Watch closely," he whispered. He shuffled the cards again and then, they changed, the symbols turning blue and purple instead of red and black.

"Wow," I said and clapped again.

He continued shuffling and they returned to black and red. He bowed his head and smiled.

My liquid courage was in full effect at the moment, plus the fact that I'd managed to get dates with some other pretty hot males this week. I hoped three would be enough, but I wouldn't be disappointed if I couldn't add him as the fourth to my phonebook.

"Would you like me to show you a trick?" I asked him.

"You, show me a trick?" he asked.

I nodded. "Yes."

He waved his hand at the bar top. "Please."

I wrote my name and phone number on a napkin, folded it in half, took the glass of water that was next to me, put the folded napkin into it, slid a coaster on top of it, flipped it over so that it was upside down, and then pulled the coaster out. This left my number in the folded napkin inside of the water with no easy way for him to get it.

I stood up and kissed his cheek. "Thanks for the show. Hopefully, I hear from you soon." Quickly, before he could say anything to me, I turned and left.

His laugh was deep, and rumbled all the way across the noisy bar as I left.

I WAS CHUCKLING TO MYSELF AS I TYPED A MESSAGE INTO THE GROUP chat with my clan, telling them about the joke I had just played on Nico. They all agreed that it was great, and if he figured out a way to get my number, he would definitely call me and I should give him at least one date. I slid my card through the reader to open the apartment building door and replied to another message on my phone, looking down as I walked inside, towards the elevator.

"Jolie!" four male voices called out at the same time.

I jerked my head up and felt a knot form in my throat. Rhys, Deryn, Fox, and Nico stood together in front of the elevator, waiting for the doors to open.

Oh no. They all know each other!

"Wait," Rhys said to the others. "How do you know her?"

"How do you know her?" Fox asked.

"What is happening?" Deryn asked.

I kept my head down and was about to head to the stairs, but the elevator arrived. They walked in first, lining up along the back of the elevator and looked at me expectantly, Rhys holding the door open for me. I stepped inside, pushed my floor, and felt as small as a mouse with all of them towering over me. Their stares were heavy, pressing upon me as the elevator moved up.

What was I going to do?

"You live here?" Rhys asked.

I nodded. "Just moved in. Which one of you live here?" I hadn't turned around, worried to see what the expressions on their faces might be.

"All of us," Nico replied with a soft laugh. "We all wondered who the new resident was. I had no idea it would be you."

"So, it seems you've met the four of us already," Deryn said. "Sort of funny, right?"

I spun around, worried they were mad and needing to defend myself.

"I didn't know you guys knew each other. I met you all randomly and..."

"It's okay," Fox said and smiled reassuringly at me.

I wasn't so sure. My floor came up and I rushed out, getting into my apartment and locking my door with a groan. What the hell was I going to do? They all lived here. They all knew each other.

My phone beeped and I wasn't shocked to see it was one of them.

Deryn: We still hanging out tomorrow?

He still wanted to hang out? Had they talked? Maybe he didn't know that I'd slept with Rhys.

Me: Yeah, if you're still up for it.

Deryn: Definitely!

CHAPTER 3

I stood outside of Deryn's apartment and fidgeted with my hair. I had told him I would come over, but now I was nervous. What if they confronted me instead of wanting to hang out?

Taking a breath for courage, I knocked on the door. *Might as well get it over with.*

Deryn opened the door and smiled. "Jolie! Come on in."

"Thanks," I replied with what I hoped was a nice smile.

His apartment was pretty large, at least two bedrooms, and had a huge living room where Fox was sitting, playing a video game.

He turned and smiled at me. "Hey, Jolie."

"Hi, Fox," I said with a little wave, shocked that he was here. Wasn't I supposed to hang out with Deryn?

Fox was playing the newest first-person shooter, a game I had been considering getting, but wasn't certain it was good enough to draw me away from *Ghost 2.*

"How do you like it?" I asked him and leaned on the back of the couch, while I watched him play. Deryn's TV was huge, at least eighty inches. I was totally jealous and possibly drooling a little at how amazing the graphics looked.

Our building had incredibly fast internet speeds as well, so the frames per second were maxed and there was no lag.

"I love it so far. I'm just doing the campaign," he replied, shooting one guy and blowing up another guy with a sticky grenade.

"Haven't given PVP a chance yet?" I asked with a smirk. A lot of the gamers I knew avoided the player versus player aspect of the game for as long as they could, because they became rage monsters. I was also one of the rage monsters when playing PVP, but it took a lot to make me rage.

"He rages worse than anyone else," Deryn told me. "We had to ban him from playing one game because he wouldn't stop breaking controllers."

"I replaced each of the ones I broke," Fox countered.

"Do you guys live together?" I asked curiously.

Deryn shook his head. "No, Fox lives across the hall. He comes over to try the new games that I get, though."

"Sweet," I said and looked at the entertainment center where my eyes widened. "You have every single console," I whispered and headed towards it. It was calling to me. All of the old consoles that I had played with as I grew up, and some I hadn't been able to get.

"Yep," Deryn said with a satisfied smirk. "Even the oddball ones that didn't really have a purpose like the Mini Sub One."

"Do you have games for all of these?" I whispered as I almost began to worship his collection.

"What do you want to play?" he asked with a smirk.

"*Road Bashers 3*?" I asked. It had been a childhood favorite of mine, but it was rare and incredibly expensive now.

"Mind if I stay and play?" Fox asked.

"Not at all," Deryn replied and then looked at me. "Okay with you?"

I smiled and nodded. "It's a party game, after all."

Deryn set up the game and I took a seat on the couch in the middle. Deryn and Fox sat on either side of me and we all grabbed a controller and prepared to play. The music came on, and I immediately got the chills.

"Oh man," I whispered excitedly. "It's been so long since I've played this."

We spent three hours playing *Road Bashers 3*, teasing and messing with each other like the three of us were old friends. They were so easy to be around. It was strange for me to feel so safe and comfortable with them when I barely knew them, but here we were. When we finally decided to turn it off, Fox kissed my cheek and then waved as he left the apartment, yawning.

"That was fun," I told Deryn. I would have kept playing except that I had my date with Rhys and I didn't want to be late for it.

He smiled and nodded. "Yeah, I haven't had that much fun playing a game in a long time."

"I should get home," I whispered and headed towards the door. He trailed behind me, then leaned against the wall next to the door. "I really did have a lot of fun tonight," I told him.

He brushed my hair behind my ear and whispered, "I'm glad." His lips were warm and soft as he slid them across mine. It was a sweet kiss, and yet, it made my hormones rage. "We should play again soon," he whispered.

I nodded and kissed his cheek once before leaving his apartment and running right into Rhys.

"Oh," I gasped.

He smiled. "Hello." He looked up at the apartment number and his smile disappeared as he asked, "Were you on a date with Deryn?"

"I played some games with him and Fox," I explained. "I had planned on going back to my place to finish getting ready." After glancing at my phone and confirming that there was still half an hour before our date, I asked, "Unless you're ready now?"

"Go ahead and freshen up. I need to talk to Deryn really quick," he told me with a smile.

I kissed his cheek and then went to the stairs to walk down to my floor. I threw open the door and almost screamed when Nico was there. I put my hand to my chest and dropped my head. "Mage's Mana!" I exclaimed.

"What?" Nico asked with a chuckle.

"You startled me," I explained and exhaled loudly. "Sorry."

He pushed open the door for me and stepped to the side. "No, my fault." I stepped past him and he whispered, "Your trick was great, but one thing you didn't know…" He snapped his fingers and the napkin I had written my number on appeared in his hand, dry and smudge free. "…I'm a mage."

My eyes widened as I stared at him in disbelief. A mage. Wow. I had no idea.

"Good to know," I whispered and smiled before skipping down the stairs to my floor.

It only took me a couple of minutes to get my hair brushed and touch up my makeup. I did a twirl in front of my floor-length mirror and then went to the living room. As soon as I sat down on the couch, someone knocked on the door.

Rhys smiled at me when I opened it. "You look beautiful."

"Thank you," I replied, stepping into the hall, and turned, closing and locking my door.

He pushed the elevator button and looked at me with a tilted head. "You're an enigma."

"What? How?" I asked.

"You're gorgeous, but single. Normally that's because the girl is crazy. However, you don't seem crazy."

"You've only spent one night with me," I reminded him. "I could quite possibly be hiding my crazy."

He smirked. "That is possible, but you're forgetting that you've also spent time with all of my friends."

My cheeks warmed and he noticed.

"All of them were raving about you," he informed me. "Deryn couldn't stop talking about how much fun he had with you today. This is the first time that I've heard him talk about a girl. It's definitely the first time I've heard him talk about a girl he hasn't slept with."

"How do you know if I've slept with him or not?" I asked defensively.

"We're best friends," he replied. "We tell each other everything."

"So, they know that we…"

"Yes, but not the circumstances or details."

"And what did they have to say when they learned I've dated all of you, but you and I have slept together?" I asked nervously.

"There were a couple high fives, and we all agreed that you're pretty awesome," he said and hit the stop button on the elevator, making it freeze between floors.

I glanced at it nervously and fought the urge to rush forward and hit the button. He walked towards me slowly, stopping a foot or so away from me.

"Why was I the only one you slept with?" he asked.

The others weren't really in situations that allowed for it.

"I just, didn't…" I replied softly.

"But you want to," he stated.

"I'm single," I reminded him. "And I had no idea that any of you knew each other, or that you all lived here. I met four sexy males at different times and they all wanted to spend time with me. I don't think it's wrong that I went out with you all. I don't think it's wrong that I had sex with you. I don't think it would be wrong for me to sleep with one, or all, of the others either. None of us are attached or taken. Am I wrong?"

"No, you are not wrong," he agreed. He reached out slowly and then pulled me forward against him. "I'm not selfish enough or possessive enough to try to make you choose. I wish I was the only one, but you have done nothing wrong and are still doing nothing wrong."

"Glad we agree," I whispered as I swallowed around the lump in my throat and set my hands on his chest, mostly to keep me balanced, but also because I *really* wanted to touch him.

"I am competitive, however," he replied and inhaled. "And you are too good to pass up." His lips were on mine and my hands wound around his neck instantly. He lifted me up and pushed me back against the wall of the elevator. He gripped my butt as he held me, his fingers digging into my skin, but not painfully.

I broke our kiss to kiss his neck and he moaned.

"Not now," he whispered and gently nipped my neck. "Though, the thought of taking you here is very tempting. Tonight, I want to enjoy our date and not lose out on it because dessert was too filling."

I chuckled and nipped his earlobe. "Okay."

He groaned and gripped my butt tighter. "If you do that again, I'll go back on what I just said."

I leaned back and held up my hands in surrender. "Okay."

He kissed me again and then set me down and hit the button on the elevator. "I'm glad that we agree."

"Me, too," I said and exhaled happily. I ran my fingers through my hair and smoothed my clothes down. "I was really worried that you guys would shut me out after you found out what happened."

"No, that's not how we are."

"Good to know."

We stepped outside and were met with several members of the media with cameras on, and bulbs flashing as they took pictures. Rhys put his arm around my shoulders and steered me away from them.

"Rhys, who is this new female? What is she doing in your apartment building? Is she part of your clan?"

"Has the Dragon Clan made a decision about the war?"

"Where was the artifact last seen?"

He didn't respond, and gently propelled me forward until we were away from the building, and across the street.

"My apologies about that. They're vicious at times," Rhys said with a soft sigh.

"Who are you?" I asked softly. "You seem to be someone important, but-"

"No one important," he replied. "They're just trying to get information out of us, but it won't work."

"You guys seem important," I commented as I looked back at the media who were now scowling at us.

He smiled. "Did you just say we are important to you?"

I scoffed, but smiled at him. "I hardly know you." It was strange, though. I did feel close to them. Was I that desperate for affection that I fell for the first guys to give me attention? Was I the crazy stalker chick? Oh no! I didn't want to be the crazy stalker chick.

He waved down a taxi and moved close to me on the back seat. His scent was a mixture of fire and something that I couldn't place, but knew it was a masculine smell. "I'd like to remedy that," he whispered to me.

"Remedy what?" I asked, sidetracked by his delicious scent and body heat.

"Not knowing each other."

"Sounds great to me," I said and looked up into his beautiful eyes. "Are you always warm or do you create extra heat when you want to?"

"I run warmer than a human, but I can create more heat if I want to," he replied.

The taxi pulled over and we climbed out onto the sidewalk. Rhys paid the driver as I stared at the restaurant we were headed into. *Simone's* was not just nice, but swanky. It was a restaurant joked only politicians and celebrities went into because no one else could afford it.

"You okay?" Rhys asked and set his hand on my lower back.

"You lied. You are someone important," I said. "Or at least famous."

"Come, our table is waiting," he replied and ushered me forward, completely ignoring what I had said. We stepped inside and the staff immediately led us to our table and brought out champagne.

Rhys smiled at me and said, "Order whatever you'd like."

The restaurant was somehow the perfect temperature. Most of the places I went to were either too hot or too cold, but they seemed to know the exact temperature appropriate. There were far less tables in this restaurant than the ones I frequented, which gave us more privacy to talk.

"Are you part of the mafia?" I asked him.

He smirked. "No."

"An actor?"

"No."

"Model?"

"Not currently, though I did model for a brief time when I was younger for extra money," he admitted.

"A member of the Summit?" I asked since I knew many of the clans had representatives who went to the Summit to meet and discuss issues with the other clans.

"I do not have a seat on the Summit," he replied.

"But you are affiliated with it somehow?"

"Yes."

"You're not a King?"

"No."

I tapped my chin as I tried to think about who he could possibly be that would allow him this much money and the eye of the media.

"Have you decided on what you want to order?" he asked, obviously trying to change the subject.

"I'm debating between the steak that costs twice my monthly

income or the chicken pasta that costs more than my rent," I replied with a relaxed and teasing smile.

He smiled back, completely at ease and relaxed as well. "I recommend the steak, medium rare."

I sipped the champagne, and my eyes widened at the delicious taste. "This is wonderful," I told him and took a bigger drink.

The waiter who came over was old, but his skin was unblemished and smooth. He also had sharp pointed teeth that came to his bottom lip. Vampire. "Are you ready to order?" he asked with a slight accent.

"My usual, Vlad," Rhys replied.

"Medium rare steak," I ordered.

"Mashed potatoes?" Vlad asked.

"Please," I replied with a nod.

"Very well," he said and bowed before leaving us to eat the bread I had not even seen him set on the table.

I took a piece and buttered it. "So, what do you do for work?" I asked Rhys.

"You asked me a ton of questions. I believe, it is my turn."

"Okay," I agreed.

"What do you do for work?"

"I write for a gaming company."

"What do you write?"

"I write the storylines for games. I've got one that I'm working on now, which I think is going to be pretty awesome."

"Really?"

I nodded.

"Do you like it?"

He was so focused on me, it was a bit overpowering, but also exciting. There was the potential for danger with him, but also for him to protect me from danger. The latter was something I desperately needed.

"I love it," I replied with a wide smile. "Not only do I love it, it was a big raise for me to move here and take the job."

"So, that's why you moved to Jinla?"

I nodded.

"What do you do when you aren't working?"

"Usually I play video games."

"Really?" he asked, eyebrows raised.

"Why is that hard to believe?" I asked him a bit defensively.

"I've never met a gorgeous woman who played video games."

"We exist," I assured him, silently pleased he had called me gorgeous.

"Clearly," he replied with a smirk. "What are your favorite types of games?"

"The kind you play," I said and chuckled. "I play a little bit of everything."

"What are you playing currently?"

"*Ghost 2.*"

"Do you play with a clan?"

"Yes," I said, shocked he knew what that was.

"Double standard," he whispered with a smirk.

"What?"

"You were shocked that someone as hot as me would know about clans."

He caught me.

"Possibly," I admitted.

"We have our own clan," he explained. "Deryn will be sad to learn that you already have a clan."

"He knows, actually. I can still play with you guys, but I've been with this clan since the first beta came out. So, I don't have any plans to leave them," I explained.

I chewed on the bread and closed my eyes at the perfect texture and flavor. How did they make bread so perfectly?

"I take it the bread is good?" he asked with a chuckle.

"Amazing," I replied and took another bite.

"What character do you main?" he asked.

"DPS."

"Really?"

I nodded. "And I'm guessing you're a tank?"

He blinked twice and then asked, "How'd you guess that?"

I smirked at him and buttered another piece of bread. "You seem like someone who would prefer a tank."

"Can you guess what Nico is?" he asked softly with a smirk.

"Obviously the DPS," I said with a chuckle. "He would be the one who wants to use magic."

"And what about Deryn?"

"That's a bit harder to guess. He seems like he would be good at all of the classes and would enjoy them all."

"True."

"If you're the tank and Nico is the DPS, then Fox is the healer and Deryn would be your additional DPS," I guessed.

He clapped softly. "Impressive."

"If I were to play with you guys, it would be beneficial if I was an additional DPS player," I replied.

Our food came out and we ate without much discussion. The food was almost worthy of the price tag and deserved to be savored. Once we finished, we didn't linger and left the restaurant, headed back to the apartment building.

"Thank you, for tonight," he told me and kissed my cheek. "I enjoyed learning more about you."

"I enjoyed tonight too," I replied and smiled happily. I was normally alone or with just one or two friends, but I had promised myself when I came here that I would be more outgoing and make more friends. So far, it was serving me well.

"Next time I get to learn more about you," I said adamantly.

"Deal," he agreed.

We waited for the elevator and I realized how tired I was. I leaned against the wall beside the elevator opening and Rhys played with some of my hair, twisting it around his finger gently and letting it fall away. The elevator opened and Deryn stepped out. His eyes widened as he took us in.

"Were you out together?" he asked.

"Yes, we were on a date," Rhys replied.

"What!" Deryn yelled.

"I told you that I wouldn't let you steal her away from me," Rhys told Deryn. "Besides, all of us are single, so there's nothing wrong with it."

"I didn't say there was anything wrong with it. I just can't believe you took her out so soon," Deryn explained.

"We had already set this date up a few days ago," I whispered, staring intently at the floor.

"Always one step ahead, aren't you?" Deryn grumbled.

"Let's get you to bed," Rhys said to me and ushered me inside of the elevator.

I put my face in my hands and sighed. What was I going to do about these guys? While I said that I didn't see anything wrong with it, part of me did feel bad. I would never forgive myself if I ended up ruining their friendship.

"Jolie," Rhys said loudly.

I jerked my head up and asked, "What?"

"It's your floor," he noted and waved at the open elevator doors.

"Oh, thanks," I said and headed towards the hallway.

He followed me to my door and kissed me goodnight. "Goodnight, my beautiful princess."

"Goodnight, Prince."

His left eye twitched. Holy monster's teats! No way!

"You're a Prince!" I screamed.

"I...yes."

My hand flew to my mouth as I held in my gasp. A Prince? He was a Prince? What had I fallen into?

"Say something," he begged.

"I'm just in shock," I explained and looked at him again. I really needed to pay attention better to the media. I would have known that as soon as I met him if I had been watching news stories or reading up on the happenings of Jinla.

"Please don't let this change anything," he whispered, his eyes downcast and fists clenched at his sides.

"Why me? You could have any girl that you want. You could have ten or twenty girls if you wanted. I'm no one. I'm nothing special. I'm just a socially anxious gamer."

"You are special. You are kind and beautiful. You are easy to be around. I've never met a human woman – any woman – who was so easy to be around. I'm so relaxed and calm with you. It's nice compared to my normally anxious life."

He was anxious? I supposed he would have a lot of duties as Prince.

"Don't worry," I told him and gripped one of his fists between both of my hands. "Knowing you are a Prince doesn't change how I feel about you."

He used my hands to jerk me forward and wrapped his arms around me in a hug. "Jolie," he whispered and sighed loudly.

"Eh?!" Nico yelled.

I jerked away from Rhys and found Nico walking down the hallway towards us.

"Nico," I whispered in shock.

"You told her you're a Prince? Why?" he demanded and stood before Rhys with a scowl.

"I didn't tell her that *I* am a Prince. She guessed that I am," he explained.

"You still admitted it though."

"I'm not going to lie to her about it. If she watches the news, she'll find out on her own."

"It's not fair. You've been out twice, while the rest of us…"

"It has nothing to do with fairness," Rhys snapped.

"Guys!" I yelled angrily.

They both turned to look at me with partially opened mouths.

I clenched my fists at my side and through clenched teeth said, "You are not allowed to fight about me."

"What?" Nico asked.

"You are friends. I'm a random chick…"

"You're not a…" Rhys began.

"I am!" I snapped. "I am a random chick and I refuse to become an issue between you friends. If that's going to be the case, I remove myself before there are any further issues."

Without waiting for a reply, I spun around, opened my door, and then slammed it closed behind me.

CHAPTER 4

I had spent my day off of work drinking and playing games in a rage.

"I think you should probably stop for the night," our clan leader said to me after I cursed for a few minutes straight when we lost the match.

I groaned. I couldn't even play video games right. I was ruining everything.

"Fine. See you guys later." I shut down my console and tossed my headset to the other couch. Playing longer would only upset me more, so I knew he was right, but it still made me mad.

The four males had been trying to contact me, but I had ignored them all, not returning any of their texts or calls. I had screwed up by continuing to see them after I found out that they were friends. I wasn't going to do it anymore. I wasn't going to cause issues between friends. I wasn't one of those girls.

I raised my bottle to my lips, but it was empty, not even a spare drop in it. "Dammit!" I growled and stood up. I needed more alcohol. After searching for a few minutes, I finally found my keys and cards, and then headed out of the apartment towards the nearest spirits store. I liked the place. The owner was a sweet old human woman with grey streaks through her hair that reminded me of lightning.

The sidewalk lurched a bit as I walked, seeming to randomly roll beneath my feet and make me unstable.

Or, I could have been drunk. Most likely I was drunk.

On the way to the store, I had to go by the park that I had met Fox in. I looked at it with a mixture of happiness and sadness. They were all so sweet. I had really enjoyed the time I had spent with them and could have seen myself becoming good friends with them

While looking at the park, I saw a huge group gathered, split into four factions, or so it appeared. At the center stood Rhys, Deryn, Fox, and Nico, each standing behind males sitting in chairs. Who brought big wood chairs to the park? What the heck was going on?

"What are they doing?" I asked myself out loud and squatted into the bushes to creep closer. They were still a bit away, but I could hear what they were saying better now. There were so many beings gathered and spread out among the trees. There had to be at least fifty, possibly more since some of them seemed to blur together and then multiply. Who were they all? I had to be extra quiet so that no one spotted me.

"It's been twenty years!" one of the men in the middle yelled. "It's been long enough! You've had long enough to return it to us!"

"What do you expect us to do?" another asked, this one standing near Fox. He had silver eyes and was definitely an elf once I focused hard enough on his features.

"I say we take over. Screw these pathetic humans. Let's kill them until we find our missing-"

"We are not killing the humans," Rhys snapped.

Hearing him defend my kind was a relief, but I did not like where the rest of them were headed with this discussion.

"Why not? They're pathetic! They don't deserve to live beside us," someone else said.

"Kill them!" another said.

My heart hammered against my chest as many began to agree.

One of the older gentlemen, who was seated in a chair at the center, raised his hand, and everyone quieted. "Raise your hand if you agree with killing the humans."

A few started to raise their hands, and I stumbled forward, tripping over the bush I had been hiding behind. Everyone turned, and the four men from my apartment all started to move towards me.

Crap. Thank you, drunken klutziness.

One of the people nearest made a grab for me. I tried to get away from him, but there were others and they were faster, grabbing my arms and stopping me. I squealed in fear and tried to break free, but their grips were too tight.

"Let her go," Rhys ordered them.

One of them released me, but the other two held on.

"Release her," Deryn ordered them with a snarl.

Reluctantly, they released me.

Tears streamed down my face, and I walked up to Rhys who reached me first, having been the closest. I gripped his shirt in my hands and said, "I don't want to die! I'm too young to die."

"Shh," he ordered me. "What are you doing here?"

"I was getting more booze and I saw you guys. Then they started talking about killing us. I don't want to die. I just met you, and I want to get to know you more."

"It's alright," Deryn told me, taking my hand and pulling me away from Rhys. "You're not going to die."

"But, they said…"

"We won't let anything happen to you," Fox said adamantly, smiling warmly at me.

"We aren't going to kill the humans," Nico assured me.

I knew that I should let the conversation drop and be reassured by their proclamations, but I was too drunk and stupid to stop. The words fell out of my mouth before I could stop them.

"I know we're stupid, and I know most of them aren't used to you, but if you give them a chance to learn, I know more will come to love you. Killing the humans won't make them like you. I only met you four, and yet I want to know more about you. If I'm dead, I won't get to learn about you and learn what makes you so amazing. I feel so content when I'm with you guys. It feels right to be with you, even if I can't anymore because you're fighting and I don't want to contribute to that. But, I don't want to be dead."

"Who the hell is she?" one of the men sitting in a chair asked. He had the same eyes as Nico.

"She's our friend," Nico told him.

"Get her out of here," he ordered him.

There was a book open in the middle of their circle showing a necklace with a pendant that looked very familiar. I pulled out of their holds and stumbled over to the book, dropping to my hands and knees to look at it.

"I've seen this," I mumbled and squinted to try to get a better look.

"Don't touch her!" Rhys ordered someone behind me.

"Don't touch the book!" someone ordered me.

I pulled my necklace out from beneath my shirt and tugged the chain over my head before setting it on the book beside the image. I was positive, it was the same necklace.

"Is this what you're looking for?" I asked and looked up at my friends who were standing in a protective circle around me. I hadn't realized how much trouble I was in until I saw that they were all using their powers at that moment to keep others away from me. All of their eyes were glowing and they all held weapons at their sides.

Everyone stopped what they were doing and turned around

to face me, and the book.

Deryn dropped to his knees beside me and looked at the book and my necklace. "It's…"

"It is!" Fox exclaimed.

"Where did you get this?" the man with Nico's eyes asked me.

"My Grandma gave it to me. She told me to keep it safe and that it would protect me from vampires." As soon as I said it, I clamped a hand to my mouth.

"Vampires? Is that who hurt you last year?" Rhys asked me.

"Maybe," I mumbled around my hand covered mouth. Maybe I should stop drinking so much alcohol.

Before I could grab the necklace back, the man with Nico's eyes snatched it.

"I need that!" I screamed. "It's the only thing preventing them from finding me!" I crawled towards him, the damp grass soaked into the knees of my jeans. "Please!"

"Jolie," Rhys whispered and placed his hands on my shoulders. "It's okay. You don't need the necklace."

"I do!" I yelled.

"This is a precious artifact to us," Fox whispered, his calming presence helping to push back the hysteria that was trying to build within me. "Please, may we have it back?"

"It's precious to you?" I asked. It was just a necklace. What was so special about it? Aside from it keeping the vampires away from me, Grandma hadn't said that it could do anything else.

"It is very precious to us," Rhys said.

"If it is yours, then I should return it to you," I said firmly. "I'm sorry for being selfish. Please, take your necklace."

A voice began laughing loudly, causing everyone to look around for the source. I already knew. I knew who was coming.

My body shook and my heart beat quickly. My palms began sweating and wrapping them around myself did nothing to help. No. How did he find me so quickly?

Rhys, Deryn, Fox, and Nico stood near me, taking protective

stances. It should have made me happy to know that they were willing to protect me even after what had happened, but it only made me worry about their safety.

"You've revealed yourself, little lamb," Demarcus said as he materialized a few feet away from us. He was tall, thin, and very powerful. His clothing was straight out of the eighteenth century, which he claimed had the best style, and refused to wear anything else.

"Who are you?" Rhys demanded.

"Oh, did you get another protector?" Demarcus asked.

"N-no," I stuttered quickly, getting to my feet.

"Do you remember what happened to the last protector you had? Do you remember how much he screamed? I'll be more than happy to do it again. Come with me now, and tell me how you escaped, and I'll leave these boys alone."

I stepped forward, ahead of the males, and started to walk towards him.

"That's a good girl. Come with me and I'll not hurt anyone," he said with a cocky smirk.

"Jolie!" Deryn called out.

Fox grabbed my arm and stopped me. "No, you can't have her."

"Oh?" Demarcus asked and quirked a brow. "You have a claim to her?"

"She's ours," Rhys growled, his eyes shifted into Dragon's eyes and his hands now had thick talons coming out of his fingertips. He came to stand on my right side and I looked at him in shock.

Deryn shifted into warrior form and stood behind me, setting his clawed paws lightly on my shoulders, his claws carefully pulled away from my skin to avoid hurting me. "Leave, or we'll take this as a challenge."

"Everyone," I whispered in shock. Even after causing them problems, they were willing to protect me?

"Do you really want me to kill these boys?" Demarcus asked me, frowning.

I turned to face the males and said, "Please. Please let me go."

"No," all four replied at the same time, not looking at me.

"You are ours," Deryn whispered. "You are our friend. You are important to us. We protect what is important to us."

"If you are hurt…"

"Don't have such little faith in us," Nico said with a smile. "Rhys isn't the only prince."

"What?" I asked, lost.

The four of them smiled at me.

"We're all princes," Fox explained.

"You may be strong, but you aren't strong enough to defeat us alone," Deryn said to Demarcus.

Demarcus smirked and five vampires materialized beside him.

"Clearly, you have a death wish," the male with Nico's eyes said. "Nico, I don't know who she is, but don't disgrace us by losing now that you've made such a claim."

"Just give me the girl," Demarcus snarled. "She's just one stupid human."

"No, she's not," Rhys growled and leapt forward, attacking Demarcus.

Nico stayed at my elbow, a staff in his hand which had a dark blue jewel on the end of it. I hadn't even seen him grab the staff. Where had it come from?

He set his hand on my shoulder and squeezed lightly. "It'll be okay."

How could it be okay? How could any of this be okay?

"Do you have a cape?" I asked softly, trying to keep my hysteria down as I watched the others fighting.

"Yes," Nico replied and added, "I'll show you it another night."

Demarcus and his vampires were ferocious and everyone

moved so fast that I couldn't keep up. Someone was going to get hurt. It was going to be my fault.

"Just give her to me!" Demarcus snarled at Rhys as they fought.

"No!" the four males yelled at him at the same time.

My legs wobbled and I dropped to my knees beside Nico. Something warm and painful at the same time spread from my chest throughout the rest of my body. What was going on? Nico stepped closer to me and began whispering something in what I was pretty certain was Greek. Air shimmered around us and a transparent bubble enveloped us.

"Tell me how you did it!" Demarcus demanded. "How did you escape?"

"It really bothers you that a human girl escaped, doesn't it?" Deryn taunted him, jumping in to back up Rhys. "How could you let such a weak being slip through your fingers?"

"You left the door unlocked," I whispered.

"What?" Demarcus asked. He leapt away from Deryn and Rhys to look at me across the park.

"You left the door unlocked. You and your men thought that leaving me broken and defeated was enough. You thought that I was too broken to have the will to run. You thought that my broken leg would keep me from trying." Fury began to build in me and I stood up, fists clenched at my sides.

"You underestimated my will to survive. You left to sleep for the day and I walked out of that building and all the way to a hospital. It was your own ego that allowed me to escape!"

Demarcus snarled. "A mistake I won't make twice."

Deryn lunged at him, but Demarcus expected the move and backhanded Deryn, sending him flying into the tree off to his right.

"Deryn!" I screamed, fear clawing its way up my throat. I couldn't lose him. I couldn't lose anyone else to Demarcus.

"Please, stop protecting me," I begged Nico. "Please, let him take me. You hardly know me. I'm not worth all of this."

"We know enough. You're our friend and someone we are all very interested in romantically. We will not let him take you and hurt you. We won't let anyone hurt you."

"You're all fighting each other already. I'm not worth ruining your friendships. I'm not worth getting hurt over. I'm just a stupid, drunk, human girl who doesn't know when to leave well enough alone."

"Ah, you're drunk. That explains a lot," Nico chuckled.

"What's that supposed to mean?" I asked with a glare in his direction. He wasn't phased by the glare, which meant I needed to work on my scary face.

"We can have this conversation another day, when you haven't been drinking. Okay?" Nico promised.

"Stop ignoring me!" Demarcus yelled and lunged towards me. One minute he was there and the next, he disappeared. My eyes widened and a small shriek escaped my lips as he appeared in front of me and tried to reach through the bubble to grab me. I jerked backward, but there turned out to be no need. The bubble exploded outwards in a flash of brilliant sunlight. Demarcus and his vampires screamed, then disintegrated before my eyes.

Nico picked me up and headed towards the apartment. I gripped the front of his shirt and stared mutely at his neck. What had just happened? It had all been so fast, that I wasn't sure what exactly occurred.

"You're safe," Nico whispered reassuringly. "We killed the vampire who was after you. He'll never hurt you again."

"He's *dead* dead?" I asked and squeaked at the end of my sentence.

"Yes."

"The artifact is returned!" someone shouted behind us. It seemed I wasn't the only one in a bit of a shell-shocked state.

"She saved the humans. She ended the war," someone nearby whispered as we walked through those in attendance.

"You hear that?" Deryn asked, walking on my left side. "You're a hero."

"I didn't do anything," I countered. "You saved me from the vampires."

"You saved us," Fox said adamantly. "Our four factions have been at each other's throats for a long time trying to locate that artifact. You found it and returned it to us."

"We need to ask her some questions," someone said behind us.

"No," Rhys snapped. "She is not well. You may ask her questions a different day. For now, be happy that this human ended the war."

"What's her name?" another person asked.

"Jolie," I replied. "My name is Jolie."

I WOKE THE NEXT MORNING TO A HALLWAY OF FLOWERS, MOSTLY roses, but all from different people, if my cursory glance at the cards accompanying them were correct. I stood, transfixed in my doorway as I looked at them.

"You're popular now," Deryn informed me from down the hallway.

I turned to look at him and saw he was not smiling, like he normally did. Instead, he radiated sadness. His eyes could not have drooped more if he was a puppy. My heart constricted.

"What do you mean?" I asked, my voice barely more than a whisper.

"Most of these are from males wanting to be your suitor," he explained. "You proved that you did not care what race we were, and that you are selfless. Those are important traits in a mate. Plus, you ended the war. You're a hero...heroine."

"I'm not a hero," I whispered. There had to be at least thirty vases here. Hundreds, maybe thousands, of dollars' worth of flowers. "What am I supposed to do with these flowers?"

"Keep them?" Deryn suggested.

"Did any of you send them?" I asked and turned my head away to avoid his eyes.

"No."

"So, if I throw them away, you won't get upset?" I asked and looked back at him.

"On the contrary, I will assist," he replied, his joyful energy returning.

I turned and he smiled warmly at me for just a moment before it wilted again. "You were avoiding us yesterday," he said matter-of-factly.

I nodded.

"Why?"

Rhys stepped into the hallway and stopped when he saw the flowers, Deryn, and me.

"I was avoiding you because I think it's best if I don't associate with you four," I admitted.

"Why?" Rhys demanded. "And you can't lie and try to say it is because we're Others."

"Because you are friends," I answered truthfully.

Fox and Nico walked into the hallway, chatting softly, but froze when they saw the situation.

What were all four of them doing in my hallway? Were they all coming to see me?

"You four are friends, right?" I asked them.

All four nodded.

"I refuse to be the girl who gets between you. I'm not like that. I hate girls like that. I spend ninety percent of my time talking with men. Half of them have stories about a girl that ruined a friendship of theirs. I won't let that happen to you four. You are princes! You have to get along so that your races get along. If I drive a wedge between you-"

"Why do you think that you will cause us to stop being friends?" Fox asked.

I slid down my closed door and wrapped my arms around my bent knees. I was a selfish woman. No matter what they said about the necklace, I was not a heroine or selfless. I was a vile, selfish creature.

"I can't choose," I whispered and placed my forehead against the top of my knees. "I can't choose between you four." I didn't know them that well, but they each offered something different. Rhys was a serious alpha, but had a soft side. Deryn was playful and strong. Fox was sweet and relaxing. Nico was silly and I could tell he was a trickster. I found that in this short time that I had known them, I was already attached to them. Thinking about being separated from them made the center of my chest hurt. Actually, ever since yesterday, my chest had felt strange.

"Does anyone smell that?" Deryn asked, lifting his nose in the air and moving towards me, stepping carefully around the flowers.

"Who said you had to choose?" Fox asked.

"Nico and Deryn both got mad at Rhys and Rhys admitted that he's competitive," I explained.

"We never said you had to choose between us," Rhys pointed out.

"Not yet, but soon you will. I've only been out with you each one or two times. Even if you let me continue to date you, eventually you will make me choose. I don't want to. I want to be friends with all four of you."

"Oh no, she's trying to friend-zone us!" Nico screeched and then gave me a smile. Yep, trickster.

I lowered my knees and picked up the nearest flowerpot. It had petunias in it. The card said it was from Anton and he had given me his phone number. Deryn had been right. These were guys trying to date me. What the heck?

Deryn continued sniffing as he went past me, but stopped and spun towards me. His eyes widened and he jerked the pot from my hand.

"Hey!" I shouted in shock.

He threw the pot out the window at the end of the hallway, shattering the glass.

"What the hell was that about?" I asked him. "Just because you don't like them, doesn't mean-"

A huge explosion rocked the building, making me scream in shock and fall to my side. Deryn picked me up and ran down the hallway.

"Run!" he yelled.

"What's-"

The next explosion made the entire building sway and Deryn stumbled a step as he raced down the stairway. My arms tightened around his neck and I closed my eyes, praying to whatever god might be listening to let us survive. I did not want to get crushed by a building.

Cold air hit me and when I opened my eyes, we were across the street from the apartment building.

"Wh-What happened?" I asked and shivered, my heart pounding and my palms damp with sweat, but still unable to release Deryn.

"Bombs," he whispered, his eyes focused on the building and a scowl on his face. "Someone sent you bombs."

"They tried to kill me?" I asked, my throat tightening as soon as I said the words.

"It would seem so," Fox whispered.

I looked around and exhaled in relief to find the four of them with me. "You're all safe," I said, feeling my back relax. Deryn set me on my feet, but kept his arm around my waist, since I didn't think I could stand up on my own at the moment.

"Why?" Fox asked Rhys.

Rhys's eyes had changed to green and gold, like dragon's eyes and he grumbled in a deep and rocky voice, "It seems some aren't happy that she ended the war."

"It will be impossible to find out who sent them," Nico whispered.

"I could have died," I whispered and looked up at Deryn. "Thank you."

He didn't smile at me. He wasn't even looking at me.

"We need to figure out what we're going to do," he said to Rhys.

Rhys nodded. "Yes."

The fire trucks came, and I stepped away from the men to sit on the curb. This was not how I expected today to go at all! I was grateful that they had saved me, but the conversation we had started in the hallway was far from over.

"Do you think my apartment is okay?" I asked them softly.

"The bombs weren't packing much explosive power, but we don't know how many of those flowers had them. We won't know the damage until we go inside," Fox said and knelt beside me. He stroked my hair slowly and it was oddly relaxing.

"I hope my games are okay," I whispered and tried *really* hard not to lean into his hand.

"If they aren't, I'm sure we can find replacements," Deryn assured me. "Your data is all saved under your login, so it won't matter if you have to get a new console."

"Right," I agreed, feeling a little better.

Fox shifted into a red fox and climbed into my lap. My brain was on overload from all of the events, so I didn't even blink at his sudden transformation. Instead, I wrapped my arms around him, moving his head to my shoulder, and buried my face in his fur.

"Cheater," Rhys whispered.

The apartment manager walked over to us and sighed loudly. "Luckily the damage isn't too bad. The door and hallway wall of Jolie's apartment are destroyed, but most of your stuff survived.

It wasn't enough to make it through the floor or ceiling of the hallway, so everyone else is good."

"Great," I mumbled into Fox's fur.

"The detectives are there now, trying to figure out who did it," the manager said. "So, you need to stay away from that floor for now."

"We can all go to my apartment for now," Rhys instructed everyone.

The group started to head across, but I couldn't move. Someone had tried to kill me. If Deryn hadn't smelled the explosive and grabbed me, I would be scattered about the hallway. There would be chunks of me with the flowers and dirt. Someone who went so far as to put explosives in flowers didn't strike me as the kind who would give up easily. What would their next attack be? Where would it be? I was in danger, and I was human. I had no way of protecting myself. There was nothing I could do. I was going to die. This was even more frightening than when Demarcus had been after me. At least with him, I knew the danger and what it looked like. This had no face. This had no warning. I was at a complete loss.

Fox leapt out of my arms, and Nico picked me up gently, cradling me against his body. "You are safe. You are alive. We are here for you. No one will harm you while you're with us."

How could he be so certain? They weren't invincible. They could be injured too.

"You'll be killed too," I whispered.

"Did Demarcus kill us?" he asked.

"No," I admitted reluctantly.

He headed to the apartment building, his head held high as he carried me, the others walked around us in a shield of protection, hiding me from the media as they tried to snap pictures.

"We will not let you die," he told me adamantly.

Something slammed into what appeared to be a translucent

shield around the five of us. On closer inspection, I realized that it was a large caliber bullet.

Rhys stepped back, shifted into his dragon form and took to the sky, disappearing into the smoke.

"Rhys!" I screamed.

The three remaining men hurried inside and to an apartment on the first floor that was unlocked. I assumed it belonged to one of them, but didn't ask.

"He'll be fine," Nico assured me.

"Bullets can't penetrate dragon's scales," Deryn said with a small smile.

A dragon's roar shook the building and I clutched Nico tighter. He sat on the couch, keeping me in his lap, and stroked my back.

"Food?" Fox asked me.

My stomach was a knotted mess of anxiety. I shook my head and climbed out of Nico's lap, sitting on a leather recliner that was unclaimed, and curled my legs up beneath me. My heartbeat quickened and I let my body fall sideways, my head resting on the arm of the chair.

"Jolie?" Deryn asked, turning to fully face me from behind the couch.

"Fine," I lied and closed my eyes.

Again. People were being put in harm's way because of me, again. I wasn't special. I wasn't gorgeous. Pretty, yes, but not a ten. Why did people keep getting hurt because of me? Maybe I needed to become a hermit. Could I get internet while being a hermit? I needed internet no matter what. There were too many games I wanted to play that required internet.

The door opened and I flew out of the chair, running to Rhys who had no visible injuries or blood stains anywhere I could see.

"Rhys!" I yelled and threw my arms around him. He hugged me back, pulling me close to his body.

"You find him?" Deryn asked.

"Yes, the police have him now."

"Did you get hurt?" I asked after stepping back from him.

He smiled. "No."

Finally, my heart unclenched and I felt the adrenaline leave me, fatigue setting in heavily. I went back to the chair and lay down again. Rhys was safe. All four of them were safe. Everything was okay for now.

"What's the plan?" Fox asked. "It's clear that they are after her and aren't going to give up."

"We're going to take shifts," Rhys said. "One of us needs to be with her at all times."

"That's a bad idea," I whispered without opening my eyes.

"Why?" Rhys asked.

"I'm bad luck. Maybe I should leave town for a while. I could take a vacation and wait for things to calm down."

"Or, they could follow you and kill you," Nico said bluntly.

True, but then none of them would be in harm's way.

"I'll watch her tonight," Rhys said. "Nico, you'll have to take her to and from work, since you have a shield. Tomorrow, we'll put the schedule together."

CHAPTER 5

Warm arms encircled me and a warm body pressed against my back. Nature called, or I would have stayed with him. I slid out of bed and stumbled into the bathroom, staring at my worn reflection. The bathroom was immaculate, not a single thing out of place. I opened the top drawer and found spare toothbrushes, the kind that had tooth-paste already on them.

"Score."

Quickly, I brushed my teeth, ran my fingers through my hair, and used the bathroom.

When I came back to the room, Rhys still lay on his bed, his shirtless torso on display for my viewing pleasure. And it was *definitely* a pleasure. He had a perfectly shaped chest, one that was all thanks to genetics. His abdominals were so defined, that I could see water getting stuck in the grooves.

His room was super tidy as well. He had a few pictures, all of them of the four princes, from toddler age all the way to the present day, during outings and events. I envied their friendship. I envied a friendship that had lasted a lifetime. I had one friend that I'd known since junior high, but we weren't that close anymore.

I crawled back into bed and lay my head on his chest, listening to the beat of his heart, and enjoying his warmth.

He wrapped his arms around me.

"Morning," he murmured.

"I'm sorry I woke you," I whispered and tried to get out of bed.

"Stay," he begged and held me tight.

I stilled and then made myself comfortable on his chest again. He was so warm and I felt incredibly safe lying in bed with him. I knew if someone busted into the room, he would protect me, no matter what the danger was.

"Thank you," I whispered. "I should have thanked you all yesterday, but I was a bit shell shocked."

"Are you ready to talk about relationships yet?" he asked, opening one eye to look at me.

"I told you guys, I don't want to come between you all. You've been friends your entire lives. If I did something to ruin that –"

"We all talked last night," he said and opened his other eye.

"Oh?" That was hardly fair. I couldn't argue with them while I was asleep.

"After you fell asleep. We all agreed that we felt a connection with you."

"A connection?"

"It's harder for humans to sense, but we all share a connection with you and with each other."

"Wait, you're bi?"

Not that I cared what they were. It honestly wouldn't change anything.

"No," he chuckled. "The four of us have a warrior's bond. However, with you, we all somehow added you to that bond."

"Warrior-"

He sighed.

"You're not a warrior. You're our…"

"Whore?"

He scowled at me.

"Absolutely not. You're like…our Queen."

"Queen?" I asked in disbelief.

"Don't give me that scowl," he teased and tapped the tip of my nose with his finger. "Generations ago, the queen would be assigned guards. The guards would develop a warrior's bond between themselves to be able to find each other and communicate easier. The Queen and her guards would develop a bond to help her call upon them in times of need and so they could sense her distress."

"I'm not a queen," I pointed out. Not that he didn't already know that.

He ran a hand down his face and sat up. "I'm sorry, I'm not very good at explaining things like this. Nico is better at it. I'll have him explain it to you as you go to work."

"My clothes-"

"I'm going to go with you to your apartment, so you can pack your essentials and clothing."

He stood up and stretched, giving me ample time to admire his muscular back and perfect ass.

"Let me brush my teeth and grab something to eat on the way out the door," he said around a big yawn.

He didn't take as long as I thought he would, but we were still pushing it and I had to rush to pack my things. He had me leave my stuff in his apartment and Nico was there waiting for me when we arrived.

"You're going to be late," he said in a sing-song voice.

"Apparently, dragons aren't morning people," I teased.

"Mornings would be better if they started after noon," Rhys said and yawned. "You got her?"

Nico nodded. "I've got it handled."

Rhys pecked me on the cheek and walked inside, yawning. "I'm going to go back to sleep now," he informed us.

Nico clapped his hands and a bubble appeared around us. A moment later, it disappeared from sight, but I could still sense it because it blocked the wind.

"Ready?" he asked.

I nodded, and we walked out of the apartment building and towards my job, passing by other males and females of various races going to their jobs as well.

"Did you sleep well?" he asked.

"I didn't even feel Rhys move me," I admitted. "I just went to sleep in the chair and woke up in his bed."

My hand flew to my mouth and I wondered if he would be upset that Rhys had slept in the same bed as me.

"Nothing happened, I-"

"Jolie, I know you slept with him already. Plus, this won't work if we all freak out when someone does something with you. We aren't like that. We aren't a bunch of jealous idiots."

"Rhys said you would be better at explaining about the bond," I told him. "He mentioned me being part of your bond, but not the warrior's one. He said something about Queens, but it didn't make sense, since I'm just a human."

He nodded. "He always gets frazzled when talking about it. So, he told you about the queen and her guards having a bond, right?"

I nodded. The light changed, so we had to stop at the cross-walk and wait. There were quite a few people walking about and many were looking at Nico. He didn't seem to notice, his hands in his pockets as he leaned against the light pole with relaxed shoulders.

"Normally, there's a big ceremony and they all make the bond as one. We aren't exactly sure how it happened, but you became part of our bond. That's not how it normally works. Normally, our bond is completely separate from the Queen's bond. I did some research on it, but haven't turned up anything yet."

"So, what you're saying is that I'm bound to you guys, but not like a queen would be, more like as another warrior, but still different?"

None of this made any sense to me.

"Sort of," he murmured and chewed on the inside of his cheek.

The light changed and we resumed walking.

"So, is there a way to remove me from the bond?" I asked and looked up at him.

His eyes grew wide and he looked at me. "What? You want to break the bond?"

"Well, if the bond isn't right, shouldn't we get rid of it?"

"It's not as simple as taking off a ring," he explained. "It's painful and it can't be repaired once broken."

"But, if you decided you wanted to bond with me later, couldn't you do it like the Queen's bond? Not that I am saying you should bond with me, since I'm not royalty or anything."

"Theoretically, yes. However, since I've never heard of this type of bond before, I don't want us to break it without knowing the consequences. For all we know, if you break it, you might die."

Nico was very blunt and straight to the point. I liked that about him.

"So, do you guys, feel me?" I asked and tilted my head to the side as I thought about how weird it must be to sense other people when they weren't near you.

"Yes," he nodded. "We can sense where you are and we can sense your mood."

"My mood?"

"Yep. For instance, right now you're anxious and confused. Yesterday, you were having an anxiety attack, but you lied to us about it."

Heat spread across my cheeks. "Oh."

"You don't have to be embarrassed. Anxiety is a common issue, mainly among humans, but Others are known to experience it as well. Next time though, you could just ask one of us to help you."

"How can you help me with an anxiety attack? They don't make sense most of the time anyway. Sometimes they just come on out of nowhere, for no reason."

"Fox is very skilled at helping people with turmoil. That's why he shifted into his fox form for you when we were outside. He could sense your anxiety spiking and knows that a lot of humans are calmed by furry animals. It did help, until we got into the apartment and Rhys went after the gunman."

"I wish you guys would see things from my side," I muttered.

We stopped in front of my office building, and he turned to face me. "So, tell me your side. We don't know anything about what happened between you and Demarcus, or what he meant about a protector before."

"I have to go to work," I said, glad to dodge the topic.

"I'll be here to pick you up at five. Please, don't step outside. Just wait for me."

I nodded.

He opened the door for me, and once I stepped inside, he removed the shield and kissed my cheek. "See you later."

I smiled and jogged to the elevator to go to work.

"You've been holding out on me," Justina accused with hands on her hips next to her cubicle.

"Uh?" I replied, smartly.

She pointed out the window. "That's Nico, prince of the Mages. He walked you to work and kissed you like you were the best of friends. What the fuck? How do you know him? Were you involved in the explosion last night at their apartment building? Are you dating him? Have you slept with him?"

I stood with my mouth open, prepared to answer her, but she

didn't stop the onslaught of questions. So, I closed my mouth and waited for her to stop venting.

She took a breath and looked at me expectantly.

"Oh? Are you done shooting questions at me a mile a minute?" I asked.

"Spill," she ordered me.

"Yes, I live in the apartment building with them. Yes, I was involved in the explosion. I'm fine though, thanks for your concern. We are friends. I have not slept with him. We are dating, I think? Maybe?"

Were we? Was what I had with these guys considered dating?

"What happened with the guy you went out to lunch with?"

"We're dating too, I think."

This was so confusing. I wished I knew more about the bond we had. How could I have joined their bond?

"You go, girl!" she said and smiled.

After rolling my eyes at her and sitting down, I got lost in my work. At noon, I realized that I hadn't made a lunch and I wasn't supposed to go outside. Justina had brought her lunch, so I didn't want to ask her to go buy me something.

People started whispering loudly and I stood up to see what was going on, to find them all looking outside. I walked to join the crowd and smiled when I saw Deryn shift from wolf to man and head into the building.

"What is he doing here?"

"He's so hot."

"That's the second prince I've seen at this building today."

Justina looked at me with a raised eyebrow.

I smiled and waited until he entered the office, a backpack in hand. He looked over everyone and then saw me, and smiled.

"Hey," he said and maneuvered around the gaping people to me. "Rhys told me he forgot to mention lunch and you were still kind of frazzled. So, I offered to bring you some food." He opened his backpack and pulled out a plastic lunchbox. It had a kid's hero character sticker on it.

"You're the best," I told him and kissed his cheek before grabbing the box from him and heading towards the lunchroom where we could sit at a table and eat.

He followed behind me and asked, "Did you sleep well?"

"Yes. I didn't even wake up when Rhys moved me," I explained. This time not bringing up waking up in his bed and hopefully avoiding that conversation.

"That's good. We were all worried about you," he whispered. He pushed open the door to the lunchroom for me and conversation inside immediately died.

I ignored it and headed to an open table. He sat next to me and turned his chair so he could face me.

"Are you going to eat too?" I asked.

He shook his head. "I already ate."

The lunch he had brought me consisted of a turkey sandwich, chips, a granola bar, and a fruit snack.

I giggled and took out the sandwich. "You packed me a kid's meal."

He smiled. "I thought you would enjoy it."

While I ate my sandwich, I looked at the others, all staring openly and not caring how rude it was.

"You learn to ignore them," he whispered to me, leaning his elbow on the table and scooting his chair closer to mine.

"Why'd you come in wolf form?" I asked after finishing the food in my mouth.

"You saw?"

I nodded. "I saw you through the window."

He scowled at me. "You shouldn't be standing next to windows. They had a sniper, remember?" he told me harshly.

The sandwich suddenly tasted like sawdust. I hadn't thought about it.

"I'm sorry. I didn't…"

He nodded and brushed my hair behind my ear. "I'm sorry for snapping. I just want to make sure you stay safe," he explained.

"Couldn't they just come into my work?" I asked.

He nodded. "They could."

"What do I do-"

"Fox said that he has a plan for that. He didn't tell us what it was, but he said he would be able to put it into play tomorrow."

"Okay," I whispered and set my sandwich down.

"Hey," he whispered and maneuvered his face in front of mine.

"Yeah?"

"You're beautiful," he said and smiled.

I laughed and shook my head. "You flirt."

His smile widened and he leaned forward to kiss me lightly on the lips. "Truth speaker."

"What's it like to be able to sense me?" I asked softly.

His eyes widened. "They told you?"

I nodded.

"It still doesn't make much sense to me," I admitted after a moment of silence.

He ran a hand through his hair and said, "It doesn't make sense to us either. Not that we would have had a problem making you our queen, eventually. It's just...there's usually a process and specific steps needed. None of us know when it happened or who did it. Well, we all did it. It's not something only one of us can do."

"Nico said if we broke it, that I might die," I said with barely any breath.

He turned his chair and draped his arm across my shoulders. "We aren't going to break it, so you don't have to worry."

"But you didn't choose this. You guys didn't choose for me to be added."

"We did, somehow. It's complicated. Like I said, we all did it. Somehow, we all decided to add you. It's just strange that it didn't create the Queen's bond between us and instead added you to our bond, but the bond isn't something that happens against the group's will."

"Will it hurt you if the bond is broken?"

"It hurts whenever a bond is broken."

"Will it kill you?"

He shook his head. "The warrior's bond was created so that if one of us dies, it won't incapacitate the others. It's designed that way so we can protect the queen. We will experience pain at the warrior's loss, but not death."

"So, then shouldn't it be okay to remove me?"

"We don't know. This is uncharted territory. Fox and Nico are in contact with their elders to try to see what they can find out from them and if they know anything. We'll know more soon."

I packed up my lunch and then leaned my head against his shoulder.

"They said you all talked about our relationship," I whispered.

He nodded.

"I'm worried that I'll ruin your friendships."

"You won't," he assured me.

"How can you be so sure?" I asked and tilted my head to look up at him.

He smiled and whispered, "Because the only thing we care about is keeping you near us. We all want you. We all care about you."

"Is that because of the bond?" I asked. Wondering if the bond made them like me more. We did barely know each other, after all.

He nodded. "Partially. We were all interested in you before the bond formed though."

"I can't choose between you four," I whispered. "I'm selfish, I know. I just...can't."

He brushed his lips across my forehead and whispered, "We

aren't asking you to choose, Jolie. We are asking you to let us all have you."

I chuckled and shook my head.

"That sounds so wrong," I whispered.

"It's not. In the days before humans ruled, the queen didn't have a king or a husband, she had her guards."

"I'm not a queen," I reminded him.

"You can be our queen," he whispered in my ear.

A shiver raced up my spine and it had nothing to do with fear or cold.

CHAPTER 6

"Jolie, are you going to introduce me?" Justina asked with a scowl on her face as she sat in the chair across from us.

"Deryn, this is my friend, Justina. Justina, this is-"

"I know who he is," she said and smiled at him. "He's the famous Prince Deryn of Clan Wolf. One of the first wolves to learn how to talk in warrior form. Beloved of his house. And, one of the most sought-after bachelors in the Others circle."

He smiled at her. "I like her. She should announce me when we go places."

Justina leaned on her elbows on the table and her eyes flashed red. "Hurt her, and I'll be the first to announce your death."

His eyes flashed gold, but the smile stayed on his lips. "Good to know."

"Justina. Deryn. We are all friends," I growled at them.

"Oh, she's got the growl down," Justina whispered. "Just how much time have you been spending with her."

"Not enough," Deryn countered and then stood up. "I have to go, but remember, stay away from the windows and wait for Nico to come get you."

"Thank you for bringing me lunch," I said and hugged him.

He hugged me back, and then spun and dipped me to kiss me deeply.

People gasped and began talking excitedly.

He helped me stand back up and then bowed to me in a grand flourish. "Until tonight, my queen."

He winked, and then we watched his great derriere leave the room.

I flopped down into the chair and sighed. I was in over my head.

"Why do you have to stay away from windows and wait for the Mage Prince to come?" Justina asked. "What haven't you told me?"

"Well…"

What could I tell her?

"…I ended the war and people weren't happy about that. They tried to kill me twice already."

Her eyes flashed red. "Why am I just now hearing about this?"

For the first time, I found myself afraid of Justina.

"I, um, it just happened last night and-"

"And you have a cell phone capable of texting," she snapped.

"A lot of shit has happened to me, Justina. I'm sorry I didn't text you, but I'm barely keeping it together right now. Please, don't add to it."

Her scowl stayed in place, but she nodded once. "Fine."

"Thank you," I said with a long sigh.

"So, how many Princes are you dating?" she asked with a smirk.

"How much do you know about magic?" I asked her instead of answering. She was a dhampir, after all. She had to know something.

"Quite a bit, actually," she admitted to me. "What's going on?"

"Do you know about the bonds that they develop with queens and guards?"

Her eyes widened. "Yes."

"Have you ever heard of one developing with the female becoming part of the warriors' bond, instead of developing a separate one?"

"What have you gotten yourself into?" she asked me softly and glanced around at the tables near us. She gripped my arm and pulled me out of the room and down the hall to one of the empty conference rooms. She drew the blinds, locked the door, and turned to face me.

"I met them all individually. I told you about my meetings with a few of them."

"How many are there?" she asked.

"Four."

"All princes?"

I nodded.

She let out a low whistle. "You met the Four Princes of Jinla. The quad of friends that every girl has been dying to break into. You broke into their group in less than a week!"

"I discovered that they all live in my apartment complex with me and they're all friends. They told me that they don't know how it happened, but at some point, they added me to their bond. They said it was not a conscious thing, but it can't be done without all of their consent. So, somehow, I joined their bond. Nico said it is possible I might die if they try to remove me from the bond."

"I've heard of it happening before," she told me softly.

"And?" I asked, my throat dry and the sad look on her face totally not reassuring.

"She removed herself from the bond and died," she whispered sadly.

Great. There went that idea.

"So, they're stuck with me?" I whispered and looked at my pathetic human hands.

"Yes. Though, with your current predicament, it will be a

good thing. They will have the uncontrollable desire to protect you."

"How did it happen for the one you know about?"

"They were all protecting the female from something and during the altercation, they expressed their interest in her. The bond formed, but since she was human, it added her to their bond and did not make a Queen's bond. The only perk, is that when she died, they didn't feel it the way they would have if she had been their queen."

"Do you think it's a defense mechanism to protect them from having a human with a shorter lifespan added? Since our lives are so much shorter?"

She nodded.

"So, does this mean the feelings they feel towards me-"

"The bond deepens the bonds of friendship, but not romantic feelings. Your friendships will grow immensely, but the romance will be something you have to work on with them separate of the bond. One positive of this, it means they won't feel jealousy towards each other when one is with you and not the others."

This was all so insane and out of control. When could this have happened? What could have-

"The park," I whispered in shock.

"What?"

"The night I returned the stolen artifact, an old enemy showed up intent on taking me back with him to torture me. They protected me. They all stood together and told me that I am important to them. They said I was their friend and they would protect me. That must be when the bond developed."

She ran a hand through her hair and thought about it. "It sounds likely that was when it happened," she agreed. "Though, as I'm not one of the participants, I can't be sure."

I pulled out my phone and dialed Nico. He answered before the first ring had even ended.

"What's wrong? You're upset," he said.

Stupid bond.

"I have answers about the bond," I told him.

"You do?" he asked, shocked.

Yes, I was capable of finding things out too. I imagined sticking my tongue out at him, but he wouldn't see it even if I did.

"Are the others working right now?" I asked.

"No, we're all at Rhys's."

"Can you come get me? I can explain it to everyone."

"What about work?"

"I can't focus on work right now," I admitted.

"I wouldn't be able to focus with four princes waiting for me either," Justina teased.

I glared at her and she laughed.

"I'll be there in a few minutes," he said and hung up.

We went to our desks and I typed a message to my supervisor, letting him know that I wasn't feeling well and would be leaving early. Luckily, I was ahead of my deadlines, so it wasn't a big deal.

"How did you meet them?" Alexandria asked. She was a short, curvy woman with a love for gossip.

"Who?" I asked, feigning ignorance.

"The princes," she said and rolled her eyes.

"Oh, we live in the same apartment building."

"How-"

She was interrupted by Nico walking inside the room and heading towards me with a determined look on his face.

"I need to go," I told her, grabbed my stuff, and met him halfway.

He hugged me and I relaxed into him, not realizing I was so close to having an emotional breakdown. I was normally really good about keeping my emotions hidden.

The emotions were easier to stuff down, once I touched him, and I smiled at him in appreciation.

"Ready?" he asked.

I nodded and walked beside him out of the building, ignoring the stares of everyone.

"What's wrong?" he asked me. "Aside from what you have to tell us?"

"You guys probably aren't going to be happy about what you hear," I whispered.

"It will all be fine," he assured me.

I wasn't sure.

Once we got into Rhys's apartment, all eyes turned to me. It was too much pressure to have four alpha males staring at me like that. Instead of sitting and letting the pressure build on me, I paced behind the couch and relayed Justina's information to them. When I finished, I continued pacing, waiting for their responses.

"It was likely the night at the park," Rhys confirmed. "We all vowed to protect her."

"Agreed," Nico said.

Tears brimmed in my eyes.

"I'm sorry," I whispered. "If I hadn't gone to the park that night, none of this would have happened. I knew I should have stayed away from you all."

"Fate cannot be stopped," Fox informed me.

"Fate? This isn't fate," I replied with a scoff. "This is my bad luck being pushed on you four. I'm a curse."

Fox stepped in front of me, making me stop walking. "You are not a curse."

"You are jaded by the bond now. You care for me as a friend because of this-"

"We cared about you before the bond was formed," Deryn countered.

"At least you guys won't be in much pain when I die," I said. The only positive thing that came out of all of this.

"You're not going to die," Rhys growled.

"Eventually, I will," I replied. "Way sooner than you all will."

The weight of everything came crashing down on me and I dropped into the leather recliner Rhys had vacated a moment ago. It was still warm from him and I curled up on it.

"Well, at least we know what happened," Nico whispered.

"It doesn't change anything, really," Rhys admitted.

Fox knelt in front of me and smoothed my hair back. "Do you want me to shift?"

I shook my head. While his fox form was comforting, I preferred his human form.

"Can you pet me?" I asked, blushing as I asked for something so ridiculous.

He didn't smirk, laugh, or question me. He just sat on the floor next to the chair I was on, and started petting my hair. "Are you hungry?" he asked softly.

"No," I whispered in response, my eyes closing at not just the soothing touch, but his reassuring presence. How could someone be so calming?

My cell phone rang on the coffee table where I had set it when I came in, but I ignored it. It rang immediately again without the person bothering to try to leave a voicemail.

"Hello?" Rhys answered.

I opened my eyes, shocked he would answer my phone, but also not really caring. I had nothing to hide with them.

"What are you talking about?" he asked. "She's not at work right now. She left early." He said to whoever was on the phone. His eyes widened and he grabbed the remote for his television. "Thanks for calling. We'll let her know you called. No, I promise, she's safe and sound. Bye."

He turned to a news station and I stared in disbelief at what was left of the building I should have been working in.

I leapt up and ran towards the door, but Deryn grabbed me and stopped me.

"Justina!" I screamed. "I have to check on-"

"There are no casualties," he said in a loud voice to get my attention.

"They evacuated everyone before it went off," Rhys said and pointed at the screen where the headline said just that.

I slumped into Deryn. "So, everyone's okay?"

They nodded.

My phone rang again, this time it was Justina calling, so I ran and snatched the phone from Rhys.

"Are you okay?" I asked her.

"Yes. Let me talk to Deryn."

"Why?" I asked a bit miffed she wouldn't want to talk to me after almost getting blown up.

"Jolie," she whispered in exasperation.

I grumbled, but gave him the phone.

"Deryn," he answered. He listened a moment and then my phone creaked as his grip tightened. "Got it," he replied and set my phone gently on the table, the screen cracked on one of the corners.

"What?" I asked.

"A package was delivered for Jolie," he told everyone. "Justina knew about the problems and smelled the package because she thought it was odd Jolie would be receiving one after starting so recently. She could smell the bomb thanks to her dhampir abilities and got everyone evacuated. The bomb squad inadvertently set it off after everyone was evacuated."

Another attempt on my life. This time, my entire building had been put at risk. Justina had been at risk. If I had still been there and received that package, I would have been blown to pieces. Why were these people always trying to blow me up?

Fox picked me up and carried me out of Rhys's apartment, despite the guys' protests. He took the elevator to his apartment and once inside, set me on a soft fur rug in front of a fire that had started as soon as we had entered. His apartment had very few decorations and hardly any furniture. I stayed in my fetal position on the rug while he did whatever he was doing in the kitchen.

A few minutes later, he came back and set a cup of hot chocolate on the ground in front of me. Hot chocolate was my favorite.

"Do you have a peppermint stick?" I asked softly, trying so hard to hold it together.

He disappeared and then came right back and put a peppermint stick in the cup.

I sat up and sipped it carefully, but it was the perfect temperature. He sat down behind me, his legs on either side of my body, and scooted close enough that I could lean back against him and still drink the cocoa.

"I know this is a lot to deal with," he whispered and pet my hair. "I know there are lots of crazy things going on. This is not how you expected your new life in Jinla to be. I know."

He was right about all of that.

"The bond is something unexpected for all of us."

"Do you hate me for it?" I asked him.

He kissed my temple. "No, Jolie. None of this is your fault. You didn't seduce us and trick us. You didn't do any of this. This, is life. This is fate. You may not believe in fate, but I do. You are meant to be with us. We are meant to be your protectors. I can feel it, deep inside of me, I know this is right."

"My life is a curse," I told him, letting the hand holding the cocoa cup fall to my lap.

"Tell me," he requested.

His phone vibrated in his pocket and he took it out, holding it far enough back that I couldn't see the screen. I didn't care. It was probably just the other guys texting to see what was going on.

"When I was eighteen, I was attacked by a vampire. My boyfriend at the time was a werewolf. He defended me from the vampire. Two years later, a witch and I bumped into each other on the street and she put a hex on me. It put me in a coma for a year until my grandma found someone who could remove it. A year after that, a human went on a shooting spree. He shot me in the leg and I almost bled to death. Last year...last year Demarcus captured me. I had been dating a human at the time. The human tried to protect me, but he couldn't defeat Demarcus and his men. Demarcus tore him to pieces, slowly, and made me watch. I thought I was going to die there. I thought I was done for. Then, I escaped. I moved here, hoping to avoid all of this. I thought it was the town I had lived in. Clearly, I'm just cursed. I'm a curse, Fox. I'll get you all killed if I stay."

"You've had a very unfair life," he whispered.

I nodded.

"Don't you think it's okay to let yourself indulge a little, then?"

"What do you mean?" I asked, tilting my head back to look up at him.

He smiled. "You deserve friends. You deserve happiness. You deserve to be loved."

"Justina could have been killed today. My coworkers could have been killed," I reminded him.

He took my cocoa and set it away from us. "They weren't. Justina is a dhampir. She is very capable of protecting herself. We are capable of protecting ourselves. We are capable of protecting you."

He did something with his phone and pushed it away from us. I watched it slide and then he turned me around to face him and brushed my hair behind my ear.

"Do you want to be happy?" he asked.

I nodded.

He brushed his knuckles down my cheek and then leaned forward and kissed me lightly on the lips. Instead of the raging fire I felt with Rhys and Deryn, I felt a slowly building fire. It was like the fire in the fireplace— small, but warming and relaxing.

I kissed him in return, and he laid me back on the rug, kissing me deeply and slowly, possessing me in a way that I had never experienced before. His movements were slow and deliberate, not rushed and demanding. It was even more of a turn on than the fast and passionate sex I'd experienced before.

He peeled my clothes off slowly and kissed from my toes to my forehead. He settled between my legs and slowly entered me, giving my body time to adjust to his size.

"You're beautiful," he whispered as he began to slide in and out of me. "Your soul is beautiful. Everything about you is vibrant and pure."

How could I be pure if I'd slept with other men before?

"You may not think you're worthy of us or of being our queen," he whispered into my ear, "but you are."

His warm lips covered mine and I lost myself to his gentle and consuming touch.

CHAPTER 7

Fox drew me a bath and while I soaked, the others came into the apartment. I closed my eyes and relaxed, completely at ease. I never knew sex like that existed. I never knew someone could fuck you into calmness.

It was incredible.

"How is she?" Rhys asked.

"Relaxed," Fox replied softly.

"What's happening tomorrow?" Deryn asked.

"Her work won't be open until they can clean up and ensure the building is safe for them to return to," Rhys explained. "Plus, a lot of employees were feeling traumatized over the experience. She's got at least the rest of the week off."

"Fox?" I called, looking for shampoo or soap near the tub.

He walked into the bathroom and knelt next to it. "Yes?"

"I can't find the shampoo or soap," I explained.

He grabbed some bottles in a carrying tray from beneath the sink and set them next to the tub. He started to roll up his sleeves, but I grabbed his hand and shook my head.

"I got it," I whispered.

He nodded and left me alone in the bathroom.

I washed quickly and then wrapped the robe he had left me around myself and tied it securely before walking out to join the guys. They were eating pizza and talking quietly. Thankfully, they didn't stop talking when I walked in. That was something I hated.

Deryn held out a plate with two pieces of pizza on it to me and I gratefully accepted it. Everyone sat on the ground, because there weren't any chairs or couches, so I joined them, sitting behind Fox and leaning against the wall. The pizza was warm and delicious, no doubt the best pizza I had ever eaten.

"This pizza is great," I whispered to no one in particular.

"It's from my parents' shop," Deryn explained.

"Your parents own a pizza parlor?" I asked, looking up at him.

"Among other things," he said.

"Well, they're great at making pizza," I praised and took another bite.

"Would you like a drink?" Fox asked me.

I nodded, but my mouth was too full to reply.

He went to the fridge and got out a bottle and brought it to me.

"What's that?" Nico asked.

"It's a cider," Fox replied.

I took a drink of it and moaned. It was a pear cider, pear was my absolute favorite.

All eyes focused on me.

I took another, bigger drink and closed my eyes as the delicious, sweet liquor went down my throat. It was perfect.

"I'll take watch tonight," Deryn said.

"I need to go to speak to my father. I shouldn't be more than an hour or two," Rhys said and stood up.

I drank more of the cider, surprised that I was still so calm and relaxed.

Rhys squatted in front of me and smiled. "You stay with Deryn and do what he says, okay?"

I saluted him. "Yes, sir."

He leaned forward and I met him halfway, kissing him lightly on the lips.

"Stay safe," I whispered to him.

He kissed my forehead and whispered, "Yes, my queen."

Part of me wanted to argue that I wasn't a queen, but I liked hearing them say it. A girl could get used to having sexy men call her their queen.

"Do you want more pizza?" Fox asked.

"No, thank you. I'm full," I replied. A small frown creased my brow. "Did you put a spell on me?"

Fox shook his head and smiled. "No. I promise I wouldn't do something like that."

"Interesting," I whispered.

"Are you ready to go?" Deryn asked me.

"My clothes are at Rhys's," I said and looked down at the robe I was in. Slowly, the euphoria was wearing off, but contentment was its replacement, which I was okay with.

Deryn picked me up and grabbed one of the six-packs of cider out of Fox's fridge. "I'm going to take this for her," he told Fox.

Fox waved as we left his apartment.

"Want to play karting when we get to my apartment?" Deryn asked.

"That sounds fun," I agreed and wrapped my arms around his neck.

"Are you feeling better now?"

I nodded. "Fox is…magical."

He snorted. "I've heard that before."

"Sorry," I mumbled, feeling bad for admitting that I had slept with Fox.

"For what?" he asked and looked down at me as we waited for the elevator.

"I just…don't know what I can and can't talk about with you guys."

"You mean about when you sleep with one of us?" he guessed.
I nodded.

"You don't have to walk on pins and needles with us," he assured me. "Plus, we all knew when we came in that you had slept with him."

"How?"

He cringed. "Uh, we just did."

"Deryn."

"We could smell that you had," he admitted finally.

"Ew," I whispered and scrunched my nose.

He laughed. "Don't worry about it."

"I can walk," I told him. "You don't have to carry me."

The elevator came, and he set me on my feet beside him. "Better?"

Now I felt cold. I wrapped my arms around myself and frowned.

"What's wrong?" he asked.

"Cold," I admitted.

He laughed and picked me up again. "I can remedy that easily."

I wrapped my arms around his neck and nuzzled my cold nose into his neck.

"Cold!" he gasped, but didn't move away.

"Warm," I purred and nuzzled him.

"None of that," he chastised.

"Of what?" I asked, but chuckled and moved my face away from him. "Sorry."

When we got to his apartment, he gave me a pair of his sweats and a shirt to change into. Once changed, I sat next to him on the couch and grabbed a controller.

"Ready to lose?" I asked with a smirk and wiggled the joysticks.

He smirked. "No one beats me at karting."

"Promise not to cry?" I asked.

"Oh! Alright. Let's make a bet. I win and you share my bed tonight. You win and-"

"I win and you give me a massage," I said.

"Deal."

The apartment was warm and I was already feeling drowsy. I had to focus if I was going to win.

The game started and I focused on the track.

"No," I screeched as I started to slide off the edge.

He laughed victoriously and slid around me.

After I was brought back onto course, I raced after him, using every trick and shortcut that I knew.

"Come on. It's like you want me to win," he teased.

Sharing a bed with him wasn't something I was actively trying to avoid, but I was very competitive.

"We've only gone one lap!" I reminded him just as I slid around him and pushed him off the edge.

"No!" he yelled and tapped his foot as he waited for the flying guy to put him back on the track.

We were neck and neck right up to the end and I would have won, but he reached over and grabbed my leg, squeezing and making me squeal and slide off the couch to get away so he couldn't tickle me more. He past the finish line first and jumped up, pumping his fists in the air.

"Woo! I won!" he yelled victoriously.

"You, cheater!" I shouted and pushed him.

He laughed and laughed and eventually, I started laughing too.

I fell onto the couch and clutched at my sore stomach. "Too much laughing," I gasped.

"No such thing," he said and sat on the ground in front of the couch, leaning his head back so that his head lay on my stomach.

"Deryn, what if-"

"Do you want to go on a date tomorrow?" he asked me.

"Huh?" I asked, shocked by the topic shift and him interrupting me.

"Will you go on a date with me tomorrow?"

"Yes," I agreed immediately. "Are we allowed to leave the apartment, though?"

He smiled. "Don't worry, I'm taking you somewhere very secure."

"Is it a dungeon?" I asked and moved away from him with a fake gasp. "Are you going to put me in a dungeon and give me lotion?"

He laughed and then stalked towards me on all fours. "Dungeons are no fun. They don't give me enough room to chase you."

I had played with werewolves before, so seeing him stalking me was thrilling instead of terrifying. My heart sped as I leapt over the back of the couch to put some space between us.

"Oh no, the big, bad wolf is hunting me. What ever shall I do?" I asked dramatically and continued walking backwards, a shit eating grin on my face.

He got onto his feet and stalked around the couch towards me. "Where will you go, little girl?"

"Well, I'd take you to Grandmother's house, but we both know what happens there," I teased.

He laughed and charged after me.

I squealed and raced around the couch, as fast as I could, and ran into his room. He pounced on me, wrapping his entire body around me as we fell onto the bed, softening the impact, so that it didn't hurt me at all.

He pinned my arms above my head and leaned down to nip the tip of my nose. "Caught you."

"Are you to eat me?" I asked with a fake accent.

He arched an eyebrow. "Very straightforward, aren't we? Most women at least have the decency to wait until I've gotten their clothes off to ask."

My heart quickened and I licked my lips. "I didn't mean like-"

He crushed his mouth to mine and he grabbed both of my

wrists in one hand. "Now, you're helpless. What shall I do with you?"

I squirmed, trying to get my wrists free, knowing full well that I had zero chance of doing so.

He wiggled his fingers and said, "I believe you shall be punished for knocking me off the track in that second lap."

"What?" I asked just before he started tickling me.

I laughed and squealed as he tickled me.

"Torturer!" I wiggled and tried to get free.

"Retribution!" he yelled as he continued.

Someone knocked on the door and he stopped tickling me. Rhys walked in and I yelled, "My savior!"

He smirked. "Am I interrupting?"

"He's torturing me!" I yelled and struggled in Deryn's hold.

Deryn kissed my forehead and then released me.

"What's up?" he asked Rhys.

"I brought her stuff here," he said and nodded at my bag that was now on the floor.

"Thanks," I replied, but stayed where I was on the bed. Feeling tired. "I think I'll sleep in this," I told them.

"Sleep in whatever you want," Deryn told me.

"Thank you, your majesty," I said and scoffed.

Rhys chuckled. "Deryn, can I talk to you for a minute?"

"No secrets!" I yelled and sat up.

"It's not regarding you," Rhys informed me. He walked over and kissed my cheek. "Go to sleep. Deryn will join you in a few minutes."

"It's still weird that you're okay with that," I whispered, but crawled under the covers.

"You'll get used to it," he assured me before leaving.

"I'll be right back," Deryn said. "Yell if you need something." He kissed me lightly and tickled my sides before running out of the room after Rhys.

I lay on the bed with a smile on my face. The smile slowly disappeared. Four men. I was dating four men who were all friends. They were all bound to me, and I brought nothing to the table, except my body.

What could I do for them? What could I offer them aside from myself? There had to be something or someway for me to prove worthy of them. The more time I spent with each of them individually, the deeper the bonds became, not on a metaphysical level or anything, but in my heart. They were great guys, and it just felt right to be with them. I felt like I was home, despite never having been with them before.

Was this what people meant when they felt like they had a soulmate? Was this feeling of home and rightness the feeling of what soulmates experienced?

Maybe Fox was right. Maybe this was fate. Maybe it was my destiny to be with them.

I scoffed and rolled over. "Right? It's your destiny to be with four men. That's called dreaming," I reminded myself callously.

For now, I would enjoy the ride. Who knew when it would end? If the people trying to kill me had anything to say about it, that ride would end sooner rather than later. It could be tomorrow or the next day and I could be dead.

Or, the men I was slowly falling for could die trying to protect me.

No, I couldn't let that happen. I couldn't let any of them die.

DERYN'S DATE ENDED UP BEING A TRIP TO VISIT HIS PACK. I practically bounced in my seat as we drove towards his pack's headquarters.

"You're lively today," he teased me.

"I'm excited to meet your pack," I said honestly. "It's been a long time since I was with a werewolf pack, but when I used to visit, we had all kinds of fun."

"How long were you dating that werewolf?"

"A year, but we lived in a small town and were friends before that. His alpha let me go on a hunt with them one time. It was so-"

"They took you on a hunt?" Deryn asked, his eyes going gold.

"Yeah," I whispered, stilling at his seriousness.

"What did you do on the hunt?"

"I rode on my boyfriend's back and watched the rest of the pack take down some deer. Then we went swimming. Why are you acting like they did something terrible?"

"Hunting is a very serious thing for packs. You're not supposed to let outsiders in."

"I wasn't really an outsider though."

"You were lucky to have found such a nice pack," he said after he calmed down.

"Maybe they're just not as uptight as you," I mumbled.

He draped his arm across my shoulders and kissed the side of my head. "My father is the uptight one. He makes sure that we do everything by the book."

"There's a book?" I asked. "Can I read it?"

Deryn chuckled. "There actually is a book, but no, you cannot read it."

"Tease."

We arrived at a huge compound, and the driver opened the door for us. I climbed out and shivered at the weight of hundreds of predators in the same place. My human brain was warning me to run, but I knew better. Werewolves were not killers, not any more than humans were. Truthfully, less than humans were, since they tried so hard to get on the humans' good sides.

We walked into the nearest building and I was shocked to discover it was a gymnasium. There were several people playing basketball and a few people in the stands. Deryn strode to the stands and took a seat, so I followed and sat next to him.

"Do me a favor?" he whispered. "Don't let anyone know we're dating."

"Okay," I agreed immediately.

"Do you want to know why?" he asked.

I shrugged. "If you want me to."

"I haven't told my father about you yet."

"Ah," I said and nodded. "Got it."

The game ended and the players walked to the sidelines to get some water. One of the players looked familiar, but it wasn't until he smiled that I realized who he was.

"Jolie!" he yelled.

I stood up and then rushed forward to meet him halfway, throwing my arms around his neck as he picked me up and spun me.

"Martin!" I squealed.

He set me down, but kept his hands on my hips. "Jolie! What are you doing here? You look amazing!"

"I came-"

"She came with me," Deryn said angrily.

I thought Martin would drop his hands, but he just turned and smiled at Deryn.

"Small world, huh? Jolie and I dated in high school. She was my best friend." He turned back to me. "What have you been up to? Why are you out here? You want to see Sharla and the girls?"

"They're here?" I asked and smiled wide. "I haven't seen them in person in a few years."

"They are up at the main house," he said and grabbed a shirt from the bench in front of us. "Sharla will be so excited to see you."

Deryn hadn't moved or said anything since his one declaration. His fists were no longer clenched as he watched Martin.

"Deryn?" I whispered.

He tore his eyes away and looked down at me. "We're going to the main house."

"Great," Martin said with a wide smile.

The house was just one building over and as soon as we walked in, the girls and Sharla saw me.

"Auntie Jolie!" the girls yelled and rushed to me. I dropped to my knees to hug the twin seven-year-old girls.

"How are my favorite nieces?" I asked and kissed their heads.

"Great!" they exclaimed in unison.

Sharla stood behind them with a smile, waiting for her turn.

I stood up and she jerked me into a hug.

"Jolie," she whispered. "I got worried when I heard about you ending the war. And your office! Are you safe? You're welcome to come stay with us."

I kissed her cheek. "Thank you, but I'm well protected." I glanced back at Deryn for emphasis.

He was looking at me with his head slightly tilted and a small frown of concentration.

Sharla stepped back and bowed to him. "Prince, my apologies for being rude. I didn't see you enter."

"You are very affectionate to a woman who used to date your mate," Deryn commented.

Sharla smiled warmly at me. "She holds no feelings towards Martin in that way anymore. We had a long talk when we came to Jolie's hometown, and became friends."

"Are you really alright?" Martin asked and set his hand on my cheek. "You look tired and stressed."

"A lot has happened," Deryn said with a bit of a growl in his voice.

The girls darted behind their mother and peeked out at Deryn.

What was with him?

"Can I talk to you, Martin?" Deryn asked with clenched fists.

"Sure."

He pecked me on the cheek, smiled at Sharla, and followed Deryn's tense back out of the living room.

The girls pulled me to the couch and climbed into my lap, sharing my lap as well as they could. I ran my fingers through their hair and the fidgety kids stilled and relaxed into me.

"We've missed you," Sharla said. "We got scared when we went back home and you weren't there?"

"I'm sorry. I'll get better about texting you." I promised.

We did video calls once a month, but I never talked about anything serious with them. most of the calls were the girls telling me things that had happened at school.

Madison shifted into her wolf pup form so I could scratch behind her ears. Tamara did the same, their heads on my thighs.

"What are you guys doing here?" I asked. They lived three states away.

"Martin was offered a job here a week ago. We came to see about finding an apartment near his job."

"So, I'll get to see you more?" I asked with a wide smile and ruffled the girls' fur.

Sharla nodded. "Much more."

I wasn't sure about that. I would visit them, but not often.

Deryn and Martin came back, both scowling.

Sharla stood up, knowing something was wrong since Martin never scowled. He waved at her and she returned to her seat.

"Girls, go to your room," he ordered them.

They whined, licked my cheeks, and obeyed.

Deryn leaned against the entryway, looking at me with that tilted head again.

Martin knelt in front of me, taking my hands in his.

"You should have called me," he chastised.

"You have your family to protect now," I reminded him.

Sharla growled at me. "Jolie. What did we talk about?"

I sighed and turned to face her. "I love you, but I won't put you in danger."

It was Martin's turn to growl at me. "You are so stubborn," he said.

Deryn had taken a step forward when Martin growled.

I took my hands back from Martin and leaned forward to kiss his cheek. "I won't curse you," I whispered to him. I kissed Sharla's cheek and walked to Deryn. "Once things calm down, I'll come visit the girls. Text me your address."

"I'm not just going to-" Martin started and stood up, but Deryn stepped into his path.

I grabbed Deryn's hand and he stepped back.

"He's my friend," I reminded Deryn.

"Why are you treating her like a mate?" Martin asked Deryn, no submission on his face at all despite Deryn outranking him.

"She's under my protection," Deryn said. "She's my friend."

Sharla quirked an eyebrow and looked at me. I found an interesting spot on the ceiling to inspect.

"Then you should understand my protectiveness," Martin said with crossed arms.

Deryn didn't reply. He took me up the stairs, away from the couple. I let him drag me, but pulled my hand free when we got close to an office with its door open and a male voice talking.

Deryn knocked on the door as he walked in. I wasn't certain if I was supposed to follow him, so I waited by the door. A huge man walked over and hugged Deryn with a wide smile.

"My boy!" he bellowed. "How are you?"

"Good, Dad," Deryn replied.

This...mountain, was his dad?

Deryn escaped the hug to grab my hand and pull me into the room to stand before his dad.

"Dad, I'd like you to officially meet Jolie."

As I looked at him, I realized that I had seen him before. He had been one of the four sitting in the park, which must have meant he was one of the Kings and the Alpha.

I dipped my head in submission. "Alpha, it is an honor to meet you."

Suddenly, huge arms wrapped around me and pulled me into a hug against the giant Alpha. He released me, but kept his hand on my shoulders while his smiling eyes met mine.

"You are welcome here anytime. If you ever need anything, just tell me. Oh, and call me Dan."

"Thank you," I whispered and glanced at Deryn who seemed as surprised as me.

"I need to tell you something important," Deryn said quietly. "It's personal."

Dan turned back to me and inhaled loudly.

I rolled my eyes. "I'm not pregnant."

Both Dan and Deryn looked at me with wide eyes.

"I dated Martin and spent a lot of time with that pack," I explained. "Their Alpha always checked if I was pregnant when I came over."

Deryn shut the door and pushed me to a couch I hadn't seen around his large Dad. I sat and he sat next to me, his body aligned with mine.

Dan sat in a huge leather chair across from us and waited.

"Jolie's become my queen," Deryn stated. "Well, sort of."

Deryn explained the entire situation, from meeting me until today. I was blushing by the end, unsure how Dan would react to finding this out.

"So, you found your queen?" he asked with his mouth hidden behind his hands as they linked in front of his face.

Deryn nodded.

"What do you think about all of this?" Dan asked me.

"I'm not sure. It's still sinking in," I admitted.

"Can you feel the bond?"

I shook my head.

"Are you certain these attacks were for her?"

Deryn nodded. "One hundred percent."

"All four princes, huh?" Dan asked and looked at me.

"I didn't know their titles when I met them," I muttered. It wasn't like I'd sought them out on purpose.

He laughed loudly and dropped his hands to his lap. "What do you need from me?" he asked Deryn.

"To keep our connection a secret. We don't want anyone knowing, but I knew I needed to tell you. And, a driver for Jolie."

"A driver?" I asked him.

"Our cars are well enforced with bullet proof windows," Dan explained. "So, they're able to drive you places without you needing the mage."

"Is this all really necessary?" I asked softly.

"Yes," Deryn said immediately.

"I agree to both of your requests," Dan said. "Would you also like a bodyguard? Martin and her seem to know each other and-"

"No," Deryn snapped a bit too quickly.

"I don't have feelings for him," I chastised Deryn.

"I don't like him touching you," Deryn snarled.

Dan tapped Deryn's nose and said, "Enough of that. Unless you take her as a mate, she's allowed to touch others."

"I know that," Deryn grumbled and rubbed his nose even though the tap hadn't been hard enough to hurt him.

"I'll also do some investigating to see if we can find out who is trying to kill her," Dan promised.

"Thank you," I said and looked at Dan. "I'm honored to have your protection."

Dan smiled. "As my son's queen, you'll have to make appearances here with the pack, once your relationship goes public. You're going to be seeing a lot more of me."

"What does that mean?" I asked.

"Nothing," Deryn said and stood up. "Let's get going. The others are probably getting antsy to confirm I've kept you alive."

"Jolie," Dan called as we stepped into the hallway. I stepped back into his office. "I'd avoid touching other males for a while.

He's too stressed out and touching others will only break his control."

"Okay," I agreed.

I jogged down the stairs where Martin was angrily talking to Deryn, who looked just as mad.

"What's up?" I asked.

"Nothing," Deryn replied tersely.

I hugged Sharla and whispered, "Love you."

"I love you, too."

"Stay safe," Martin ordered me and hugged me.

"Love you," I told him instead of responding to his order.

"Love you too," he whispered.

Deryn was already outside of the house, so I jogged to catch up to him. A car pulled up and he climbed in without saying anything to me. The silent treatment lasted all the way to the apartment building and up the elevator.

We walked into Deryn's apartment to find the other three males playing video games together on his couch.

"How was your trip?" Rhys asked.

"My trip was great, except for the green monster who unexpectedly tagged along," I said with a pointed look at Deryn.

"What?" Fox asked, looking away from his game.

"Deryn got super jealous of my friend hugging me," I explained.

"He wasn't just hugging you. He had his hands on you for longer than is acceptable with a female who isn't his mate."

I rolled my eyes in response. "You're being ridiculous."

"Did you sleep with him?"

"Yes."

The pen in his hand snapped and the ink splattered on his clothes. His eyes didn't just flash yellow – the wolf remained.

"Why didn't you tell me that before?"

"Would it have made you less jealous?"

"No, but I wouldn't have let him touch you at all."

"You can't tell me who I can and can't be friends with. Or, who I can and can't hug. I've known him much longer than I've known any of you. He has saved me multiple times. His daughters are my nieces."

"Okay. Everyone, calm down," Nico said, coming to stand between us.

I pushed past Deryn to the kitchen, grabbed one of the ciders and chugged it.

"How did it go with your dad?" asked Rhys.

"Great. He loved her, which was expected. He gave her permission to return to the pack whenever she wanted and also gave her a driver and car whenever we need it," Deryn replied as he took his ruined shirt off and tossed it into the trash.

"Wow, that's pretty generous of him," Fox commented.

"I think the fact that she had two wolf pups in her lap and calmed them down better with scratches than he has been able to with intimidation had a big part to play in his decisions. She's unexpectedly great with werewolves," Deryn explained.

I stopped guzzling my cider long enough to ask, "He saw me with the twins?"

Deryn nodded. "He has cameras everywhere."

"Is that why he hugged me when I met him?" I asked sheepishly.

"He hugged her?" Rhys asked and looked at me. "The Alpha hugged you?"

I nodded. "Big bear hug."

"Holy shit, Deryn. Was your dad high?" Fox asked and chuckled.

"I know," Deryn muttered.

"He hugged Deryn when he walked in," I muttered, feeling uncomfortable that they were making such a big deal out of it. He seemed to be pretty affectionate.

"Dan is very affectionate to his pack, but outsiders he is

extremely cold to. He still won't give us his full attention and it's been over two decades," Rhys explained.

"Maybe that's because you're all alphas and threats. I'm just a small human girl," I suggested.

"No, he just likes you," Deryn said. "Dad is never affectionate to outsiders."

"Well, I am pretty special," I mumbled and tossed my now empty cider into the trash and grabbed another. "Can we order pizza?"

"Why don't you wait to drink that until it comes?" Nico suggested.

I glared up at him. "No."

He sighed, but didn't say anything else as I popped the bottle cap off and started drinking it. I sat on Fox's lap and ran my fingers through his hair. It was incredibly thick and as was usual when it came to Fox, it was calming.

"Want to play a game?" Fox asked me and motioned at the controllers on the table.

I shook my head. "Not right now. Have we heard anything about when my apartment will be ready for me to stay there again?"

"Manager said at least a week," Nico replied.

I let my head drop forward to rest on Fox's shoulder. "Dammit."

"Thought you could get rid of us, didn't you?" He whispered and chuckled.

"No, just not used to not having privacy," I whispered back.

"We can give you privacy," Deryn said. "If you want to be alone, you're welcome to use my spare room."

He was being nice, probably because he realized what a jerk he was earlier.

"Okay," I replied, but didn't move.

Seeing Martin and his family had been a huge surprise and knowing they were nearby made me worry. I didn't want them to get caught up in my problems. I meant it when I told him that I wouldn't come see the girls until after all of this was over.

I finished my second bottle and started to trace Fox's pointed ear, but he grabbed my hand and looked at me with silver eyes.

"That is very sensitive," he whispered to me. His eyes were glued to my mouth and I realized that there was a new part of his body pressing against my lower body.

"Oh," I gasped and jerked my hand away. "Sorry."

He smiled. "You didn't know. It's okay."

"Pizza should be here soon," Deryn called from his bedroom.

Nico was engrossed in the video game he was playing next to us and it appeared Rhys hadn't heard what had happened.

I exhaled in relief, glad they hadn't witnessed my embarrassing action and climbed off Fox. He kissed my cheek and said, "I'll be back."

I took his vacated spot and let my head fall into my hands.

"Need to vent?" Nico asked me, eyes still glued to the TV as he shot his way through a horde of zombies.

"No," I whispered. "Need to hide."

He chuckled.

"Nico, what do you like? I don't really know much about you."

I felt terrible about it too. I barely knew them and yet they were already bound to me and protecting me.

"I like video games. I like learning new things and read a lot of books and magazines…"

"He likes science, a lot," Rhys added.

"Really?" I asked, shocked that a mage would like science.

He nodded. "I love science."

"Even though you can use magic?"

"Science explains a lot of things that we don't understand."

"Too bad science can't explain males," I mumbled and walked to get another bottle of cider.

"What about you?" I asked Rhys as I struggled to get the bottle cap off.

He took the bottle and opened it for me before handing it back. "I like video games. I like sports cars too."

"What do you like to do?" I asked, leaning my hip against the counter while I faced him. He was sitting on a stool and it made us almost the same height.

"You," he said with a wink.

I rolled my eyes and walked back to the couch with him laughing behind me.

"Is Deryn hiding?" I asked Nico softly.

He nodded, but didn't say anything.

The doorbell rang and Rhys went to answer it, opening the door so the pizza guy could deliver the ten boxes they had ordered.

"Did you get pepperoni?" I asked, set my drink on the coffee table, and walked over to the pizza guy and Rhys.

Rhys nodded. "Yes."

"Here's your change," the pizza guy said to him, but his eyes kept darting to me.

Rhys carried the pizzas to the counter and I went to shut the door, but the pizza guy grabbed my arm and jerked me out of the apartment. He slammed the door shut and ran with me down the hallway and down the stairs.

"Let me go!" I screamed at him.

"Shut the fuck up," he ordered me with a growl.

I couldn't believe that the guys hadn't caught up to us. This guy wasn't running *that* fast. Were they not even aware that he had grabbed me?

He threw open the door on the bottom floor and ran right into Rhys. Deryn grabbed me away from the guy while Rhys held him up by his throat with one arm.

Did it make me twisted to be turned on by seeing Rhys strangle someone with one arm? Most likely. Did it stop me? Nope.

"You okay?" Deryn asked me, blocking me with his body from

the guy.

I nodded and smoothed down my clothes.

"Who sent you?" Deryn demanded.

The guy was turning purple and opened and closed his mouth with no sound.

"He can't answer when you're strangling him," I reminded Rhys.

Rhys dropped the guy and he crashed to the ground in a heap, gasping in breaths. "I don't know," he said quickly. "I got the job by text and they wired the money."

"What was your job?" Deryn asked.

"Grab the girl and take her outside," he said and started to stand up.

"Nico!" Rhys yelled.

Nico appeared next to us. "You bellowed?"

"Can you create a protective shield around her if you can't see her?" Rhys asked him.

He nodded. "I can create one that will last about five minutes, will that work?"

"Perfect," Rhys said with a smile.

Nico leaned down to kiss me lightly on the lips and when he stepped back, a translucent shield was around me.

"Last kiss in case the shield doesn't hold?" I asked with a smirk despite the fear I felt, knowing that Rhys was going to make me go outside.

Nico scowled at me. "That's rude."

"Alright, pizza boy. Go ahead and grab our girl and head outside."

"What?" he asked and looked between us all.

"Go on," Rhys ordered him. "Go finish your job."

Pizza guy grabbed my arm and pulled me towards the exit, a scowl on his face. I had a feeling that whoever hired him hadn't planned on him living past getting outside, and the guys likely assumed that as well.

"Rhys," Deryn growled as I moved closer to the door.

"She's protected," Nico assured him.

"What if someone grabs her?" Deryn asked.

"Then I'll grab her," Rhys assured him.

"I don't like this," he growled.

I smiled and blew them a kiss. "At least if I die, you won't have to worry about the bond anymore."

"Not funny!" Deryn snapped, but his voice was drowned out by the sound of traffic and people as I stepped outside.

"Now what?" I asked pizza guy who had stopped as soon as we stepped outside.

His phone rang and he answered it. "Yes?"

The person said something and pizza guy nodded along and then started walking in the direction of the park.

"Got it," he said and ended his call. "Looks like you'll be going on a trip," he informed me.

A blue dragon dropped out of the sky and landed in front of me. I screamed and tried to get away, but pizza guy was deceptively strong and held me. The dragon shifted into a female who grabbed me and tossed a sultry smile towards pizza guy.

"Pleasure doing business," she told him. She shifted again and flew up into the sky with me in her claws.

I screamed again, hating heights and being dangled in a dragon's claws was not the way to get over that fear.

A dragon roared below us and I recognized it instantly.

"Rhys!" I yelled.

The dragon carrying me growled and flapped her wings harder. She got up out of the city skyline and a red circle appeared in front of her nose. She blew red mist out of her nostrils and the circle changed into a weird symbol and then we were flying through a portal into a place with lush green grass and mountains.

The portal closed and I stared in disbelief at the land we were in. It reminded me of home, but it couldn't be...

"Why are we here?" I asked loudly, hoping she could hear me. She didn't respond.

We flew towards the Arle River and I knew without a doubt that we were back in my hometown. Why did shit always happen here?

We flew past the small city where the diner, police station, post office, and city hall sat. We flew over Mr. Archer's fields of corn, past Ms. Fritz' strawberry patch, and straight to the place of nightmares, my childhood home.

She landed and shifted as she did, ending up carrying me in her arms, which was highly awkward since we were the same height.

"Why the fuck are we here?" I demanded and tried to get out of her arms.

She gripped me tighter and snarled, "Shut up and stay still."

The front door opened and my pulse skyrocketed. A man of average stature with dazzling red eyes and a heart blacker than the midnight sky smiled at me. His jeans were streaked with what was most likely blood, his shirt the same, but his duster was clean. He loved that duster more than anything else in the world.

"Hello, daughter."

"Why the fuck am I here?" I demanded.

The dragoness set me down and bowed to him. "I've done as you asked."

He tossed a pouch to her and she left as soon as she caught it.

"You're hard to get ahold of," he told me as she walked down the steps of the house towards me. His cowboy hat was pushed up slightly, so he could look at me without tilting his head at all.

"I moved. Everyone knows I moved."

"I don't have your address," he said.

I glared at him. "You have no right to fucking do this."

He turned to mist and closed the distance between us in less than a second. His hand gripped my jaw painfully and he glared into my eyes. "Watch how you talk to me, child."

"Fuck you," I snapped. It wasn't smart to antagonize him. It would be better to bow to him, gravel at his feet. I had done it for twenty-three years. I wouldn't do it any longer. I refused to bow to him.

He backhanded me hard enough to make me fly backwards four feet. I landed on my back and knew the entire right side of my face would be bruised tomorrow. "You disobedient, brat!" he yelled. "You think that just because you're an adult that you can do as you please. That's not how this works!"

Slowly, I pushed myself up to a standing position and wiped the blood from my mouth. He'd held back on that hit, which meant that he needed something from me.

"What do you want?" I asked him quietly.

He smiled. "You're smart, despite being impudent."

I didn't rise to his bait.

"You ended a war that I've been working very hard to keep alive," he told me. "I don't know where you found the artifact, but obviously I need to learn to hide things better."

Him? He was the one who had stolen the artifact?

"Why do you want the war?" I asked.

"The more those four factions fight, the more time I have to raise my army without them coming to look for me."

"Army for what?" What the hell was he scheming now?

"You don't need to worry about that," he assured me. "What you do need to worry about is figuring out how you are going to help me."

"I'm not," I stated bluntly.

His jaw clenched and it took a minute for him to respond. "You're going to use your connections with those four princes to restart the war."

He'd gone insane. Even more insane than after he was turned into a vampire and gained his powers.

"No," I stated firmly.

He was choking me just like Rhys had done to the pizza guy

and I realized that it was definitely not sexy. It hurt. A lot! Especially when you didn't have a chance to prepare for it since the other person moved faster than your eye could track.

"Do not tell me no!" he growled, the human façade he wore breaking as his true self came out. He wasn't human any longer. No, he was a demon in human skin.

"Fuck. You," I gasped out.

He tossed me into the gravel driveway and I screamed in pain as the rocks scraped my arms and hands and a few got stuck into my skin.

"You will do this," he ordered me.

"Or what?" I asked with a gasp. "You'll kill me? Do it. Just fucking put me out of my misery, because I won't betray them."

"Do you need incentive?" he asked with a smirk. "I heard your former werewolf lover moved to Jinla. I could pay his adorable family a visit and-"

"Touch them and I'll kill you," I threatened him.

I knew the blow was coming, but knowing it was coming didn't stop it from hurting. I clutched my side, sure that he'd broken one of my ribs again, and took shallow breaths.

"You are suicidal, aren't you?" he growled.

"I won't do what you want," I whispered. "I won't betray my friends."

"I'll kill them all," he threatened me.

"You can't kill the princes. They're too powerful. Plus, that would put your head right on the chopping block," I reminded him smugly.

He growled and stalked away to pace across the porch.

I took the reprieve to pull out my cell phone and send a message with my location in the group text that Rhys had created.

Dad walked back towards me and I slid the phone back into my pocket while doubled over, so he wouldn't see it before getting up to my knees. He grabbed me by the hair and dragged me into the house. I cried out and tried to grab his arm to take some of the pressure off my hair, but couldn't get a grip. My scalp was on fire and tears filled my eyes.

"Let's see how some time in here treats you," he snarled.

"No! No! No!" I screamed and struggled as hard as I could to get away from him and the closet under the stairs. It was the place of my nightmares. The place he had tortured me and punished me as a child and teenager.

He shoved me in, slammed the door closed and locked it, laughing the entire time.

"Let me out!" I screamed and slammed my body against the door. "Let me out!"

"You can come out when you're ready to do what I ask," he said, his voice fading as he walked away. The front door opened and closed and I knew I was alone.

I curled up into a ball and rocked myself back and forth. The cupboard was small, only big enough for me to be on my knees. It was pitch black.

"You're alive, Jolie. You're alive. He can't hurt you when you're in the closet. They're coming. They'll come for you." I whispered.

It didn't help. No matter what I tried to tell myself, I couldn't stop the panic as it set in. My breathing became rapid and before long, I passed out.

CHAPTER 8

"Let me out!" I screamed for the fiftieth time and kicked the door.

I thought the guys would have been here by now, but I was still locked in the closet. I checked my phone and the group message. My message had gone through, but I hadn't gotten a response and now, I had no service. Figures that the place of my nightmares wouldn't have reception. Even having the phone to brighten up the cupboard so it wasn't pitch black didn't help.

I wasn't a child anymore, but I couldn't convince myself not to be terrified.

I had texted the guys hours ago. Why weren't they here? What were they doing?

The house door opened.

"Fuck you!" I screamed loudly. "I fucking hate you! I hope you die!"

Maybe if I provoked him, he would take me out and hit me or something. At least I would be out of the cupboard.

"That's not very nice to say," Fox whispered from outside the door.

"Fox!" I screamed and then lowered my voice. "Fox, please fucking open the door. Let me out. Let me out!"

"Easy, I'm working on it," he assured me. "Deryn, a little help? There's no key."

The door creaked and then it was gone and light blinded me. Fox sat off to the side and Deryn held the door, which he had ripped out of the stairway.

I scrambled out and ran to hide behind Rhys who was furthest away from the cupboard, next to the door. My body was still trembling and I couldn't get it to stop.

Deryn tossed the door off to the side and they all turned to face me.

"The fuck happened?" Nico asked.

Rhys pulled me in, and I sobbed into his chest. His arms wrapped around me. "What happened?"

"We need to go," I sobbed. "He'll come back."

"Who?" Deryn asked. "Who took you?"

"Boys, this is incredibly rude," Dad chastised them. "When you come to meet the father of the girl you want to date, you shouldn't destroy his property. It makes a very bad first impression."

"Who are you?" Fox demanded.

"Fuck you!" I screamed at him and stepped away from Rhys. "I'm done! Don't ever fucking talk to me again. I'm not yours. I'm not going to do what you want. You can torture me all you want, but I won't help you. I'd rather see you turn to ash."

His smile wilted and he said, "You can leave tonight, but this isn't over."

"I won't help you," I told him. "I'd sooner die."

He moved and I was across the room, pinned to the wall by his arm. The guys moved towards me, but Dad held up his hand to them and they stopped.

"You help me, or I kill them," Dad whispered.

"You can't defeat them all," I gasped.

"No, I can't defeat them all at once, but I can kill them one by one. Which should I start with? The wolf seems mighty fond of you. Perhaps I should start with him? Maybe after I break a few legs, you'll be more obedient."

"Let her go," Rhys ordered Dad.

"Boy, be quiet when family is talking," Dad ordered him.

"Kill me," I ordered him. "Kill me and get it over with."

Dad sighed and shook his head sadly. "I had hoped it would never come to this. Very well, if that's your wish." He drew a blade from his back and I took one last look at the guys and awaited my death.

Death didn't come. The princes attacked as one. Dad cursed, dropped me and then disappeared, tucking his tail between his legs as he ran away to stay alive.

I fell to the ground and screamed as my broken rib hit the hardwood floor.

"Jolie!" Fox yelled and rushed to me. He started to move me, but I held up my hand to stop him.

Slowly, I pushed myself up into a sitting position and took several breaths with my eyes closed.

"He won't give up," I whispered with tears in my eyes. "He's going to try to use me. He'll hurt you to force me."

Rhys folded his arms across his chest. Deryn squatted down in front of me, next to Fox. Nico looked around the house.

"That was my dad," I whispered.

All of their eyes widened and Nico focused on me.

"He was turned after I was born," I explained. "He's very powerful."

"We know who he is. We just didn't know you were related," Nico said.

"Why did he kidnap you?" Fox asked.

"He wants the war to resume. He wanted me to use my connections with you to start the war again. He wanted me to betray you. I refused."

"How badly are you injured?" Deryn asked.

"I think at least one of my ribs is broken. It hurts *really* bad to talk or breath. Or move."

"Then shut up," Fox ordered me with a scowl.

The normally happy elf was incredibly angry and it caught me off guard.

"Fox-" I started, but he looked up and glared at me, so I shut my mouth.

"We need to take her to the hospital," Deryn said, despite the fact that all of them already knew that.

"There isn't one for an hour," I said quickly before Fox could tell me to be quiet again.

"I'll heal her," Fox whispered and put his hands on my sides.

"You sure?" Deryn asked, a crease in his brow.

"Just protect me if someone comes," Fox ordered him.

Deryn stood up and spun around so that he was facing away from us, watching for danger.

Fox closed his eyes, inhaled, and his hands started glowing.

"Healing takes a lot of my energy," Fox explained. "I'll be useless in a fight after I'm done, so I don't heal others often."

"You all heal fast anyway," I whispered.

"Shush," he snapped. "No more talking."

I obeyed.

"When I first learned how to heal, I didn't understand the energy it would take. I healed Deryn's broken leg and slept for two days. Deryn thought I'd killed myself by fixing him and freaked out."

"Did not," Deryn mumbled.

"He cried," Rhys said.

"We were four!" Deryn growled.

"My parents spent a lot of time with me to teach me to heal properly. I'm still not anywhere as great as my mother. She can heal a hundred soldiers and just needs an hour nap afterwards. She's amazing."

"And hot," Rhys replied with a smirk.

Nico and Deryn nodded their heads with the same smirk.

"Shut it," Fox growled, but it was obviously a conversation they'd had several times before and he didn't really care.

My breathing became easier and my side stopped hurting completely. I leaned forward and kissed him, just a brush of lips across lips. "Thank you."

"Where else are you hurt?" he asked.

"Everything else is just bruised," I told him and stood up.

"Where?" he asked and saw my cheek.

"Leave it. It's not life threatening," I said and moved away from him.

"Let's go," Rhys said and headed outside.

We stepped outside into an ambush. Fifty vampires stood in a loose semicircle around the porch, their eyes glowing in the moonlight.

"Fuck," I whispered.

"Ready?" Rhys whispered.

"Yes," the three others replied.

Deryn picked me up and tensed, waiting for something.

"Give up and we won't kill you," a tall vampire with shoulder length dark hair said.

Rhys flipped him off and then shifted into his huge dragon form and immediately sent out a wave of fire at the gathered vampires, making them jump back several yards.

Deryn leapt up onto Rhys's back, as did the other two, and then Rhys took to the sky. I clutched Deryn tightly and buried my face in his chest as we flew.

What were the odds that I'd be carried by a dragon twice in one day?

"It's okay," Deryn assured me. "Rhys is an excellent flyer."

I didn't respond.

"Why were you so scared when we found you?" Fox asked me.

He was lying on his back on the center of Rhys's back, which was just wide enough for it.

"It's stupid and embarrassing," I whispered, "but he tossed me in there for days at a time as a kid with no light or anything. It's terrifying."

"It's not stupid," Nico assured me.

"He's the one who had the artifact," I informed them. "He wants the war because he said that while you are all fighting each other, he can grow an army."

"For what?" Deryn asked.

"I don't know," I admitted. "To take over? He's always been power hungry."

"We need to let the elders know," Nico said and pulled out his phone.

I looked around at the men, sitting or lying on the back of their friend in dragon form, texting and playing games on their phones. I couldn't believe what I was seeing. I burst into laughter and all of them looked at me questioningly, even Rhys's large dragon head turned to look at me.

"What?" Deryn asked.

I waved my arm at all of them. "This scene," I gasped out between laughs.

They looked at each other and slowly smiles took the place of the scowls that had been there.

"Thank you," I whispered and looked at them each in turn. "Thank you for rescuing me, again."

Deryn kissed my cheek. "You don't have to thank us."

"We wish we could have been here sooner," Nico said. "We were attacked as soon as we stepped outside of the apartment building by a group of vampires. That's why we were delayed."

"We came as fast as we could," Deryn assured me.

Rhys snarled.

"Rhys flew as fast as he could," Deryn amended with a smirk.

"So, Lamar was the one who stole the artifact to start the war,"

Fox whispered. "I shouldn't be surprised. I am surprised that he is your father though."

"Only by blood," I grumbled.

"We felt your pain multiple times. What happened?" Nico asked me.

"Well, I talked back and he didn't like that. So, he hit me a few times. Then I told him I wasn't going to help him by betraying you and that really pissed him off. I told him just to kill me, but he decided torture was better and threw me in the closet. He would have left me in there for days before coming to get me to see if I would agree to what he wanted."

"Has he always been like this?" Fox asked softly.

I nodded. "Yes. He started when I was eight...nine? Somewhere around there."

"And you didn't know about the artifact?" Deryn asked me.

I shook my head. "My Grandma gave it to me after I escaped from Demarcus. She just told me it would keep my location a secret from him and keep his group from finding me."

Now I wondered if Grandma had known more than she let on. Maybe she had hoped I would return it to its rightful place.

"Your cheek is going to be really bruised tomorrow," Deryn whispered.

"I know, but at least he held back that hit," I said and sighed. "He may be psychotic, but he won't kill me. I know that much."

Or, at least I hoped that much. He had seemed like he was planning to kill me at the end there.

Rhys landed and we climbed off of him. He switched forms, walked into the apartment building, and then hugged me. "I'm sorry we weren't faster."

I scoffed. "I'm just glad you came."

He kissed the top of my head and tears started to fall. Damn him. I had held on during the flight here.

We got into the elevator and the guys crowded around me,

placing a hand each on me as I cried. I cried surrounded by four males I was falling for deeper and deeper.

"Who's watching her tonight?" Rhys asked.

"Me," Deryn said.

"I need a shower," I whispered and brushed some gravel off of my arms.

"You have dirt in your hair," Fox pointed out.

I sighed and dropped my head. "Movies are so unrealistic. No one gets rescued looking perfect. They need to show the princesses covered in dirt and grime, not having showered for days."

"You're still beautiful," Fox assured me and kissed my cheek. "Even covered in cobwebs and dirt."

I chuckled and followed Deryn to his apartment, straight for the bathroom. I stood in front of the mirror and looked at myself. My cheek was swollen and I was covered in dirt with leaves and rocks in my hair.

"Gorgeous," I scoffed.

"I think so," Deryn said.

I turned to glare at him in the bathroom doorway. "Sneaking up on people isn't nice."

He smiled. "You just didn't notice me. I've been here for a few minutes." With long strides, he walked across the bathroom and turned the shower on. Steam began to rise and I couldn't wait to get into it.

Without turning around, he took his shirt off and his pants.

"Uh," I said intelligently.

He turned to look at me. "Mind if I join you?"

"No," I replied immediately, waiting expectantly for the last piece of his clothing to be removed.

I was not disappointed when he did.

Blue rupis! He was fucking perfect. How could they all be so perfect? It had to be against the law for them to be perfect and friends and all available for me to touch.

I shed my clothes and got into the shower behind him. The shower was large, big enough that four people could comfortably stand in it and shower together. There were jets in the walls that sprayed your body and a huge sprayer in the ceiling.

I stepped into the water and hissed in pain from the tiny cuts being hit by the water. Deryn turned around and looked me up and down slowly, his mouth curving upwards as he finished.

"See something you like?" I teased and reached for the soap.

He nodded and slid his hands along the tops of my hips. "All of this," he responded and kissed me.

I opened my mouth to him, and he slid his tongue along mine. Damn he tasted good. The kiss deepened and I moved closer to him, squishing his erection between us while I ran my hands along his chest and abs.

"Why were you so jealous of Martin?" I asked him, stepping back and putting shampoo in my hair to distract me for a moment. It didn't take long for the overhead spray to rinse my hair and I cringed when I saw the amount of dirt and debris going down the drain.

"Because, you're my queen," he replied, putting more shampoo in my hair and massaging it in.

"But you don't get jealous of Rhys or Fox," I reminded him.

"You're their queen too."

"So, if another male who isn't part of our fivesome touches me, it's going to make you jealous?" I asked and rinsed my hair.

When I opened my eyes, his face was level with mine. "No one else is allowed to touch you."

"What if I want to be touched?" I asked breathlessly and backed away from him, towards the wall of the shower.

He rested his hands on either side of my head and leaned close to whisper, "Then you tell me." He dropped one hand and slid two fingers inside of me, making me gasp and spread my legs wider for him.

"What if I want-"

I didn't even get to finish the question. He dropped his head and took my nipple into his mouth, twirling his tongue around my nipple and then sucking on it while he continued to finger me.

"Yes," I whispered and let my head fall back.

"What else do you want?" he asked me.

Instead of responding, I dropped to my knees, warm water sliding over my back, and took him into my mouth, surprised at his girth, but luckily able to accommodate it and still take most of him in before drawing back again.

"Fuck," he groaned and watched me.

His dick would feel amazing inside and I couldn't control my selfish desire any longer. I stood up, wrapped my arms around his neck, and climbed on him like a horny monkey, wrapping my legs around his waist.

He adjusted the angle and slid into me, groaning at the same time that I screamed.

"I'm sorry," he whispered as he withdrew.

"For what?" I asked, confused.

"For being a jealous asshole. I'm not usually like that," he replied.

I dropped my hips to pull him back into me. "You can fuck me in apology," I suggested.

He gripped my hips and smiled. "I've never done an apology fuck before."

"We can be each other's first apology fuck," I said with a smile and wiggled my hips.

He groaned and said, "If you keep that up, this will be a short apology."

I chuckled and he gripped my hips tighter before slamming into me.

"Yes!" I screamed.

"You're beautiful," he told me and kissed me deeply.

"Deryn!" I screamed as he pounded into me over and over

again, bringing orgasm after orgasm. I had never orgasmed so many times in my life.

He lay me on my back on the floor of the shower, water pelting us from every direction, and flicked his tongue across one nipple while playing with the other at the same time that his hips moved. Everything had become warm and wet, inside and out.

I reached down and rubbed my clit and moaned at the overload of sensations.

"Damn, you're glorious," he growled. Adjusting his position, he gripped my hips and slammed into me harder and faster, bringing another wave of pleasure that had me gripping his shoulders and screaming his name again.

He pulled out of me and orgasmed a moment later.

"Your…"

"Good?"

"Apology is accepted," I replied and closed my eyes, lying on the floor in euphoria.

He chuckled and kissed my cheek as he helped me stand up. Then, we washed each other, taking turns using the bar of soap. When we were done, we dried off and I put on one of his shirts and a pair of underwear.

We sat on the couch and I climbed into his lap, letting him cuddle me while we watched a comedy.

"I'm sorry we let that guy take you," he whispered in my ear. "We hoped we would find out who was behind it all. We didn't think a dragoness would come and steal you away using a portal."

I kissed his cheek and snuggled closer to him. "We found the culprit of this attempt, so it was probably for the best."

"You being injured was not for the best," he growled.

"I'm alive. That's all that matters," I whispered.

"We still don't know everyone who is after you. It obviously wasn't your dad who was trying to kill you. So, we're back to square one."

I hadn't thought about that. He was right.

"Are you hungry?" he asked. "You didn't get to eat any pizza."

"No," I whispered, my thoughts swirling away. "Sleepy."

"WE HAVE TO GO SEE THE ELDERS," RHYS TOLD ME. WE LAY IN Deryn's apartment together, facing me while I sat on the couch, Rhys's hands fisted on the back of the leather recliner.

"Okay," I replied, not sure why all four were looking at me so strangely.

"We can't take you," Deryn said, frowning and leaning forward like he was prepared to punch something.

"So, you'll be here alone," Fox explained, putting a calming hand on Deryn's shoulder.

"Oh," I whispered. Being alone wasn't a terrible thing, but having been with them constantly made being alone seem, well, lonely.

"We aren't sure how long we will be. Maybe an hour or two," Rhys said. "We'll try to hurry back."

"I'll be fine," I said, pulling the blanket I had wrapped around me even tighter. "I'll just play some video games."

They all fidgeted. Rhys shuffled from one foot to the other. Deryn stuck his hands in his pockets. Fox chewed on his bottom lip. Nico scuffed the toe of his shoe on the hardwood floor.

"What?" I asked and stood up, letting the blanket fall on the couch.

They glanced at each other and had some type of silent communication go on between them.

They obviously wanted to say something or ask something, but were hesitant to. I stepped forward and hugged Rhys, then went down the line, hugging each of them. They relaxed slightly and they turned to leave.

"Deryn?" I called.

He turned. "Yeah?"

"Can I add my account to your system?"

He smiled and nodded. "Yeah, go ahead."

"Thanks," I replied with a smile for him in return.

"Don't let anyone in," he ordered me.

I locked the door behind them and went to the fridge, grabbed a bottle of cider, and returned to the couch to play some games. It took a bit to get my profile set up on his system, but once I was logged in, a smile plastered itself on my face. I didn't like being away from the guys, but it had been far too long since I'd played games with my clan.

"I've returned!" I said when I joined the party chat.

"Jolie!" four male voices yelled joyously.

"We've missed you," Dragonknight told me.

"Sorry, things got crazy over here. So, are we playing *Ghost 2,* or what?"

"Duh!" Orphan, one of the crazier ones of our clan, said.

"I'm going to be rusty," I said with a sigh. "So, don't expect too much out of me."

"We never do," Turbo said.

Everyone laughed, even me, at his taunt.

The hours past as we played, my mind focused on the game and joking with my online friends. I didn't realize how late it was until Orphan said he was getting off for the night. He was in a different time zone than me, two hours ahead.

"I should get off too," I said, worried since the guys still weren't back and hadn't text me either.

"Night!" everyone yelled as we backed out of the chat lobby.

They said they would be an hour or two, but it had been four. I didn't want to seem needy, but I was worried about them. Sending a text to the group chat seemed the best option.

Me: You guys okay? You've been gone awhile and I haven't heard from you, so I was worried.

To distract myself, I heated up some of the leftover pizza and scrolled through the movies, trying to find one that would distract me enough not to worry about the guys. Thirty minutes past and I still hadn't received a text or call. Something was wrong. They wouldn't go silent like this and not respond to my messages.

I stood and paced. I didn't know where they had gone. The elders were not people I had been introduced to. Plus, I couldn't go outside on my own. Maybe Martin knew where they were.

Me: Hey, have you seen Deryn tonight?

Martin: No. I thought he was with you.

Me: He went to see the Elders. No idea where that is.

Martin: The Elders have a place in the center of all of the territories. I've never actually been there. Is something wrong? Do you need me to come over?

Me: No. No. I'm fine. Just being a worry wart because I haven't heard from him in a few hours.

Martin: He's really strong, Jolie. I'm sure he's fine.

Me: You're right. Sorry for bothering you.

Martin: If you need me to come over, just tell me.

Me: I'm fine. Thanks. Night.

Martin: Night.

I didn't think Deryn would be okay with coming back to his apartment and finding Martin with me. Hitting play on the movie, I tried to focus on the story and forget about the boys. They were princes. They were strong and I was just being paranoid.

What would I do if they didn't come back? I hadn't known them long, but they had quickly become part of my life. A big part of my life.

Shouldn't I be able to feel the connection between us? Hadn't they said that it was just harder for humans to use magic, not impossible?

Try as I might, I couldn't feel anything.

I'd fallen asleep at some point, because when they did come back, I was on my side on the couch. I jolted up and jumped over the couch, hugging the first one who came inside, which turned out to be Deryn.

"Hey," he said softly and hugged me back.

I pushed away from him with a fist to his chest, glad that he was back, but also pissed that they hadn't messaged me. Glaring, I asked, "Why didn't you text me?"

"We don't have service there," Rhys said softly, approaching as though to hug me.

I stepped back and said, "Whatever."

They frowned at me. It was frustrating to have four males frown at you at the same time.

I glared at them. Then, turning, I went to the spare room and climbed into the bed. They were safe, which was what I cared about. I wanted to touch them all, but I was letting my anger take over instead.

The four of them stood in the doorway to the room and looked at me.

"We're sorry," Fox apologized. "We would have messaged you or called if we could."

"It's fine. You don't need to apologize," I muttered and pulled the blankets up to cover the bottom of my mouth.

"We do," Nico said adamantly. "If the roles had been reversed, we would have been frantically trying to get ahold of you."

"I'm weak. You guys aren't."

They moved forward, and to my shock, all of them climbed onto the bed so they could all surround me in a square.

"What?"

They didn't talk, just placed their hands on my legs, arms, shoulders, whatever they could reach and closed their eyes. Almost instantly, Nico's breathing evened out as he fell into a deep sleep. Obviously, they weren't going to talk, so I got more comfortable and fell asleep too.

∾

I SAT BETWEEN NICO'S LEGS ON THE COUCH WITH RHYS AND Deryn on either side, and Fox sitting between my legs on the floor in front of the couch. They'd been overly affectionate ever since they returned from the Elders three days ago. Every night, they slept in a square of protection around me, making sure to touch me as they slept. No one tried anything sexual, not even more than light kisses were exchanged.

It was frustrating to be celibate again. Okay, I was being childish and selfish since it had only been about a week since I'd slept with one of them, but I was surrounded by gorgeous men and none were trying to fuck me.

The guys laughed at the comedy we were watching, but I wasn't really paying attention. There had been a search for my dad by the four clans, but of course, they hadn't found him. He was exceptional at hiding and disappearing when he needed to.

Nico slid his arms around my waist and squeezed me in a hug. "What's wrong?" he whispered in my ear.

"Nothing," I lied.

"Liar."

He stood up, disturbing the other three, but they didn't complain, just moved out of his way as he carried me to the spare bedroom. He set me on the bed and stood in the doorway, leaning against the doorframe.

"What's up?" he asked, his brow slightly furrowed in worry.

"I don't want to tell you," I muttered in embarrassment and looked down at my hands in my lap.

His hands covered mine and he squeezed them. I looked up into his eyes. He knelt in front of me and smiled. "You don't need to be embarrassed. You can tell me anything."

"You've all been exceptionally affectionate lately," I whispered, staring at his chest. "Which is great. But, none of you have done more than kiss me. What changed? Did I do something?"

His warm hand slid along my cheek, and he rubbed my cheek bone with his thumb. "You've done nothing wrong. We all agreed that we would be okay with all of us sleeping in the bed together and touching you at the same time. However, having other males so close, does make arousal nonexistent for us. That's just not something we are into. We are all wildly attracted to you still."

"I'm being needy and self-conscious," I muttered. "I tried to cure myself of that when I was a teenager. I thought I had, but clearly-"

He kissed me deeply and slid his hands into my hair, gripping the back of my head so that I had nowhere to go except to surrender to him. His tongue slid across mine and I moaned into his mouth, but immediately pulled away, surprised that he let me go.

"The others are right there," I reminded him. "They likely heard that."

Nico flicked his hand towards the door and it shut and locked on its own. He held his fist in front of him and blew into it. A bubble formed out the other end, continuing to grow in size the more he blew on it. The bubble slid along my skin as it engulfed the bed. When it went past my head, I could no longer hear the TV in the living room. Nico stepped into the bubble and pulled his shirt off.

"The others-"

"This bubble keeps the sounds we make from being heard by others. It also keeps the sounds from outside from being heard by us. We can be as loud as we want and they won't hear us," he explained. To prove his point, he yelled loudly and then smiled.

No one came running.

The sight of him shirtless was making it harder for me to remember why I was objecting in the first place. Crawling across the bed, he leaned over me, his bare chest right there for me to touch. Without even thinking, my hands went to touch his chest and stomach, stroking the muscles there.

"You're so handsome," I told him and looked up into his eyes.

He smiled and leaned down to kiss me while his hands slid up beneath my shirt and frustratingly stopped at the bottom of my bra. I sat up and ripped my shirt off over my head, then unsnapped my bra. His eyes lowered as the bra slipped off my arms, my nipples already hard from my arousal. He unbuttoned my pants and slid them off with my underwear in one motion. Cool air hit me and I shivered. His pants were still on, which was definitely not what I wanted. Before I could voice my objection, he opened my legs and his tongue swept across my most sensitive parts.

I arched up into him and gasped in pleasure. The amount of sexual frustration and desire I had been feeling made his tongue only necessary for a few swipes before an orgasm ripped through me. His eyebrows rose and he pulled his pants off.

"You should have told us you were so horny," he chastised me.

"Then what, you ro-sham-bo for who gets to fix me?" I asked breathlessly.

His pants gone, he pushed himself into me in one quick movement. The task easy since I was so incredibly wet.

"Yes," he replied. "Or we ask if you have a preference between us."

His mouth closed around one of my nipples just before he slammed into me hard enough for our skin to slap and sting a bit. Too worked up for it to matter, I could only moan my pleasure at the movements. His tongue swirled around one of my nipples while his fingers squeezed and teased my other one. It had been a long time since I'd been so far gone that my orgasms came so quickly. He was gentle with my nipples, but hard with my lower body. He pounded into me so hard that I knew I would be sore tomorrow, but I didn't care. It felt amazing and I was screaming his name and moaning louder than I ever had before.

"I'm really close," he admitted to me. "If you want to switch positions, now is the best time to tell me."

I pushed his chest and he leaned back, letting me get up. He put a condom on and sat back in front of me. Pushing his chest again, he lay on his back and I climbed on top of him, lowering myself until he was fully sheathed inside of me.

He groaned loudly and gripped my hips with his eyes rolled back in his head. I shared the sentiment and took it slow, moving my hips back and forth.

"You are fucking gorgeous," he told me as I rode him.

I smiled at the compliment and rode him harder and faster.

"Goddess, yes!" he moaned.

I screamed as another orgasm tore through me and he groaned.

"You're so wet," he told me. "It's amazing."

With a few more movements, he and I finished at the same time and I lay forward, my head resting on his shoulder with him still inside of me.

"I don't know if I'll be able to tell you when I want one of you," I admitted to him. "I don't want to hurt anyone's feelings or make you guys think that I have a favorite. I don't."

He rubbed my back and said, "We know you don't have a favorite."

"It's still weird," I told him. "Four males all bound to me. I don't even feel the bond."

"How do you feel about us?" he asked, turning his head so he could look at me.

"Way more than I should for only knowing you such a short time," I admitted.

"Come on," he groaned. "Give me more than that."

I cared deeply for them. I was falling in love with all of them. Admitting it out loud wasn't something that I wanted to do though. I didn't want to admit that I had developed such feelings for them.

His phone rang in his pants and he rolled us over until he could stand up and answer it. "Yeah? Okay. We'll be out in a minute."

"Who was that?" I asked, glad for the distraction from the conversation that we were having.

"Rhys. We're going to go out for dinner and he wanted to also check to make sure that you were okay."

I blushed and whispered, "Doesn't he sense my feelings through the bond?"

Dressing took a bit because my legs were jelly-like. Soreness was already setting in, which did not bode well for tomorrow.

"Yes."

"So, he knows that I was, uh, happy a minute ago."

Nico laughed and kissed my cheek as he put his pants on. "Yes, Jolie. They all know what we did in here, even if they couldn't hear us."

My face was on fire. How could I go outside and face them? This was not something I was going to get used to.

We finished dressing and he pulled me into a hug, resting his head atop mine. "It'll take some getting used to, but eventually, we will all grow accustomed to this and it won't be awkward at all."

Eventually? Even though I knew the bond wasn't something I could break without dying, I hadn't really thought about them being with me for the rest of my life. "You're all stuck with me for the rest of my life?" I asked him softly.

"Not stuck," he said adamantly. "We all chose this."

"Not really," I reminded him. "You all did it, but not really on purpose."

"We all care deeply for you," he whispered. "None of us regrets it."

Not yet, but what would they feel in six months or a year or three from now?

CHAPTER 9

"We're going on an overnight trip," Fox informed me with a wide smile as soon as I answered his knock at Rhys's apartment. He and Deryn came in at the same time, while Nico lounged on the couch. Rhys had taken a call in his bedroom and had yet to return.

"Really? Where?" I asked, excited to get out of the apartment.

"Camping," he said.

"Camping?" I scrunched my forehead.

"What's wrong?" Deryn asked.

"I've never been camping," I admitted. The thought of sleeping under the stars was nice, but being surrounded by bugs was not something I particularly had any interest in. Didn't mean I wouldn't go and enjoy myself, but I was definitely taking bug spray.

"When are we going?" I asked, already making a list of supplies I'd need in my head.

"Today," he said and smiled wide. Fox was perpetually playful, reminding me of a puppy a lot of the time. He was also incredibly smart and quiet most of the time, letting the others make decisions and only voicing his opinion if he really felt strongly about it.

I blinked. Scratch going to the store. "Can you take me to my apartment?" I requested.

"Sure," he agreed. "Rhys! I'm taking her to her apartment!"

"Okay!" Rhys called back from his bedroom. It wouldn't surprise me if he was already packing.

Fox and I took the elevator and walked to my apartment in silence. His aura and presence were incredibly relaxing and I preferred being alone with him.

"Fox?"

"Hm?" he asked and turned towards me.

"How do you feel about this whole situation? Being bound to me and the others?" Aside from not talking much, he rarely expressed his feelings.

"I would prefer to have you to myself," he admitted with a smirk. "However, I love my brothers, and sharing you with them isn't so bad."

"So, you're fine with sharing me as long as it is with them?" I questioned.

He scowled. "Are you wanting to see other men?"

The absurdity of his question made me burst out laughing. I had to stop walking, resting a hand on the wall as I doubled over in laughter until tears streamed down my face.

"What's funny?" he asked.

"Foxfire, I feel terrible for being shared among the four of you. There is no way in hell I could even begin to consider other men."

He pinned me to the hallway wall and all of my laughter died at the sight of the heat in his eyes. "It makes me very happy to hear you say that," he whispered. His eyes searched mine a moment and then lowered to my lips.

We hadn't kissed in too long, and he seemed to waver on his decision, so I stood up on my tiptoes and kissed him, sweeping my tongue along his lips so he would open them. He pressed me into the wall and returned my kiss, opening his mouth to me and surrounding me in his scent, jasmine and freshly cut grass.

The kiss ended too soon for my liking, but the beautiful smile on his face made it all worth it.

"Come, we need to get you packed quickly so we can be on our way."

The hallway was still burned and there was just a tarp stapled over the hole of my apartment.

"Do you think anyone stole anything?" I asked nervously.

"No, the apartment manager is very good about not letting anyone inside who isn't supposed to be in," he assured me. "If you're worried, you can put whatever you want inside of my apartment. We've been staying in Deryn's apartment most of the time anyway."

"I would appreciate that," I replied and pushed aside the tarp that now made up my door. I longingly gazed at my gaming console, but since Deryn already had one and had agreed to let me put my log in on his, I looked away.

"Would you like me to take your games and console over?" Fox wrapped his arms around my shoulders and whispered in my ear.

I chuckled. "Am I that obvious?"

"No, but it's probably the most expensive thing you have, so it makes sense that you would want it to be safe," he explained, squeezing me once and releasing me before heading toward my games.

He was right, the console and all of the games were the most expensive things that I owned. Was that sad? Should I have other more expensive things? I had never been obsessed with jewelry or makeup. I liked wearing dresses, but hated shopping for them or anything else really. I liked buying presents for people, but hated buying anything for myself.

I was ecstatic that I hadn't had anything against the wall that had been blown up, so I hadn't lost anything in the explosion. Except my privacy.

I headed toward my bedroom and realized that I had nothing on my mental checklist for camping, but the bug spray. "What the hell am I supposed to bring?" I yelled into the other room.

"Clothes!" he yelled back and then laughed.

"Asshole," I muttered. Packing took me a long time, but I figured out to pack jeans, t-shirts, warm pajamas, and underwear.

When I walked out to the living room, I realized that I was alone.

"Fox?" I called.

"Coming!" he called from outside of my apartment. The tarp moved a minute later and he was there.

"What were you doing?"

"I was putting some of your stuff in my apartment," he explained.

I looked around and was shocked to see that all of my valuable items were gone now.

"Wow. Thanks, Fox. I really appreciate you doing that."

He kissed my cheek. "Anything for you, my queen."

He pulled my bag from me, and pressed a finger to my lips when I went to protest. He hurried back under the tarp before I could say anything. I sighed and followed him to the elevator where I took my bag back. Amused, Fox put up his hands in surrender before we stepped out on the first floor. When we walked into Rhys's apartment, the other three standing in the living room, with a pile of supplies between them.

"Got your stuff?" Deryn asked, looking at my black duffle bag.

"Yep," I said and tossed the bag onto their pile. "I'm sure I'm forgetting something, though."

"Always happens," Nico said with a chuckle. "You get there and realize that you've forgotten something important."

I hadn't noticed until then, but all of them were wearing jeans and t-shirts. Damn they looked amazing. Deryn had the largest biceps, and his shirt accentuated them nicely.

Rhys's chest was the most sculpted, visible through his shirt.

Nico and Fox were sexy too, and I couldn't stop staring.

"Jolie?" Rhys asked.

"Huh?" I replied, looking up at their faces.

They were all smirking.

Shit.

"Ready to go?" I asked and turned towards the door.

"Our eyes are up here," Deryn whispered as he walked by me.

They all laughed and grabbed the supplies. I walked down in the middle of them, glad to be getting out of the apartment. There was a SUV waiting for us outside the apartment building with Martin leaning against it.

I pushed past the guys and rushed towards him. Martin pushed off the SUV, a wide smile on his face, and pulled me into a tight hug.

"What are you doing here?" I asked from within his hug.

"Deryn called in the request for a driver, and I was the only one available, so Dan asked me to come," he explained.

"Jolie," Deryn growled.

Martin kissed the top of my head and released me to face the four angry males behind me. It seemed that Deryn wasn't the only one who had jealousy issues. Fox's jealous face was the most surprising of all.

"Guys, this is Martin, my best friend. Martin, you know Deryn. This is Rhys, Fox, and Nico," I introduced them.

"Martin, your ex-boyfriend?" Fox asked, taking a step closer to me.

It seemed the best thing to do would be to ignore them. So, I turned around, putting my back to the foursome.

"Do you know where we are going?" I asked Martin.

"Yeah. Deryn sent me the address beforehand. I've actually been there a couple of times. It's a gorgeous place. You'll have a ton of fun," he told me and opened the passenger door of the SUV for me.

Before the guys could object, I climbed inside and buckled my belt. The four jealous males climbed into the back, glaring daggers at Martin who climbed in the driver's seat with a wide smile on his face.

"All set?" he asked them, draping his arm across the back of my seat to turn around and look at them.

"Martin," Deryn growled in warning.

"Great!" Martin said and started the car. "Jo, do you want to pick the music?"

Martin was obviously doing this to rile them up. Why? I wasn't sure, but I was sort of enjoying it. As twisted as that was.

"Thanks," I told him and started shifting through the various stations. "Hey, remember that time that we snuck out of town and went to the country music concert?"

His driving had always been great, so I didn't worry about distracting him. He tugged on my hair and then twirled it around his finger. "Oh, you mean that night that you got so hammered, that I had to pull you off of the stage and you almost puked in my truck?"

"Was that the night that we ended up sleeping in Mr. Archer's corn field?"

He nodded. "We woke up covered in dirt and leaves," he said and laughed. He turned to look at me while we were stopped at a red light. "You still looked beautiful, even covered in dirt." He winked and there were at least two growls behind us.

"Oh," Martin whispered and reached into the center console. "The girls sent this for you." He pulled out a bracelet of braided hair.

"What is this?" I asked, confused.

"It's their tail hairs. They took turns plucking hairs from each other's tails and then braided it into a bracelet for you," he explained.

I gingerly took the bracelet and felt tears stinging my eyes. "Oh, wow." It was very soft and was made up of a few different colors.

"They told me to tell you, 'we love you, Auntie Jolie and we hope to see you soon'. They wouldn't stop talking about seeing you for like, a week."

"I wish I could see them more," I mumbled and sniffed against the tears threatening to spill.

"No reason you can't," Martin reminded me. "We're living in the same city now."

"I told you. You know why. And don't for a minute act like a part of you doesn't agree with me."

He sighed and set his hand on my knee. "I'm sorry. I didn't want to start a fight."

"Get your hand off of her," Rhys ordered him with a snarl.

I turned and faced the four, incredibly angry, males. "Hey! You four need to chill out."

"Stop flirting with him," Fox accused.

I rolled my eyes. "I'm not flirting with him. We are talking as friends. He is my friend. He has a mate who he loves and two daughters with said mate. His mate is my other best friend and I love his daughters. I would never come between them, even if there was something between us. But, there isn't! You all are being incredibly jealous, and I don't appreciate it. Not one bit."

Thankfully, the four of them had the decency to look cowed, even though I knew that they likely weren't done being jealous.

Martin had removed his hand, but as he faced forward, watching the road ahead, I saw the smirk on his lips. Did Dan have an ulterior motive in sending Martin to drive us?

"How long will it take to get to our destination?" I asked Martin, turning to face the front.

"About an hour," he answered.

An hour of awkward silence between my males and me. Mine.

When did I start thinking of them as mine? They did call me their queen, and the bond made, them my guards.

"Jolie," Fox whispered.

I turned slowly towards him, and found them all staring at me with various expressions, but luckily none looked mad.

"What are you thinking about?" Fox asked.

"Nothing," I mumbled and turned away, looking out the window to my right to avoid all of their gazes.

"She's always been a terrible liar," Martin said to the guys. "She thinks she is good at it, but she's quite terrible."

"We know," Nico replied tersely.

No more words were spoken on the rest of the drive. Our destination turned out to be a gorgeous field of green grass with a few trees and a beautiful lake not far off. Martin helped the guys unload everything and then hugged me tightly before leaving.

Standing alone, I looked out over the sea of grass and watched it sway in the breeze.

"We're sorry," Fox whispered behind me.

"It's fine," I whispered back and headed towards the lake.

"Can I walk with you?" Rhys requested.

"Sure," I replied, but still didn't turn to look at him. This land was beautiful, but it reminded me a bit of home.

His fingers laced through mine, and he walked by my side silently. I stopped at the edge of the lake and looked out at the clear water. I could see all the way to the bottom, even far out from the beaches.

"We didn't realize how much it would bother us to see you with another male, since we all share you so easily," he whispered to me.

"I wasn't *with* another male," I reminded him. Seriously, what type of girl did they think I was? Oh, right. A girl that slept with one of them the first night she'd met him and went out with them all in the same week.

"Seeing you touch another male," he amended. "We all laughed at Deryn for his fit of jealousy, but then we all felt it. I understand that you and Martin are simply friends, but it doesn't change how it feels to see a male hugging you."

"So, I can't touch any other males?" I asked.

He sighed. "I would prefer if you didn't, but we of course aren't going to do that. It would help if you would just keep our feelings in mind when you do touch other males. We don't touch other females and wouldn't if you asked us to."

"I'm not going to apologize for hugging Martin," I told him and turned to face him.

He smiled and rested his hand on my cheek. "We don't want you to."

"You keep saying, 'we' instead of 'I'. Why?"

"Because we all agree on these topics. We've all discussed them."

"How could you have discussed this when we were silent in the car?"

"Text message," he replied with a chuckle.

I rolled my eyes, but laughed too. "I should have known."

He lowered his head towards me, seeking a kiss, but hesitated. "Are you still mad?"

"No," I replied honestly.

"Can I kiss you?"

"You may."

His lips brushed mine and then he kissed me firmly.

"You said you won't touch other females. Does that mean ever? Like, you four won't sleep with other women the rest of our lives?" I asked him softly.

He nodded. "You're our queen. You're my queen. You are the only female for me. If I took another lover, it would divide my attention and you could be hurt or killed due to my distraction. Plus, I care about you and I wouldn't want to hurt you by being with another female."

"What if I said you could?" I asked him. I truly didn't want to know or see them with other lovers, but it just didn't seem fair to them.

"You want me to have another lover?" he asked, his hand still on my cheek.

"No, but you four are sharing one female between you. It's hardly fair."

"As long as you are in my life, and I get moments like this, I will be happy."

His statement made me ridiculously happy and made me feel even more selfish. It should be wrong for me to be so happy that they only wanted me. I was an incredibly selfish creature and I didn't deserve any of them.

"Rhys, can I see your dragon form?" I requested. "I didn't really get a chance to admire your other form the other day since we were running away from vampires."

He kissed the back of my hand and bowed. "As my queen wishes." His body glowed and then he became a dragon, easily twice the size of an SUV. His scales were red and shimmered in the sunlight with an almost pearlescent quality to them. He had horns on his head and his nostrils were huge. He was magnificent.

I stepped forward and slid my hands along his scales, which were smooth, but very thick. his tail had a few spikes on it, reminding me of a dinosaur I saw in a museum. Did he use it in fighting?

He exhaled and smoke puffed out of his nostrils, drawing my attention. It was definitely warmer up by his head and I waved my hand through the smoke, giggling like an idiot. He lowered his head and I stared into his large dragon's eye, seeing not a dragon, but Rhys.

"You're gorgeous," I admitted to him.

He shifted back and smiled. "I'm glad that you think so. I was worried that you might be scared of me in that form."

"Would you ever hurt me?" I asked him.

He smirked. "Only if you wanted me to."

I laughed and playfully pushed his arm. "Brat."

"Jolie, why did you and Martin break up? You two are very close."

"That's not a story I'd like to relive right now," I whispered and felt my chest tighten as panic started to set in at the onslaught of memories.

"Okay, we don't have to talk about it," he promised and pulled me into a hug. He smelled like he always did and it made me instantly relax.

"Hey, you going to help us set up the tents?" Nico called.

"I guess we should get back to them," Rhys said with a sigh.

"We should," I agreed.

Rhys took my hand, and we walked back to the others to help get camp set up. Once everything was ready, we went to an open area and all of them, except Nico, shifted.

I leaned against Rhys's massive side with Deryn's wolf head on my lap, and Fox lying on my chest with my arms around him. Nico sat next to me, his side touching mine from shoulder to ankle.

"I could get used to this," I whispered as I dozed happily with them.

"We could do this more, but Rhys is a bit too large in his dragon form," Nico replied.

He was right, but I hadn't wanted to say it.

Rhys huffed and smoke rose from his nostrils. I chuckled and patted his scaled side. "It just means we will have to make more trips away from the city, so I can spend time with you in this form."

My butt was starting to hurt, so I set Fox to the side and stood up, stretching my arms up over my head. Deryn stretched and then dropped his front paws down and wagged his tail in an invitation to play.

I reached out and tapped his shoulder before running away. "You're it!" I yelled back to him.

He yipped and charged after me, his long strides ate up the ground between us and he bumped his nose against me.

I turned and ran back after him, but tapped Fox who was just watching us. He squawked in shock and then started chasing after me.

Deryn ran with me, but at the last second, Fox bumped Deryn, making him it. He ran over to Nico and bumped him with his nose and then hightailed it away.

Nico stood up slowly, but then reached back and touched Rhys before running as fast as he could towards us. Rhys growled and charged us, his massive size made each step shake the ground and I stumbled, falling into the grass as he rested his nose against me.

Groaning, I leapt up and raced after Nico, who was the closest to me. He was fast and nimble though, so I couldn't get him, but focusing on him had made Deryn drop his guard and I slapped his shoulder as I ran by, hiding behind Nico.

For at least an hour, I played tag with my guards, only stopping because I was too tired to run more and dropped onto my back, my chest heaving.

"I give!" I told them and raised one arm. "I surrender. I'm too tired to do more."

"Here," Nico said and handed me a bottle of cold water.

Greedily, I gulped it down and exhaled loudly after finishing it. "So, what's for dinner?"

"I guess it is dinner time," Deryn replied after shifting back to his human form. "I'm always hungry, so I wasn't really thinking about it."

"I'll start the fire," Nico said and headed towards the rock circle that we had made for the fire pit.

Rhys shifted back and lay on the ground beside me, his arms

behind his head. "That was fun. I can't remember the last time that I played tag."

"Me neither," I admitted and snuggled closer to him, putting my head on one of his arms. "Turtle," I said and pointed up at the sky.

"Turtle?" Fox asked and looked up where I was pointing. "Oh, the cloud shape!" He laid his head on my shins and pointed in the distance. "Monkey."

"That's an octopus," Deryn argued.

"It's clearly a squid," Rhys argued back.

"Rhys, come cook the meat!" Nico called from the campsite.

We all went with him, and I sat on a log that they had carried over, drinking ciders that Fox had brought for me. The four of them went about making dinner, bantering with each other and acting like they would have, if I hadn't been there. It was nice to see them happy and doing something without me being the center of attention. Could it be like this after we defeated my dad and the strangers who were trying to kill me? Could we have a life like this all of the time?

My number one worry was that they would try to make me choose. *I couldn't choose. I loved them all.*

Wait? Love. Had I just admitted to myself that I loved them?

"What is it?" Fox asked, kneeling in front of me. "Why are you scared?"

Stupid bond!

"Nothing," I whispered and knew I was blushing as I looked away from him.

"You can't lie to us," he reminded me. Gently, he picked up my hand and kissed my knuckles. "What is it, Jolie?"

I shook my head and walked away from them, headed towards a set of trees not far away so I could think without them being near me.

Love? Did I truly love them? Wasn't it too early to be in love?

The bond had accelerated our feelings, so it was hypothetically possible.

I pictured my life without them and immediately felt fear, anxiety, and a few other things swirl within me that I didn't like. No, I couldn't live without them. Not any of them. There was no possible way to choose between them. And, I didn't want to live without them all either. Thinking about them being hurt sent a pang of pain through my entire body.

Dammit. I was in love with them. All four of them.

"Talk to me," Fox whispered and slid his hands and up down my arms. "What's going on in that head of yours? Your emotions are all over the place."

"I can't live without you," I whispered. "Any of you. You all mean so much to me that thinking of living without you now, hurts."

"We feel the same way about you," he told me. His arms wrapped around me and held me in a warm hug. "You are our world, Jolie. Nothing else matters, but you."

Was he saying what I thought he was? Did they love me too?

"Dinner is ready!" Rhys called to us. "Get it while it's hot."

Dinner turned out to be hamburgers and hot dogs, which I was perfectly fine with. I made my plate and sat on the log with them all around the fire on other logs.

"What would you be doing right now, if I wasn't in your life?" I asked between bites of my burger and drinks of my third or fourth cider. I had lost count already.

They all tensed and it took a minute for one of them to reply.

"We would be playing games online together, most likely," Fox replied.

"Would you be with females?" I wasn't stupid enough to think they were virgins before me, but thinking about the with another female made my blood boil.

"Perhaps," Rhys agreed.

"Why are you asking this?" Deryn asked, his shoulders tensed.

"It just seems like I have changed your lives too much," I admitted. "Like I've stolen what your life should be like."

"You've invaded our life for sure," Nico agreed. "If we went back in time and could change things, we wouldn't change meeting you or you entering our lives. We are happy with you."

"Our lives were boring before we met you," Fox said.

"You mean it was quiet because you didn't have to keep saving or rescuing a human girl," I said and chuckled. "My life has definitely been noisier since meeting you all."

"What would you be doing right now if you hadn't met us?" Rhys asked.

I shrugged. "Playing games with my clan, most likely. Or trying to find someone to date."

If I hadn't met them, I wouldn't have gotten them tangled in the cursed web of my life.

"You've become entangled in our hearts," Deryn told me. "There is no way for you to leave, no matter how much you might try to hack at the vines entangling you."

I was envisioning myself standing within a heart with vines covering it and wrapped around me.

"You make it sound like it is a prison," I said and smirked. "Being with you guys is anything, but awful."

"We are glad to hear that," Fox said with a smile.

"So, is this what you usually do when camping?" I asked. "You play games, eat some food, and hang out?"

They nodded.

"We also make s'mores," Deryn said and grabbed a bag of marshmallows and sticks.

"I've never had one," I admitted. "I've heard about them, but since I have never been camping before…"

"They're amazing," Fox said and came to sit next to me. "I'll help you make the perfect one."

"There's a way to make them wrong?" How could you make it wrong?

"No, but the marshmallows are best when they're lightly toasted on the outside and melted on the inside. You have to put them in the fire just right."

"You need to light them on fire for a minute to get them crispy," Rhys said and sat on my other side.

"I'm surprised that you use this fire and not your own," I teased.

"He has used his fire when he was craving them and we weren't camping," Deryn told me.

"That was one time and I was hammered," Rhys argued.

"You still did it," Deryn said and pointed at him.

I laughed as the guys made the marshmallows. The first time I tried to roast mine, it melted right off my stick and fell on the ground. They laughed at my pout and told me more stories about times they had gone camping.

S'more in hand, they all watched me with bated breath as I took a bite. The cracker crumbled, but I was able to catch most of the crumbs in my hand as I chewed on the s'more. It was divine!

"It's amazing," I said with a full mouth of smore.

They all beamed proudly, like they had made it for me personally.

"I know you'd like it," Fox said and ate his in two bites before reaching and grabbing another marshmallow to make a second one.

"What's your favorite color?" Rhys asked me.

"Teal."

"Favorite flower?" Deryn asked.

"Cherry blossoms and hibiscus."

"Favorite holiday?" Fox asked.

"Halloween!"

"Favorite drink?" Nico asked.

"That's hard," I admitted. "I love cocoa, margaritas, and iced tea with a lemon wedge."

"Favorite male?" Rhys asked.

I rolled my eyes. Nice try. "It's so hard to pick," I replied with a groan. "I have so many to choose from."

"So many?" Deryn asked.

"Who is your favorite female?" I asked them.

"You," they said at the same time.

"Do you want to sleep outside or in a tent?" Nico asked me.

"Tent," I replied instantly.

They looked at each other and then back at me.

"What?" I grumbled.

"Why did you say it like that?" Fox asked.

"I don't like bugs," I admitted to them. "I've always been creeped out by bugs."

"Are you scared of certain bugs or animals?" Rhys asked.

"Yes," I mumbled, not wanting to reply.

"And those are?" Deryn prompted.

"Why does it matter?" I asked grumpily. Every girl I knew was scared of bugs.

"If we know what you're afraid of, we can make sure to keep it away from you," Fox explained.

"I'm afraid of losing you four," I mumbled, staring at the last half of my s'more in my hands.

"Why would you lose us?" Rhys asked and squatted down in front of me. He set his hands on top of mine, where I was twisting my s'more around.

"If you wise up and realize I'm not a queen. Or you try to make me choose. Or you find someone better suited to being a match for a prince. Or if you get hurt or worse, killed, trying to protect me. Or...damn this alcohol. I wasn't supposed to say any of this out loud."

Quickly, I stood up and stumbled away from the fire and them. Away from the fire and their eyes, I felt cold and rubbed my arms while looking up at the stars overhead. We were such small creatures in the universe. None of us truly mattered in the grand scheme of life.

"You aren't going to lose us," Rhys whispered from behind me.

I turned around and all four of them stood side by side just behind me.

"You can't say that for sure. You don't know what will happen in the future," I argued.

"We know that we all love you," said Fox.

"We all know that you are our queen," said Deryn.

"We all know that we will do whatever we must to keep you safe," Nico said.

"And we all know that we will do whatever we have to, to keep you in our lives," Rhys said.

"You love me?" I asked softly, feeling like I was flying and falling at the same time.

"We do," Deryn replied and the other three nodded their heads in agreement.

"And you won't make me choose between you?" I asked softly.

"Never," Nico promised.

"I love you, too," I said as I looked at each of them.

They moved forward and surrounded me in a group hug.

"You're stuck with us forever, now," Deryn whispered against my neck.

"Now that you've admitted you love us, we won't let you go," Rhys murmured from my right side.

"Together forever," Fox whispered as he stood in front of me with a wide smile.

I smiled back at him and said, "Sounds like a great plan."

CHAPTER 10

"What do you mean they've summoned me?" I asked Rhys and looked at the other three who were wearing identically blank expressions. They only used blank expressions when they were hiding their true emotions from me.

"The Elders want to meet and talk with you," Fox explained.

"We'll be with you the entire time," Nico assured me.

"Will they hurt me?"

"No," Deryn said adamantly and picked up one of my hands, squeezing it in reassurance. "We won't let them hurt you."

It had been over a week since they had visited the Elders without me. In that time, I'd gotten used to staying in Rhys's apartment, where I was safe and together with all my boys. Even though the room was warm, I felt a chill.

"But, they're the Elders and they can tell you what to do, right? They could order you to kill me?" I'd seen it in a few anime shows and I did not want to end up like those poor women.

"They could order us, but we have free will and none of us would ever harm you," Deryn promised.

"Then you'll get killed for not obeying them," I said and threw my hands up in the air.

Rhys chuckled and took my face in his hands, forcing me to meet his eyes. "They won't do anything like that. They just want to talk to you and meet you. They said they may be able to help you learn to use the bond, which I know is something you want help with."

I looked at them, standing together in front of me. They always dressed like they were going to go out. I had gotten a little dressed up earlier on a whim, even though we hadn't left the apartment since our camping trip. Now I was glad I had.

"Okay," I agreed. "As long as you'll be by my side the entire time."

They nodded in agreement and I reluctantly followed them out to the car. Martin smiled at me as we approached, but when he saw my face, his smile wilted.

"What's going on?" he asked me after getting into the driver's seat.

"She's nervous about going to meet the Elders," Deryn informed him.

"They'll love you. Everyone who meets you loves you. The Alpha can't stop talking about you," Martin said with a smile.

"Will the kings be there?" I asked and turned to face my Guards.

They all nodded.

"Great. Not only do I have to meet the Elders, but the other fathers too," I grumbled, folded my arms, and slumped in my seat.

"They met you once already, remember?" Fox reminded me.

"Oh yes, when I was hammered and interrupted your meeting," I said, my scowl deepening.

We drove in silence, my mind supplying all kinds of situations which ended with me dead. Martin rested his hand on my knee, where the guys couldn't see it. Even his touch wasn't enough to reassure me.

I envisioned us driving to a dark and gloomy castle, but it was the furthest from the truth. Martin stopped the SUV in front of a gorgeous country estate with perfectly trimmed hedges and a beautiful rose garden.

Martin squeezed my knee for reassurance and I climbed out. No point in delaying the inevitable. My guards took their places. Rhys in front of me, Deryn on my left, Fox on my right, and Nico behind me. I touched each of their hands briefly and then we walked inside.

Inside, paintings by famous artists lined the walls, each worth hundreds of thousands of dollars.

The guys seemed to know where they were going, making a few turns, going down two flights of stairs, and then stopped before two metal doors. So far, we hadn't seen a single person. Where were they?

"We're with you," Rhys reminded me without turning around.

"We love you," Deryn whispered.

"I love you all, too," I replied, surprised that my voice did not wobble with emotion.

Rhys pushed open the door, and we walked inside. The room was humongous, large enough to hold a concert in, easily. At the moment, there were seven people at the end, all males. I recognized the four kings from the park, but the other three were definitely no one I had met before. They were old, bent with age, but their eyes held an intelligence and authority that made it clear they were the Elders.

We stopped before them and all bowed. The guys had worked with me on this move a few days ago, for the purpose of meeting the alphas, but we hadn't gotten a chance to do so before today.

When we stood up, I glanced at the alphas and Dan winked at me. That helped me loosen a bit and I faced the Elders with no tremors.

The Elders were all different races. The one in the middle had the telltale pointed ears of an elf. The one on the right was the tallest, with a full head of grey hair, and a matching beard. His eyes were golden, a werewolf. The Elder on the left was the shortest, but most muscular, with forearms of a much younger male. He smiled at me and his eyes shifted to a bright green with a slit down the center. A dragon.

"Great Elders," Rhys began, "we present to you our queen, Jolie." He stepped to the side, taking a place beside Deryn and exposing me to them.

"You are human?" the elf Elder asked.

"Yes, sir," I replied. "I do have a thirty second Gorgon in me, but no powers or anything."

"Your father is the vampire king, correct?" the dragon Elder asked.

I nodded.

"When was he changed?" The wolf Elder asked.

"A few months after my birth," I answered and then quickly added, "Sir."

All three Elders smiled and the wolf Elder said, "we appreciate your respect, but you need only answer, not add 'sir' at the end."

"Yes, sir," I agreed and then cleared my throat. "Okay."

"The princes indicated that you discovered the vampire king had stolen the artifact to start the war," wolf Elder said. "Yet, it came to be in your possession without his knowledge. How?"

"My grandmother gave it to me. I'm…" I paused, unsure how to describe myself. "…I say I'm cursed, but I'm not literally cursed, I don't think. So, unlucky might be better. I've been attacked on multiple occasions by Others. One attack was by vampires who captured me and…hurt me. I escaped and when I told my grandmother what happened, she provided me with the artifact. She said it would keep the vampires from finding me."

"Did it?" elf Elder asked.

"Yes. The vampires hadn't been able to locate me, until I removed it and relinquished it to the kings."

"Not without a bit of a fight," the mage king commented.

"And your guards protected you and killed the vampires, correct?" dragon Elder asked, ignoring the comment.

"Correct," I agreed.

"And that is when you believe you created the bond?" wolf Elder asked and looked at my guards.

"Yes, Elder," Deryn replied.

"Yet, it wasn't a completely conscious decision, correct?" Dragon Elder asked.

"Yes, Elder," Rhys replied.

"Do you feel the bond, Jolie?" elf Elder asked.

I shook my head. "No. I've tried, but can't sense it."

"Jolie, please come forward," elf Elder ordered me.

Determined not to upset them, I didn't glance back at my guards. Despite really *really* wanting to. I stepped forward and my guards moved with me.

"Only Jolie," elf Elder ordered them.

Out of the corner of my eye, I saw Deryn's hand curl into a fist.

They didn't seem like they would appreciate being made to wait, so I walked to them and wondered if I should bow again or drop to one knee.

The three Elders' eyes shifted and began to glow. They covered me in glowing magic of three different colors. Red for the dragon, white for the elf, and green for the wolf. The colors highlighted a rope that went from my chest to the four guards behind me. There was no doubt about the bond now.

"We can remove the bond without hurting you," dragon Elder offered me. "It won't harm your guards either, but you will be removed and unable to develop a bond with any of them in the future, should you desire to, aside from a mate bond."

"I-"

Did I want to remove the bond now?

"Jolie," the four said at the same time.

"You could be free," I whispered to them. "Free to find a princess worthy of you. Free of my curse."

"You are cursed," elf Elder agreed and waved at my chest. "A witch's curse."

"We don't want anyone else. We told you this on our trip," Fox reminded me.

"You are more than worthy," Deryn told me. "Right, Father?"

All eyes turned towards Dan who had been scowling. He looked at me and said, "You are worthy."

The other kings' eyes widened and they turned away from Dan to focus on me. No doubt, trying to understand what he saw in me.

"What's your decision?" dragon Elder asked.

I chewed on my bottom lip and looked at my four guards. What to do? Free them, or keep them? Was it selfish to keep them?

Definitely. They had said that they wanted to keep the bond, though. If I freed them from me, they could return to their normal lives. They could be free of the chaos that I brought with me. And I would be miserable. Even though I couldn't feel the bond, just knowing it was there made me happier and safer than I had in years. Plus, I truly loved them. I didn't want to be without them.

"I'll keep my bond," I replied.

All four exhaled and their bodies relaxed, tension leaving them in a rush.

"Would you like us to teach you how to use the bond?" wolf Elder asked.

"Please," I begged.

Then, I decided to ask for something else, since they were offering to help me.

"Can you remove the curse?"

The three Elders looked at each other, some type of silent communication going on.

"We can," elf Elder finally said.

"But it will hurt you, a lot," dragon Elder explained.

"What is the curse?" Dan asked.

"Curse of Antalia," elf Elder replied.

Dan said something under his breath and looked away. When I looked at the guys, they were all scowling and whispering to each other.

"Breaking that curse will have repercussions," The dragon King said. "She may not be able to handle them."

Dragon Elder shrugged. "True."

"Don't do it," Rhys ordered me.

"What? Why not?" I demanded, spinning to face him.

"You might die from the backlash. It's not worth it," Deryn explained.

"Listen to them, girl," the dragon King said.

"Let us show you how to use your bond," wolf Elder said. "Our offer will remain open and you can return, should you want to remove the curse."

"Thank you," I said, feeling irritated to be so close to being able to remove it and yet being told not to.

The Elders took an hour to show me how to find the bond. Finally, I could sense the bond and with it, feel the guys and their presences. Even a slight sense of their feelings.

"The more you practice, the easier it will become and the stronger your sense of them will be," elf Elder told me.

I bowed. "Thank you."

"What will your father do, now that his secret has been exposed?" dragon Elder asked me.

"He is power hungry. I have no doubt that he will still grow his army and attack at some point."

"Vampires can't defeat dragons," the dragon king replied confidently.

"He never said his army was vampires," I pointed out.

That had every one of them focused on me again.

"Do you have information you haven't shared with us yet?" wolf Elder asked.

"This isn't a certainty, I just know how he works. He has worked with other races before. I could see him doing so again. To defeat mages and dragons, he would need more than vampires, and he knows that."

"You five are dismissed," dragon Elder ordered us. "You may return if you change your mind about the curse, or your bond," he told me.

I bowed and the guys did the same. "Thank you, Great Elders," I said.

Dan grabbed my arm gently before I turned to leave. "Come see me tomorrow," he ordered me.

"As you wish, Alpha," I replied and dipped my head in submission.

He bent close to me and whispered, "Stay close to your guards. I want you to stay safe."

I nodded once and he released me to return to my guards who immediately herded me out of the building and into the SUV.

Martin drove us out and waited until we were off the grounds to ask, "How'd it go?"

"Good," I replied softly, my brain spinning with everything that had happened. Most of all, Dan's warning words. Did he know something? Or was he just worried?

And I knew I was cursed!

"What's the Curse of Antalia?" I asked out loud, hoping one of them would respond.

Martin looked at me and then had to swerve back into his lane on the road before running into another car.

"How'd you hear about that curse?" he asked, his words tumbling out almost on top of each other.

"It's what I'm cursed with," I said and turned to smirk at him. "I told you I was cursed."

He glanced in the rearview mirror. "Please tell me she heard wrong or is confused."

Deryn shook his head. "The Elders informed us that she has the curse."

"Fuck," Martin replied.

"Anyone going to fill me in?" I asked, but received no response. Pulling out my phone, I searched the internet for the curse and got a ton of results.

Curse of Antalia
Performed by a witch. High level curse.
Curses the victim with a propensity to self-sacrifice, increases likelihood of Others finding them, increases the odds of attacks by Others, decreases moral...

Blah, Blah, Blah. Ah! Here it was.

Removal can be done, but the magical backlash has been known to cause paralysis, coma induction, and even death.

Well, fuck.

My door opened and I jumped, barely holding in a scream. I hadn't noticed the car had stopped.

Rhys unbuckled me and tugged me out of the SUV by my hand.

"Bye," I said to Martin, but he wasn't even looking at me.

We took an awkward elevator ride up to Deryn's, reminding me of the day that I had found out they knew each other and lived with me.

Deryn ordered pizza and they all stood stiffly around the living room. I could barely sense their feelings, but anger and fear prevailed.

"That went better than I thought it would," I said cheerfully with a wide smile.

"You were going to break the bond," Fox whispered. He felt sadness and fear. "Why?"

"I didn't break it," I reminded them.

"It took you quite a while to decide not to," Nico pointed out.

"You're all mad at me," I realized.

"Wouldn't you be?" Deryn snapped.

I shook my head. "No. I would know that you were thinking of me and what would be best for me. That you were trying not to be selfish."

"Selfish?" Rhys asked.

"It's selfish of me to keep the bond. I know that. Especially, now that I know what the curse is."

"You know?" Fox asked. "How?"

I held up my phone. "Internet."

"You were going to break the bond, even though we told you that we love you," Nico argued.

"Yes, I contemplated it."

"Don't you love us?" Fox asked.

"Of course I do!" I yelled. "That's why I was trying to save you. To free you. But, ultimately, I couldn't do it. I couldn't give you up. I can't imagine my life without you in it."

They relaxed, but now I was frustrated, so I stormed off to the spare room, and shut and locked the door. Head in my hands, I sat on the bed.

How could they not understand what I meant? It had nothing to do with my love for them.

"Trouble in paradise?" Burton, my father's right-hand man asked.

I opened my mouth to scream, but he hit me on the back of the head, knocking me out.

CHAPTER 11

"Killing her would weaken them," Burton said angrily.

"We need her as bait and as a bargaining chip. If she is dead, they won't bargain with us," Dad told him.

"They're going to kill you," I mumbled from the chair they had tied me to. At least he had not thrown me in the closet.

"They won't risk your life," Dad replied smugly.

"They're here," Justina said as she entered the room.

"Justina! Help me!" I yelled at her.

"Don't worry, Jolie. You'll be let go once the princes do as our king asks," she told me with a soft smile.

"Our king? What are you talking about? I don't have a king."

She looked at my dad and then at me. "You may think you don't, but he is our king. It would be smart of you to accept that and join us."

She was working for my father? Why? How? She had never said anything about having a king when we worked together. How had he gotten to her? Dhampirs usually hated vampires.

Dad brushed his hand down her cheek and her eyelids fluttered.

"Oh, fucking gross," I gagged.

"Let's go greet our guests," Dad said with a smile.

Burton untied me from the chair and retied my arms before I could get away. He pulled the ropes extra tight and pushed me forward.

I stumbled, almost falling on my face, but caught myself at the last second and followed Dad and Justina out of the room we had been in, down the hallway, and out onto the porch.

My four guards stood in a line on the front lawn, fists clenched and fury etched into their faces. They saw me and took a step forward, but Burton put a knife to my throat.

"No closer," Burton ordered them.

"Are you hurt?" Rhys asked me.

"No," I replied.

"I wasn't sure you would come," Dad told them, spreading his arms in a welcoming gesture. Then he shook his head and gave them a look of pity. "I'm sure you're likely tired of rescuing Jolie by now."

"What do you want?" Deryn demanded, his eyes boring into Justina who was standing slightly behind Dad, letting him shield her.

"You four are the most powerful, next to your fathers. I need your power," Dad told them. "If you want my daughter back in one piece, you will go to the dedication ceremony tonight and kill the President."

"No!" I yelled. If they did that, their clans would be forced to kill them.

Burton dug the knife into my neck, cutting me enough to make a small line of blood trickle down my neck.

"Quiet," he ordered me.

"We would all be dead before we made it back to get her," Nico told Dad.

"I'm sure you will figure something out. Though, time is

running out. You only have two hours before the ceremony starts."

"Are we coming back here afterwards to retrieve her?" Rhys asked.

No! They couldn't seriously be thinking about doing it. It was suicide!

"No, call Jolie's phone after you've done it, and I will give you the location," Dad said, a wide, evil grin on his face.

"How do we know that you won't kill her while we are gone. Or run off?" Deryn asked, bearing his teeth.

"You don't, but you can track her with your bond," Dad said with a smirk.

How did he know about that?

"Not if she's dead," Nico pointed out.

"You'll have to take that risk. Or, Burton kills her right now," Dad said.

Burton dug the blade in deeper, making the blood flow faster.

"Fine!" Rhys snarled. "We'll do it. Stop hurting her."

"I knew you boys would see things my way," Dad said smugly. "Off you go."

My four guards turned to face me and as one, they bowed to me and then spun around and left.

I was crying and didn't care if my dad saw or not. Those idiots were marching off to die. They hadn't even taken a moment to debate it or not. They just agreed and left. They were going to lose their statuses and lose their clans, because of me. It was stupid and asinine.

"Let's move," Dad ordered us. "We have a long drive ahead of us."

Burton withdrew his blade from my neck, allowing me to take a deep, stuttering breath. Dad licked his finger and then brushed it along my cut, healing it. If only other pains could be fixed so easily.

The four of us climbed into a truck, and Burton drove

towards the city. We parked at an old, abandoned factory, much to my surprise. Dad hated places like this. He avoided them if possible and would rather kill everyone in a hotel to use that as a base of operation. So, why were we here? Was it because it was so unlike him?

Inside the factory was nothing except two couches and a television set.

Burton shoved me down on the couch. "Get comfy. The show will start soon."

They couldn't do it. They had to be smarter than that.

Dad turned on the television and settled on the couch beside me. "Think they'll do it?"

"I hope not," I muttered.

"You better hope they do. For your sake."

"How'd you know about the bond?" I asked him angrily. Only the alphas and Elders knew.

"I have my ways," he said cryptically.

I rolled my eyes in response and looked at the TV where a crowd was gathering in front of a stage which had a podium on it. There had to be thousands of people there. There really was no hope for them.

The President took the stage and started his opening speech.

No sign of the guys. Maybe they were just going to abandon me. That hurt to think about, but it would be better than them dying. I would much rather they left me to my father than to put themselves in such a dangerous situation. I wasn't worth it. I wasn't worth this. The price was too high. I should have let the Elders remove the bond, so that they wouldn't feel compelled to protect me. To ruin everything.

No, it was my dad who was ruining everything. Once again, he was ruining my life.

The crowd began to scream and soon we saw why. The four princes walked down the center of the crowd, bodies glowing with power. Deryn was in warrior form, half wolf and half man.

Rhys was also in warrior form, though I had no idea Dragons could do it as well. Nico had a staff with a glowing crystal on the top in one hand and I realized, he wasn't walking, but floating. Fox had his hair pulled back and in his hands, he carried two swords. They looked scary as shit and hot as hell.

Fuck.

The President held his ground, and stood facing them boldly. His guards had run off. What cowards.

"We're sorry," Rhys said. "We must protect what is ours."

Nico raised his staff, freezing the President in place.

"They're really doing it!" Burton exclaimed in shock, standing up from the couch.

Rhys shifted into his full Dragon form and in one swoop, swallowed the President.

"Fuck!" I screamed. How could they do this? What was wrong with them?

"I knew you'd come in handy, eventually," Dad told me, smiling victoriously.

The camera turned off and a screen announcing technical difficulties appeared. Dad turned off the television.

It was over. They were going to be killed. The life I had finally started to love, was just swallowed up with the President. If there was any hope of the guys getting away, I prayed they would survive. Even if I never saw them again, I wanted them to survive.

My phone rang and Dad answered it. "Hello?"

"Let me talk to her," I heard Deryn say.

Dad put the phone to my ear.

"What have you done?" I asked, tears making my throat constrict and making the words difficult to say.

"I love you," he whispered.

Fuck. No!

"This is not goodbye," I growled.

"Is the TV off?" he whispered so softly that I barely heard him.

"Yes."

What did that have to do with anything?

"Good, put your dad on."

"They want to talk to you," I told him.

Dad took the phone back. "Yes, you can come get her." He gave them an address and then hung up, putting the phone back in my jacket pocket.

Burton tied me to one of the beams in the center of the building.

"What are you doing?" I asked him, trying to get free of his hold.

"We can't be here when they show up, or they'll kill us," he explained. He taped C4 above my head on the beam and hit a button, starting a countdown.

"Dad!" I screamed.

"You said she wouldn't be hurt!" Justina reminded him.

"If they get here in time, she won't be hurt. Or, they'll all die together," Dad said and waved as he walked away. "Bye, Jolie."

"Don't do this!" I screamed at him.

There was no way the guys would make it in time. They were probably in a battle right now, trying not to be killed by their fathers. They had done what he had asked and it didn't matter. I was going to die anyways.

Closing my eyes, I reached down the bond to each of them, only able to brush them with my essence, but I knew that they had all felt it. At least I was human, so I wouldn't hurt them like losing a true queen would when I died.

I let myself sob, a truly ugly cry, since no one would see me. I wailed my despair, knowing they would die for no reason. I was the cause of their deaths.

"I'm sorry," I cried. "I'm so sorry."

No one answered.

I glanced up, checking the timer. One minute and forty

seconds. Pulling on my restraints, I tried to break free, but they were too tight and I was too weak.

"Fuck me!" I screamed and closed my eyes.

"Now doesn't seem like the appropriate time for that," Rhys said.

I opened my eyes and gasped. All four were standing in front of me.

"I'm hallucinating, right? You're all most likely dead now. I will be in less than a minute too. This has to be a hallucination. My mind, trying to give me one last goodbye?"

I was rambling, but I couldn't help myself or stop the words from tumbling out.

Nico removed the tape from the C4, took the C4, and ran outside with it. Rhys unbound my hands and then the bomb exploded.

"Nico!" I screamed.

"What?" he asked, coming back into the warehouse.

I dropped to my knees on the dirty floor and asked, "Is this real?"

They huddled around me and there was no mistaking their body heat and touch.

"You ate him," I whispered.

They all laughed and Rhys said, "I didn't. We just made it look like I did."

"You didn't kill him?"

"Nope."

I turned to him and punched his arm as hard as I could.

"You scared the shit out of me! I thought you were all going to die!"

The tears returned and Rhys pulled me into a tight hug. "We are all alive and well, my queen."

I kissed him and then hugged and kissed each of the other three as well.

Dan barged into the warehouse with the other three Alphas.

We all stood up off the floor and I waited to find out why they were here.

Dan shoved Rhys aside, so he could get to me. Deryn moved forward, but before they could react, he grabbed me in a huge hug.

"You're alive," he breathed.

I hugged him back as much as I could with his size, my arms barely making it around him.

"I am," I agreed.

He set me on my feet and set his hand on my cheek. "When they told us what was going on, I feared the worst."

"Thirty seconds later and I wouldn't be here," I admitted to him.

"You can come live with my pack, in my house, if you wish to," he offered.

"What?" mage king asked.

"She's an outsider," dragon king reminded him.

"She's human," elf king added.

"She's my son's queen, which makes her basically, my daughter-in-law."

"I appreciate the offer," I whispered. "I'm honored to receive such an offer. However, I can't leave my guards."

"Are we sure she isn't a witch?" dragon king asked.

"It would explain everyone's infatuation with her," elf king said.

"I'm not a witch," I snapped at them and then remembered who I was talking to. "Sirs."

They all laughed at me.

"Why are you all here?" I asked the kings.

"The princes weren't sure who would get here faster, since we didn't know where you were going to be. So, we all came," Dan explained.

I bowed. "Thank you."

After standing up straight again, I asked, "Is anyone going to tell me what the fuck went on? I saw you swallow the President, Rhys."

"We called in some favors," Dan said. "You save the city, and country, enough times and they'll do almost anything you ask."

"Everyone, except those watching through their televisions, were warned ahead of time what was going to happen," Fox said.

"You guys shouldn't have done it," I chastised my guards. "You could have died."

"Our lives are yours," Deryn whispered. "Nothing else matters."

"We should go," Dan said. "You sure you won't come live with me?"

"I'm sure."

Dan's phone rang and he answered it quickly. "Yes?"

"We're under attack!" Martin yelled so loudly that even I heard him.

"Martin!" I gasped.

"We're on our way," Dan said immediately and took off.

The other three kings' phones rang, all with similar news.

"This must have been his plan," I realized. "He got the kings and princes away to attack the clans at their bases."

"Let's go!" Rhys growled.

"We can't go to four places at once!" I reminded him. "I'll go with Deryn and you three go with your fathers."

"I don't-" Nico started, but I took his hand.

"Protect your people. Deryn will protect me," I said.

He kissed me deeply and whispered, "Stay safe."

Fox kissed my cheek before darting by with his father.

Rhys's jaw was clenched, as were his fists. "I don't like this."

"I love you," I whispered to him. "And I won't be the reason your people die. They need you, much more than I do right now."

"She's right," dragon king said. "Obey your queen, Son."

Rhys pulled me to him and kissed me passionately. "I will come for you," he whispered as he pulled away.

"I can't wait," I replied with a smirk.

He let out a bark of laughter, kissed my forehead, and rushed out.

"Let's go," Deryn said and picked me up in his arms. "Put your face against my chest, so the bugs don't get in your mouth."

I obeyed, having had that exact thing happen once when Martin ran with me. He took off at a sprint and I gripped him tighter. He made a few turns and I realized that we were very close to the werewolf pack.

Deryn flew, making it within a few minutes. Utter chaos greeted us. Werewolves were fighting ogres, trolls, vampires, and goblins.

"You were right about it not being just vampires," Deryn said.

"I wish I wasn't right," I muttered.

"I'm going to take you to the house," Deryn informed me. "Go inside and hide. There is always one person to guard the house, so you should be safe."

I nodded and didn't put up a fight about it. He needed to be able to focus so that he could save his people. He ran me to the door, kissed me deeply, and then shifted and charged at the nearest enemy.

"No!" Madison screamed.

Turning, I caught sight of Madison and Tamara cowering against the side of the building nearest us with an ogre moving towards them.

"Maddy!" I screamed. "Tamara!" Without thinking, I raced towards them. I couldn't defeat an ogre, but I might be able to distract it long enough to get them away from it. I slid around the ogre's side and stood between him and the girls.

"Auntie Jolie!" they shrieked at the same time and clutched at my legs.

The ogre growled at me and then roared in my face.

I couldn't let anything happen to the girls. They were my only nieces.

My stomach and chest were hot, way hotter than usual, but I couldn't focus on that. I had to protect the girls.

The ogre roared at me again, spittle flying from his mouth.

I opened my mouth to roar back, but instead of sound coming out, fire did. The ogre screamed in pain and ran off.

What the fuck?

I had just breathed fire. How? Now wasn't the time to think about that. I needed to get them to safety.

"Come on," I ordered the girls. "We need to get inside the house."

They nodded their understanding and the three of us ran to the house. The door was locked, so I banged twice on it. "It's Jolie and the twins, Madison and Tamara!" I screamed as loud as I could.

The door opened and Sharla screamed as the girls tackled her. She hugged them and they all rubbed their faces on each other. I shut and locked the door and she pulled me down to hug me.

"I couldn't find them," she told me through her tears. "I was going to go out and search for them. Thank you. Thank you."

I kissed her cheek. "No need to thank me."

"Auntie Jolie breathed fire," Madison told her excitedly.

"Shush," I ordered them. "That's not something we need to tell everyone. We need to keep it a secret until I can figure out how the hell it happened and why. Okay? It's very important that we not discuss it."

They mimed locking their lips closed and I smiled at them.

"Who is guarding the house?" I asked Sharla.

"Me," she replied.

"I can't believe he is doing this," I told her sadly.

"Who?"

"My father. It's his army attacking. They're not only attacking the wolves, but the mages, dragons, and elves as well."

She gasped and asked, "Are they going to be okay?"

"I hope so. The princes and kings went back to help fight. Deryn is outside fighting right now," I explained.

She gripped my hand, and we cuddled closer together on the floor of the entryway.

Please be okay. Please let my guards be okay.

There had to be a way to defeat my dad. I knew he wouldn't be here, he preferred to send his minions to do his bidding instead of coming himself. That way, if they lost, he was still safe. What was he hoping to gain by this attack? Was he really trying to defeat the four main races with his army? There hadn't seem to be *that* many attackers here. There were a lot, but not so many that I would think the werewolves would be overrun.

Something else was his goal. But, for the life of me, I couldn't figure out what it was.

I sat on the floor, huddled with the girls and Sharla, for what felt like hours. We all jumped when someone knocked on the door.

"It's me, Deryn," he said through it.

Sharla got up and checked through the peephole before opening it and letting Deryn in.

He rushed over to me and picked me up to hug me when he saw me. "You're okay?"

"Yes. You?" I asked as I hugged him back.

"I'm fine."

"The other guards?" I asked nervously.

"No one has been hurt significantly," he told me.

"Who got hurt?" I asked.

"We'll find out when we get home," he said. "Let's head home."

The door opened and Martin came in. His family rushed to him, hugging, kissing, and rubbing their scents on each other.

"Do you need me to drive you?" Martin asked from within the arms of his girls.

Deryn shook his head. "Console your girls. I'll drive us and someone can come pick the car up later."

Deryn led me outside, to a building I hadn't gone into before. Dan was there, talking with a few other people. He turned around when we approached and hugged me. "Did you get hurt?"

I shook my head.

"Good. Take the car over there," he said and indicated a black car. I had zero idea what kind of car it was.

"Send someone to get it later," Deryn told his dad.

Dan nodded and waved to us, resuming his conversation.

There were bodies all over. Thankfully, I didn't see any werewolf bodies among them. Blood and body pieces were everywhere, on the walls, the grass, the concrete, hanging from trees. It was disgusting and terrifying.

The entire drive, I felt like I was going to explode with nerves. Someone had been injured. One of my Guards was injured. Deryn wouldn't tell me who or how bad it was, which was making it even worse. Who was it?

Knowing that they were all alive was a huge relief, but I was still worried about the injury. Others healed so quickly, that injuries were not discussed unless it was serious. Like, an arm being cut off, which they would not be able to grow back.

When Deryn parked, I jumped out of the car and raced to the elevator. It seemed to take twice as long for it to come than it usually did.

I burst into Deryn's apartment and looked over the three inside. Rhys was the only one with a bandage. I rushed to him and he immediately pulled me into his lap.

"I'm fine," he assured me.

"A shifter with a bandage is not fine," I accused him.

His right arm was bandaged, at least half of it covered.

"It's just a scratch," he said.

"Down to the bone," Nico muttered.

Rhys growled. "Not helping."

I rested my fingertips over the bandage, being sure not to let the pressure hurt him. "You're okay?" I asked softly.

He kissed my cheek and nodded. "I'm okay."

"The battle isn't over," I told them. "This was too easy a win and there weren't that many beings."

"You think this was a test?" Nico asked.

I nodded. I had been thinking about it on the way here.

"Also, I need to tell you something," I mumbled without looking at them.

"What?" Rhys asked and slowly ran his fingers of his good arm up and down my arm.

Getting out of his lap, I stood behind the couch and said, "I, uh, breathed fire."

Silence was not the reaction I had expected.

"Come again?" Rhys asked quietly.

"When we got to the pack, I heard the twins scream. An ogre was attacking them. I couldn't let them get hurt, so I ran over and stood in front of them. the ogre screamed at me and my stomach and chest felt really hot. Then, when I tried to scream back at the ogre, fire came out instead."

"You put yourself in front of an ogre?!" Deryn shouted.

"My nieces were in trouble," I growled at him. "Should I have left them to die?"

"No, you should have yelled for me," he growled back.

"You were fighting already."

"Do you think you can do it again?" Nico asked, stopping our argument.

"I don't know. It wasn't a conscious decision. I wasn't trying to do it. It just…happened," I explained.

Rhys walked to me and said, "Picture a volcano. Then, imagine the fire of the volcano erupting, but out of your mouth."

"You really want me to try?" I asked. "What if I light something on fire?"

"I've got it covered," Nico assured me.

This seemed like a really bad idea.

"Okay," I conceded.

Closing my eyes, I pictured a volcano like Rhys had instructed. I imagined the fire coming from my belly and erupting from my mouth. My stomach grew hot, just like it had earlier, and when I opened my mouth, fire came out.

Nico used a spell to contain the fire, but all of them were staring at me instead of the fire.

"Her eyes," Deryn whispered.

Rushing to the bathroom, I looked in the mirror and the blood drained from my face. I gripped the sink to keep from falling.

Dragon's eyes. I had Dragon's eyes.

"I've never heard of something like this," Rhys told everyone.

"We should contact the Elders," Fox said.

"What if it is something bad? They could order her to be contained or they could kill her," Deryn said.

That sounded like a terrible option.

Nico pried my hands open and turned me to face him. "Breathe," he ordered me.

A big breath whooshed out of me and I fell into his arms. What was happening?

Nico held me tightly. "It's going to be okay."

"It's the stupid curse," I whispered and pulled away from him. "You're all in danger by being with me."

"Jolie-"

Someone knocked on the door and everyone went silent. Deryn opened it to reveal the apartment manager.

"There you all are!" she exclaimed. "I've been going to each of your apartments trying to find you. Great news, Jolie. Your apartment is fixed."

"Great," I said with a wide smile, glad that my eyes had apparently returned to normal since she wasn't freaking out. "Thanks for getting it taken care of for me."

She waved and left, but before Deryn shut the door, I walked out of it.

"Where are you going?" Deryn demanded.

"My apartment," I replied without turning back to look at him. I pushed the button for the elevator and waited.

Nico stopped next to me.

"What are you doing?" I asked him.

"Coming with you."

"I don't need a guard in my apartment."

"You were stolen from Deryn's apartment," he reminded me.

"Can't I have some privacy? Some alone time?" I asked angrily. My hands were clenched and felt tingly.

Nico tried to pull me into a hug, but I pushed him back. Or, that had been the plan. Instead, he went flying down the hallway and slammed into Rhys who had just stepped out of Deryn's apartment.

I looked down and gasped at my glowing hands.

"I'm sorry. I didn't-"

Booth stood up and shook their heads.

"What was that?" Rhys asked.

"Mage powers," Nico said. "Somehow, she's using our powers."

The elevator opened and I climbed in, mashing the close button as Nico and Rhys raced towards it.

"Wait!" Rhys yelled.

"Jolie!" Nico called.

Instead of going to my apartment, I went to the ground floor and ran outside. Everything was going to shit. Why was I using their powers? I could have killed Nico.

My phone rang and I was surprised to find Martin calling instead of the guys.

"Hello?"

"Where are you?"

"Why?"

"Because Deryn called me, upset, because you ran off. What's going on?"

He was genuinely worried about me. I couldn't let him come near me.

"I can't involve you."

"Just tell me where you are."

"No. the whole point of me leaving is to stay away from them. You'll just tell them where I am, so they can find me."

"They are freaking out," he said. "Deryn said, 'please' to me. Think about that."

He hung up, which shocked me almost as much as Deryn saying please to Martin.

My stomach was growling and I was a good distance from the apartment building now, so I went into the first restaurant that I saw. It was a chain diner that offered a variety of food. Usually, the food wasn't very good, but most of the people who ate there were either old or drunk.

I was neither of those, but I *was* very hungry and it was really dark now. I hadn't realized how much time had past since we had seen the Elders. It was definitely past dinner time.

There were only a handful of people seated, half teenagers eating fries and drinking soda, and the other half were clearly drunk.

The waitress looked tired, but she still feigned a smile as she took my order and set a cup of hot chocolate in front of me.

It was childish of me to run away. Maybe it was the curse. The website had said the curse increased my self-sacrificial tendencies. If I could just stop worrying and trying to leave them, our relationship would be better off. I needed to text them.

Me: I'm safe.

Nico: We know.

Me: How?

Deryn: Look behind you.

I turned around and the four waved at me from a booth they were sitting at. Instead of getting mad, I laughed. I had forgotten that they could track me. Dad had mentioned that.

Grabbing my cocoa, I walked to their table. Rhys stood up and let me slide in to sit between him and Nico.

"Did you know that dragons love hot chocolate?" Rhys asked me.

"All of them?" I asked, skeptically.

He nodded. "Yep. We have cupboards full of it and every meeting, all of our scariest and most powerful members, drink cocoa while making important decisions."

"Will I get to see your clan or your home?" I asked him.

"Once our relationship is official, then you will."

"Why isn't it official now?" I asked, my eyebrows furrowed. How did you make it official?

"We don't want to put you in anymore danger than we already are. Once we find the people responsible for hunting you, then we will make it official," Rhys explained.

"How did my dad know?" I asked with a frown and shook my head.

"We were trying to figure that out as well," Fox said, his frown mirrored mine.

"Here's your sandwich," the waitress told me as she set it on the table in front of me. "Your orders will be up soon," she told the guys.

"Thank you," Deryn replied with a charming smile that would make most girls, me included, melt in their shoes.

She left without even caring. She was the first female I had seen who didn't care about them.

Rhys reached for one of my fries, and I smacked his hand.

"Mine," I told him.

I poured ketchup onto my plate and took a bite of my sandwich.

"Feisty," Rhys teased me.

Ignoring them, I ate my food, cleaning my plate completely.

"I didn't know you could eat that much," Fox whispered. "I'm impressed."

The waitress had to make three trips to bring out all of the food the guys had ordered. I sat back and watched them. Four princes, all different races, that got along like brothers. They were all hot, sweet, and incredibly powerful.

"When I saw you on the TV, walking down the crowd, powers on display, do you know what I was thinking?" I asked them.

They paused eating and turned to me.

"What?" Deryn asked.

"You all looked hot as fuck," I replied with a wide smile. "Also, Rhys, I had no idea that dragons had a warrior form."

"You're teasing us at a restaurant," Nico chastised. "Not nice."

"I'm not teasing you," I replied defensively.

"Most dragons aren't powerful enough to have a warrior form," Rhys explained. "It's a unique skill."

The waitress set the bills on the end of the table and before I could grab mine, Rhys did.

"Hey, one is mine," I said and tried to grab it.

He held it up above my head, high enough that even if I jumped, I couldn't reach it. "I'll pay. It's my turn."

"Your turn?" I asked. What was he talking about?

"We rotate who pays for food when we go out," Deryn said and draped an arm across my shoulders.

I snuggled into his side as we walked out of the restaurant. There was no point in arguing with them, they were the most stubborn males I had ever met. We waited for Rhys to pay on the sidewalk with people milling about, going on their ways.

If I was able to use their powers, could I shift into a wolf? Outside the restaurant in the middle of the city was probably not the best place to try.

Rhys came out and we started towards home. We walked by an ice cream shop and I stopped, making Deryn stop walking with me.

"Ice cream?" he asked.

"Please," I requested. I was abnormally hungry, wanting to eat again, even though I had just eaten a full meal.

We crowded into the already busy shop, and I immediately regretted my decision. There was a swarm of teenage girls inside, who all stood up and squealed when they saw the princes. The girls rushed over, asking to take pictures with them.

One particularly pushy girl, shoved me out of the way so she could take a picture with Deryn. I laughed at her bravado and went to the counter to order my ice cream.

The guy behind the counter was in his mid to late twenties, attractive, and had a ton of tattoos on his forearms. They were gorgeous, well done tattoos and I wanted to ask about them, but didn't.

He smiled at me, putting on the charm. "What would you like?" he asked, and I realized that he was flirting with me.

Hadn't he seen me walk in with the guys?

"What do you recommend?" I asked, returning his smile. Flirting was harmless fun, especially with the guys behind me.

"My place, dinner, and dessert."

Damn he was bold. And his offer reminded me of Rhys when we first met.

"Sorry, I already have plans."

"Well, then I recommend the Sunny Sundae," he said, not fazed by my rejection at all.

"Okay, no nuts," I ordered after looking at the ingredients on the menu. I turned and asked, "You guys want anything?"

They were still surrounded by the girls, but didn't seem bothered. It probably happened a lot.

"Strawberry on a sugar cone," Fox ordered.

"Vanilla sundae," Nico ordered.

"Peanut Butter Rush," Rhys ordered.

"Two scoops of chocolate with caramel sauce," Deryn ordered.

"Got all that?" I asked when I turned back around.

He nodded. "I'll get started."

"Who is she?" one of the girls whispered to her friend while looking at me.

"She is our friend," Deryn informed them.

"Lucky bitch," one of them muttered.

I was. Bumping into the guys was the greatest set of accidents I had ever experienced. Even with the attempted bombing and sniper, I didn't regret it. They were stuck with me now. The bond was permanent, and I would never try to get rid of it.

A sudden wash of magic swirled in me and as it dissipated, I felt all of the guys and their emotions clearly for the first time.

They all turned to face me, feeling as I touched them through the bond.

"You accepted it," Nico said happily.

"What are they talking about?" one girl asked.

I nodded.

Deryn walked to me and pulled me into a deep kiss.

The girls gasped and began talking in whispers.

"We're supposed to keep this a secret," I reminded him after he released me.

"We still are," he replied.

"Totally unfair," Nico grumbled.

"Rude," Fox said.

We got our ice cream and walked back towards the apartment, eating in a swirl of bliss.

"We were discussing having a schedule," Rhys said between bites of his ice cream.

"A schedule for what?" I asked.

"For us to be with you," he explained. "So that you don't have to have all of us in your apartment at once. We would each take one day during the week and the rest of the week, you could choose who you wanted to protect you."

"A schedule of who will guard me?" I asked, thinking this was a sex schedule. Both of which I was okay with.

"Yes," he replied. "And, so we can get some alone time with you."

"Would I be able to hang out with all of you, even if it was one of your days?"

They nodded.

"Why this decision?" I asked.

"We don't want to suffocate you," Nico said. "This way you have more freedom."

"But, if you go outside of the apartment, you have to take one of us with you," Deryn ordered me.

Shocked wasn't the beginning of my feelings on this development.

"Thank you."

They led me to the park, which was abandoned this late at night, instead of straight to the apartment.

"Why are we here?" I asked.

"Try to shift," Deryn ordered me.

"Oh. Okay."

He took my ice cream cup, which was empty, so I had my hands free.

I had no idea how they shifted, but I closed my eyes and pictured all of the times I had seen a werewolf change. My entire body began to tingle, and then I felt it change.

"Holy shit," Fox whispered.

"Shift into a dragon," Rhys ordered me.

That shift was easier, but becoming a huge Dragon was startling and a bit disorienting. I looked down at them, their eyes wide in disbelief.

My scales were a beautiful purple color, a color I had never heard of a dragon having. I shifted back and collapsed on the wet grass, panting.

"This is crazy," Fox whispered. He sat down next to me and said, "Tomorrow, I want you to try some elf stuff. Though, I'm sure you will be able to."

"What should we do?" Nico asked Rhys. "This is a huge discovery. The Elders should be told."

"We could have two go and tell them while the other two stays to guard her," Deryn suggested.

"Will it be safe for the two who go?" I asked.

They looked at each other, and I knew the answer.

"I can take her to my dad's," Deryn offered. "He'll help protect her."

"Are you sure?" Nico asked. "She can shift into a wolf. That's likely to set a few people on edge. It makes her a potential threat."

"We're going to need to start teaching her how to control the powers," Rhys said. "The last thing we need is for her to shift in a restaurant or something."

"Why am I so tired?" I asked.

"You used a lot of magic," Fox explained. "You have to learn to pace yourself and figure out how much you have. We'll have to increase your stamina too."

"Like, by running?"

He nodded.

"I hate running," I groaned.

"Let's get back to the apartment," Rhys said as he looked around. "I don't like being out in the open with her for this long."

Fox helped me stand up and kept his arm around my waist as we headed home. "You're truly an enchanting creature," he whispered into my ear.

I blushed and said, "Thanks."

He kissed one of my flaming cheeks and chuckled.

CHAPTER 12

"We got them to agree to speak to us, with the promise that they would allow us to leave and to return home unscathed," Rhys informed everyone.

"Really?" Nico asked.

Rhys nodded.

"They're not going to kill me, are they?" I asked softly. I was a potential threat to all of them, at least in their eyes. I would never do anything to hurt my guards or their clans, but they didn't know that.

"We won't let them," Fox whispered adamantly.

"When do we go?" Deryn asked.

"Now," Rhys said. "Martin is on his way and should be here shortly to drive us."

"Have you guys finally gotten over your jealousy of Martin?" I asked with a smirk.

"No," they all said at the same time.

"What?" I asked and laughed.

"He has slept with you," Deryn reminded me. "We won't ever not be jealous of someone who slept with you. Especially, not the one who took your virginity."

"Males," I grumbled.

"He's here," Rhys said and headed towards the door.

The schedule had become a great thing for us. I got three days to myself, but usually spent it with all of them, or had one of them come over to have some more alone time. Alone time was a rare commodity for us and it was incredibly necessary to keep everyone sane. Unknown to them, I kept a record of who came over on my off days, so I could make sure that I wasn't favoring one of them over the others. I didn't have a favorite and I wanted to ensure that they all knew that.

The Elders were alone in the giant room this time, but I was still terrified. The guys stood around me in protective stances before the Elders.

"What have you come to discuss with us?" wolf Elder asked.

"There's been a recent development in our bond," Rhys started.

"She's using your abilities, right?" dragon Elder asked.

Our surprised faces made him laugh.

"We know it is possible for humans to do this when they are part of the warrior bond. We did a lot of research into it, after we learned of Jolie joining you four," dragon Elder explained.

"Uh," Rhys said, stumped since I was certain he had planned out exactly what to say to the Elders.

"Do you have any instructions for us or recommendations?" Nico asked them.

"You need to announce your relationship soon. If someone sees her change, or use the powers, before you announce it, it could be disastrous for you," elf Elder ordered them.

"We haven't found out who was trying to kill her," Rhys explained.

"It's likely not one person. It's most likely that it is several individuals from all of the clans," Wolf Elder told us. "I would not fret about that specifically and instead just focus on keeping her safe, no matter the circumstances."

"Also, Nico, you should have a talisman made for her, to store some magic power. She is human and her body can't handle using too much magic at once. If she runs out of magic in an emergency, the talisman will provide her an additional source, though it will be tiny," elf Elder said.

"Thank you," Nico replied. "I will have one created."

"Will the others think I'm a threat?" I asked them. "Will this make them uneasy with me?"

All three nodded.

"However, most will understand that as their queen, you are not seeking to destroy the Princes' clans, but unite them," elf Elder said.

"Will you take them as mates?" dragon Elder asked.

"What do you mean?" I asked him back. Weren't they already my mates? I was sleeping with all of them.

"You are their queen, yes, but you can also be their mate. You would need to create a mating bond with each of them individually," dragon Elder explained.

"It comes with risks," wolf Elder added. "After you create the mate bond, if one of them dies, or if you die, they will feel it tenfold compared to you being a part of their warrior bond."

"And you have a higher chance of getting pregnant," elf Elder added. "We aren't sure why, but after a mating bond is created, couples get pregnant much easier, even when using contraceptives."

"Good to know," I whispered.

"Think about it. If you don't take them as mates, they may be required to take a mate by their clans. The princes are often given mates by other clans in a business marriage to unite clans or packs," wolf Elder told me.

"Wouldn't that distract them from protecting me?" I asked, since they had told me that before.

"Yes, but in this case, the mate wouldn't be as important as you," he said. "And the mate would know that."

That was incredibly crass. I couldn't imagine being someone's mate and knowing that another woman would take priority over me for protection in an emergency.

Deryn told him. "We've already discussed this with our kings."

They had? Why hadn't they talked to me about it and what their decision is?

"When times are tough, royalty is forced to do many things that they do not like and had not planned to do," elf Elder said.

"Any other advice?" Fox asked respectfully.

"Learn to control your abilities as fast as you can," dragon Elder told me. "Once you do, you will be able to protect yourself, until your guards show up, should they not be with you."

I nodded. "I will."

"Ruminate over everything we said. Especially, about announcing it soon," Wolf Elder said.

"Have you made a decision about whether to remove the bond or the curse?" Dragon Elder asked.

"I won't be removing the bond," I said adamantly. "I'm still debating about the curse."

"We are glad to hear about the bond," he said.

"Thank you for your time," Rhys told them.

We bowed and returned home.

"Well, that went much better than expected," Rhys said as he plopped down onto Deryn's couch next to me.

I wanted to ask them about the mate bond, but decided I would do it individually over the next four days, when I was going to see them separately.

"I'm glad they already knew about it," Nico said with a sigh. "My fingers were tingling with magic, worried they might attack us."

"During the days that we are alone with her, we should teach her about each of our powers," Fox suggested.

The other three nodded in agreement.

"Jolie?" Rhys asked. "What are you thinking about?"

"Everything," I muttered.

"It's a lot to take in," he agreed.

"What are we going to do about the announcement?" Deryn asked Rhys. "Should we announce it soon, or hold off?"

"Let's hold off for a bit," he said. "I want to get her powers under control and talk things over with my father before we do the announcement."

"All of the poor maidens are going to be crushed when they hear that you have a queen," I said with what I hoped looked like a true smile as I tried to lighten the mood and stop focusing on my worries.

"They will be," Nico agreed with a smirk at me.

"My brother can stop being jealous of me once that happens," Fox grumbled. "Once I'm not the top bachelor, he will get more attention from the ladies."

I laughed and they laughed with me. This was better. Laughing and joking was much better than being scared or worried. It was a constant issue with the curse, but it seemed that I might be able to get a handle on it and suppress it a tiny bit.

"Who's hungry?" Deryn asked.

"You're all always hungry," I teased them.

"True," he agreed.

"Let's get Chinese food tonight," I requested. "We always get pizza."

"We haven't had that in a while," Rhys agreed. "Sounds great."

"Let's play something," Deryn said and walked to his video game shelves.

I rushed to stand by him and grabbed the game I had been dying to play. "What about this one?"

"Rumble?" he asked.

"It's four players, so we can take turns with just one person not playing. Plus, it's a lot of fun."

"Oh, I haven't played that in a long time," Fox commented with a wide smile. "I'm totally going to own you all."

"What game?" Rhys asked from the kitchen where he had his head buried in the fridge.

"Rumble," I told him.

He spun around. "Oh, yeah! I'm going to destroy you, Fox."

Fox rolled his eyes. "Bring it on."

After hashing out the order, we all sat on the couch and grabbed a controller. The point of the game was to defeat the other players so that you are the last one standing, by beating each other up. It was a 2D game, but oh so fun.

The game started and everyone immediately went after Fox, since he had claimed that he could beat everyone. He was out of the game quickly, which left three of us. I attacked Rhys, who was defending himself against me when Deryn came up behind him and attacked him.

Suddenly, both turned to me and attacked me, killing me.

"No fair!" I yelled and set my controller down.

They focused on each other again and Deryn ended up winning.

"Take two," Fox said.

Nico took the controller I had set down and joined the game.

"No, you don't!" Fox yelled when they tried to defeat him first again. He jumped over them and defeated Deryn.

"Damn it!"

Fox attacked Rhys, but ended up dying instead.

"No!" Fox yelled.

Nico swooped in at the last moment to defeat Rhys and claim victory. "Yes!" Nico yelled. "Finally!"

"Crap. He finally won for once," Rhys said.

"It won't be the last either," Nico said confidently.

After five more matches, our food came, so we set the controllers down to eat together. We all sat at the dining table, plates and silverware out instead of using the paper plates the store had provided.

"This is nice," I whispered. "I've never had a family meal like this before."

"You've never had a meal at a table with your family?" Deryn asked.

I shook my head.

"What about Thanksgiving?" Nico asked.

I shook my head. "I've always wanted to have a Thanksgiving dinner. Like they have in the movies."

The guys looked at each other and then returned to eating.

"What about Christmas?" Deryn asked.

"My Grandma and I used to trade gifts, but that was it." Though, the idea of buying presents for the guys sounded fun.

"We're going to show you what these celebrations are supposed to be like," Deryn promised me.

"Definitely," Rhys agreed.

∼

RHYS AND I STOOD TOGETHER IN THE PARK, MY BODY COATED IN sweat from his training, and my clothes stuck to me.

"Done for the day?" Rhys asked.

I nodded. "Please. I am so tired." To accentuate my statement, I dropped to sit on the ground.

There were a few joggers out, but most went by without stopping. That surprised me since Rhys was standing there in a pair of tight sweatpants and a shirt that accentuated his muscular chest. He looked damn good.

He dropped down to sit next to me and kissed my cheek. "You did really well."

"Thanks," I replied and leaned my head on his shoulder.

"What do you want to do next?" he asked.

"Actually, I wanted to talk to you," I admitted.

"Uh oh," he grumbled. "Whenever a woman says they want to talk to you, it's not good."

I rolled my eyes at him and stood up. "Come on, let's go home and shower."

"A shower sounds wonderful," he whispered and slid his arms around my waist. He pulled me back against his front. "You're so beautiful."

"We're in the park, in the middle of the day," I reminded him with a blush.

"Then we best hurry home," he whispered, picked me up, and ran.

I squealed and clutched his neck as we flew down the side-walk, somehow avoiding all of the people who were walking around. He didn't stop until we were in front of my apartment.

I gasped in a lungful of breath and he set me down to open my door.

"Next time, I would suggest that you don't hold your breath," he chuckled.

"Noted," I whispered.

He shut the door behind us and followed me to the bathroom, but before I could climb into the shower, he grabbed me and pulled me against him again, kissing me passionately. I kissed him back, glad to have some alone time with him where I didn't feel bad about focusing on one of them with the others around.

He slipped my shirt off and moaned when he slipped his hand under my sports bra. He almost tore my pants, ripping them off of me in his haste. I tugged at his shirt and he removed it and his pants.

I stepped back from him, putting a hand on his chest so that he would stay still as I admired him.

"I'm so lucky," I whispered, finally meeting his gaze.

"That's my line," he replied, swooped me up, and dropped me onto the bed, ravaging me and making me scream his name countless times.

"Rhys," I whispered after we were done and cuddling in bed.

"Hm?"

"About the mate thing…" I wasn't really sure how to ask what I wanted to ask.

"The decision is up to you," he whispered and kissed the top of my head. "I would be honored to have you become my mate. Nothing would make me happier."

I jerked my head up and looked at him. "You want me to be your mate?"

He nodded. "Yes."

"What did you talk to your dad about then?"

"The fact that I won't take anyone but you as my mate. Even if you don't want to become my mate, I won't take one. I won't allow my attention to be divided from you. You are my queen, my love, and I won't let anything happen to you."

"What do we have to do, to become mates?"

"I mark you with a bite and some magic, and we have glorious sex, and then our bond should snap into place."

"But, when I die, you'll feel it so much more," I reminded him.

"You're not dying."

"I will die before you. I have the lifespan of a human," I said.

"Not once you become my mate," he argued. "You'll have the same lifespan as I do after we are mated."

That definitely changed things. If I could live as long as them, then most of my worry was gone.

"Don't answer today," he said. "Think about it during the week and then decide."

I nodded in agreement and then we took our shower.

"You've been scowling all day," Nico said and tapped my nose. "What's going on in that head of yours?"

We were sitting on his bed, having just finished an amazing love making session.

"Do you want me to become your mate?" I asked outright.

Nico was so blunt all of the time, I figured it was best to be blunt with him as well.

"Yes," he replied instantly and turned all the way so he was facing me completely. "I would be the happiest mage in the world, if you became my mate."

"What if I became everyone's mate? Would that bother you?" I hadn't asked Rhys about it, but planned to do so soon.

"I don't care if you become mates with the other three as well," he said honestly. "As long as I get moments alone with you, like today, then I'm fine."

"Swear?" I asked, surprised he would be so fine with it.

He nodded. "You are what I want."

"How does one become a mate for a mage?"

"A spell, of course," he replied with a smirk.

"Of course," I giggled. I lost my smile and said, "Can I have the week to think about it?"

"You can take as much time as you want to decide," he replied and kissed me lightly. "I'll be here."

"You're too good for me," I whispered and kissed him.

"What happened to your mother?" he asked.

"I don't really know," I admitted. "She died when I was a baby, but my family refuses to tell me how she died. Dad had really loved her and her death took a big toll on him. I think that was part of why he became a vampire. I think her death broke the last bit of humanity he had and he truly became evil."

"I wish I could go back in time and save you from your awful childhood," he told me and rested his hand on my cheek.

I smiled and said, "I appreciate the sentiment. However, changing my past, might mean that I wouldn't be where I am today. I wouldn't change anything, as long as it meant I got to be with you."

"Ditto," he replied and kissed me roughly, laying over me and pressing our naked chests together.

"Nico," I whispered.

"Hm?" he asked between kisses on my neck.

"You're squishing me."

He chuckled and leaned up on his arms, taking his weight off me. "Sorry."

"When do I get to officially meet your dad?" I asked him. "I haven't gotten to really meet him or speak to him."

"Whenever you want to," he said. "Though, he's not the warmest guy. You'll like my mom better. She has been asking to meet you."

"Then, why haven't we?"

Was he embarrassed by me? Did he not want to introduce me to them until we had decided about being mates?

"We've been a bit busy," he chuckled. "Plus, I wanted to get your powers under control before we went to meet with them."

"Oh."

I supposed that made sense. It wouldn't look good to meet his parents and turn into a wolf or dragon suddenly.

"Then, we should get back to work on my powers," I suggested and climbed out of bed.

~

DERYN SURPRISED ME BY TAKING ME TO THE PACK ON HIS DAY, straight to the house where Tamara and Madison were waiting to leap on me for hugs.

I hugged the girls and Sharla, but was pulled away by a giant arm, attached to an equally giant alpha.

He hugged me tightly and said, "I'm happy to see you're safe."

"I am safe," I agreed.

One of the great things about alphas, is that they can make you feel very safe and loved. Dan was incredibly good at that.

He pushed me back to look at me and asked, "Do you need anything?"

"No, I just came to visit with the pack," I said even though Deryn hadn't told me we were coming here.

"Well, most of the pack are at the sports complex right now. They're finishing up a tournament they had started about a week ago," Dan told us. "Why don't you take her and I'll meet you over there?"

Deryn nodded his head and opened the front door for me. "Come on, you're going to love it."

The sports complex turned out to be a legit complex with a full-sized baseball diamond, soccer field, and a few other things that I wasn't sure what sport they were used for.

There were several wolves on the field, playing what looked like baseball, but they weren't using bats. They were just using their hands to hit the ball.

To the right of the field, was a set of stands with a ton of spectators.

"Are they all werewolves?" I asked Deryn softly as we approached.

He nodded. "Yes. The pack loves these types of games and come to watch them, even if they live away from here."

That was a lot of predators in one place. Deryn took us to the stands, and we sat next to two identical looking guys with long beards and clothes that reminded me of lumberjacks.

"Stan. Clark. I'd like you to meet Jolie," Deryn introduced us. "Jolie, this is Stan and Clark."

"Hi," I said and waved.

"Hello, Jolie," they greeted me in unison.

"The twins here are two of our top fighters," Deryn told me. "If I'm ever incapacitated, you just run to one of them and they'll keep you safe."

"If you're incapacitated, most of us would most likely be dead," Stan, or was it Clark, joked.

"Good to know," I said and watched the game.

"Is that a human?" someone in the stands asked.

"What's a human doing here?" another asked.

Deryn sat up straight and looked around at all of the stands. Everyone tensed up, people's backs in front of us were barely moving as they breathed.

"Jolie is my friend," Deryn said. "And if anyone has a problem with that-"

"They can take it up with me," Dan finished.

For such a large man, he was sure quiet when he moved. He stood beside me and all eyes were fixed on him, even the game on the field had stopped.

"Jolie is an unofficial member of the pack," Dan told them.

"Dad," Deryn said in shock.

Several members gasped and a few started whispering to each other.

"Despite being human, she stood between an ogre and two wolf pups, saving their lives. She has earned her place as an unofficial pack member." He turned to me and smiled. "Hopefully, you'll become an official member soon."

What did that mean?

"Continue the game," Dan ordered them and sat next to me.

"Dan, I…" I didn't know what to say.

He smiled at me and said, "You don't have to say anything, Jolie."

The game didn't last much longer, but it was exciting and fun to watch. Deryn took me back to the apartment and I asked, "What do you have to do to become an official pack member?"

"You would have to mate with someone in the pack," he replied.

"Do you want me to become your mate?"

He laughed. "I thought I had made that clear. I one hundred percent want you to be my mate."

"Even if I'm mates with the other three?"

"Yes."

So far, it seemed that they all wanted me.

"Would we have to wait until after we announced our other bond to become mates?" I asked.

"Either we wait until after, or we mate right before so that we can reveal you as our mate and our queen."

"I'm still not used to that title," I admitted to him.

He chuckled and pulled me to lay on top of him on the couch. "You'll get used to it, eventually."

"If you could have one thing for Christmas, what would you want?" I asked. It was a random thought I had been thinking lately.

"You, with just a red bow on," he said with a smirk.

I laughed and kissed him. "Besides that."

"I don't know. I haven't really thought about it since Christmas is still a few months away," he admitted.

"I'm glad I finally got to go back to work," I told him. The company had found another building to work out of and I had started back yesterday. "I'm going to need to save up money to buy you four presents."

"You don't have to get us anything," he told me. "As long as we have you, we'll be happy."

"I appreciate that," I said.

I had to get them something. I knew they were going to get me something and I didn't want to feel like an ass for not having a present in return. Plus, I loved giving presents to people. I loved seeing their reactions to the presents.

"What do you want?" he asked me.

"You, nude and on my bed," I replied with a smirk.

"You can have that right now," he replied and kissed me fiercely.

～

FOX WAS THE LAST ONE I HAD TO TALK TO ABOUT THE MATING. Despite him being the sweetest, and quietest, I was most worried about what his answer would be. He had his spurts of seriousness that always threw me off.

We sat in a quiet café, eating breakfast before I had to go to work. He was sipping some tea while watching me eat my omelet.

"You've been wanting to ask me a question for a while," he commented. "Are you going to?"

"How'd you know?" I asked him and set my fork down.

"I just did," he said with a shrug.

We were alone, outside of the café and there were very few people walking down the sidewalks who might walk by us, so I didn't have to lower my voice.

"Do you want me to become your mate?"

"Duh," he said and rolled his eyes.

"I'm being serious, Fox."

"Me too," he replied. "I only want you, Jolie. Even if that means sharing you with my best friends, I want you. I want you to be my queen, my mate, and my best friend."

"What do elves do to become mates?" I asked him.

"I perform a spell that binds us together for eternity," he said nonchalantly.

"Oh, only for eternity?" I asked with a smirk.

He laughed and held one of my hands on top of the table. "One lifetime isn't enough for me to spend with you. I need at least five or more, but would prefer to be with you for eternity."

"You're so good at flirting," I whispered, a blush covering my cheeks and possibly my entire face, and squeezed his hand.

"Just speaking the truth."

"I love you."

He leaned forward and rubbed his nose on mine. "I love you, too."

We didn't generally say it in public, but sometimes I just felt it too much not to say it to them.

"Ready to go to work?" he asked.

"I wish I didn't have to work today," I told him with a pout.

"You could quit and we could go play in the park together," he tempted while waggling his eyebrows.

I laughed and shook my head. "No, you naughty elf. I have to work to get money."

"We have enough money for you," he said.

"No, I have to earn it myself."

"Alright, but let it be known that I offered."

"The offer is appreciated, but I wouldn't feel right not doing something to earn money," I explained.

"Well, I could pay you for-"

I smacked him before he could finish his sentence. "Rude!"

He laughed and pulled me against him, making me tilt my head back to look up at him. "When will you decide about becoming my mate?" he asked me softly. His thumbs were beneath my shirt, rubbing against the skin just above my pants. If I let him continue much longer, I wouldn't make it into work.

"Soon," I promised.

He bent his head and brushed his lips across mine. "I look forward to your reply."

There he was again, serious Foxfire.

"Pick me up after work?" I requested.

"As my queen orders," he said and bowed to me before walking away.

I watched his lovely backside walk away from me with the stupidest smile on my face.

"Who is that?" someone nearby on the sidewalk asked.

One lucky bitch. That's who I was.

CHAPTER 13

An entire month went by with no attacks or incidents. The guys were just as vigilant as ever in their guarding duties, saying they didn't want to fall into a false sense of security because that was when the enemy would attack.

They were likely right.

"There's a meeting today," Rhys informed me as soon as I opened my door to them. I thought they were just coming over for dinner, but their serious expressions said otherwise.

"Oh? With who?" My heart raced, and my nerves were already on edge.

"Everyone," he replied. "All four clans."

"Why?" I asked. "What's the meeting about?"

"Officially signing a peace treaty," Fox replied.

"You have to sign one? You can't just not be at war with each other anymore?" I asked. It seemed a bit ridiculous to me.

"It's in our rules," Nico explained. "We sign a declaration of war and we have to sign a peace treaty when it's over."

"Okay. So, I need to stay in my apartment until you get back?" I guessed.

"No, we want you to come with us," Rhys explained.

"But, all of your clans will be there. We aren't sharing our relationship yet."

"You'll be attending as our friend, and the one who ended the war," Deryn said.

"You're all tense," I noted and it was true. Despite us being at my apartment and them all sitting around, they were rigid and stiff. Worried about something.

"We think someone might try to attack you while you're there," Deryn said.

"You'll be there to protect me, right? So, we shouldn't worry about it. Plus, if they did attack me in front of everyone, it would be a death sentence for them," I replied.

"You want to go?" Nico asked.

"Duh. I keep trying to get you guys to take me around your clans. I want to get to know your worlds better and learn more about you and where you come from."

"One more thing before you completely agree to come," Rhys said.

"It's a formal event. So, you would need to wear a dress," Nico said since Rhys seemed nervous about it.

"I don't have a formal dress," I reminded them. They had all seen my closet and all of the clothes that I owned, which weren't many.

Fox held out a bag that I hadn't seen him holding with a wide smile on his face. "I got you one."

"You bought me a dress?" I asked as I looked inside. The dress was a dark blue, that would go well with my skin color and hair.

"Yes."

"You know how I feel about you buying-"

"You can repay me by letting me remove it later tonight," he said with a wink.

Tilting back my head, I laughed, and shook my head at him. "Incorrigible."

"You love me."

"I do," I agreed. "Fine, give me an hour to get ready."

They nodded and headed towards the door, but Fox ran back and set a box on my coffee table. "Those are your shoes! Love you!"

Before I could say anything, all four of them were gone and I was alone in my apartment.

"Brat!" I called, since I knew he could hear me.

I showered and took the time to curl my hair. Then, I actually did my makeup for once. It took me thirty minutes, but I knew it would be worth it once the guys saw me.

The dress lay on my bed where I had set it after pulling it out of the bag and gasping at its beauty. Fox had exquisite taste and the designer tag on the dress told me just how expensive it really was.

The dress fit me perfectly, hugging my curves and high-lighting all of the areas that looked good being round. It was tight enough that I didn't need to wear a bra, and that I had to remove my underwear so there wouldn't be a line in the dress.

Since I never went to things like this, I didn't have jewelry to wear, but I didn't think they would mind.

The shoes fit perfectly as well, which made me wonder if Fox had gone snooping through my clothes and shoes to find sizes, or if he was just great at guessing.

"Jolie!" Rhys called from my living room.

"Coming!" I called back.

I did one more check in the full-length mirror and smiled happily at the woman I saw there. Who would have thought that I would find four perfect males who would fawn over me and meet every wish and desire that I had?

When I stepped out of my room, all four of them froze and stared at me with an intensity that was slightly frightening. Their gazes roamed along my body and four sets of eyes bore into mine. My eyes were doing their own roaming. All four wore black suits with white shirts and I desperately wanted to tear the suits off of them with my teeth.

"So?" I asked, since none of them had said anything.

Rhys was suddenly in front of me. "You would put Aphrodite to shame," he whispered and kissed my cheek.

"You look beautiful," Nico said with a smile.

"I knew that would look amazing on you," Fox said with a wide smile. "It will look better on the floor tonight."

"Alright, stop rubbing it in just because today is your day with her," Deryn growled at him.

I couldn't help laughing at that, but dabbed at my eyes to keep them dry, so my makeup wouldn't get ruined.

"Let's go," Rhys ordered everyone.

Standing in the elevator, all four of them found a place to touch me, their hands rubbing me and driving my hormones insane.

"Unless you want a five-way in the car, you should stop touching me," I threatened them.

Instead, their eyes brightened at the prospect.

"No," I said despite the warmth I felt in my core at the thought. I had meant it to be a threat and a joke.

Their hands moved away and I immediately missed their touches.

Martin whistled from his spot against the SUV when he saw me. He walked to me and bowed. "You've never looked more perfect."

"Hey, no flirting with her," Nico ordered him.

"Not flirting," he replied and kissed my cheek. "She knows what my flirting is like."

I blushed, and Deryn got into the front seat, so that I couldn't sit next to Martin. Martin chuckled and got into the driver's seat. I climbed into the back seat next to Fox. He immediately put his arm around me and began caressing my shoulder with his fingertips.

"You know what her outfit is missing?" Rhys asked.

"What?" I asked him.

He leaned back, draping himself across me and touching my neck. When he sat down, a gorgeous diamond necklace lay around my neck. It was shaped like flowers and vines and had to be worth our apartment building.

"This is too-"

"She needs earrings too," Nico said and put a pair of diamond earrings in my ears before I could object.

Deryn smirked at me and said, "My gift is on your wrist."

What? I looked down to find a diamond bracelet on my wrist. When the hell had he put that on me?

"I'm worth more than half the city right now," I whispered.

"You're worth more than anything on this world combined," Fox whispered and kissed me.

"We give her presents and he gets the kiss," Nico scoffed.

I leaned forward and kissed him and then Rhys. Deryn was looking at me expectantly, so I blew him a kiss with a wink.

He pretended to catch it and tuck it into his suit pocket.

My smile was instantaneous.

"I love you four," I told them. "More than anything else."

"Alpha said he expects a dance with you tonight," Martin informed me with a glance in the rearview mirror.

"I'll happily dance with Alpha," I replied honestly.

"You have to dance with us too," Deryn reminded me.

I rolled my eyes. "Oh no, how will I ever cope with having to dance with you four."

That earned laughs from all of them.

To my surprise, we drove to the estate where the Elders met with us.

"Here?"

"Yes, there's an area behind the house which was designed for events like this. It has enough room for all of our people, as well as a dance floor," Nico explained.

"A bar?" I asked hopefully. I did not doubt for a minute that I would need some alcohol to get my nerves calmed.

"Yes," Rhys said with a smirk.

We climbed out of the SUV and walked together around the side towards the bright lights, music and loud voices. Rounding the corner, I was surprised to see close to a thousand people stretched out over a huge concreted area. White lanterns with a strange blue light lined the area, providing mood lighting. The silvery full moon shined overhead, brightening the area better than anything electric could have.

A DJ was set up off to the side with several people surrounding his table.

As promised, there was also a bar, but not just one - four.

"Booze," I drooled and headed towards one.

Fox stayed by my side and chuckled at me. "Alright, we'll go get you a drink, but once the music starts, you and I are dancing first."

"Very well, Guard," I teased him.

His body tensed and his face dropped all emotion.

"I, uh, I thought I could call you that, since you are...I'm sorry."

He relaxed and whispered, "I've just...you've never called us it before. It was a shock to hear. That's all."

"I won't call you it again," I promised, feeling like an idiot.

He grabbed my hand, stopping me from walking. "No, please. Call me that as much as you want. I loved hearing it."

"Oh," I exhaled. "I thought you were mad at me."

He released my hand and bent close to whisper, "If we were alone, I would show you how much I enjoyed you saying that."

When I glanced down, I could already see what he meant as his erection strained against his pants. My cheeks warmed, and I quickly turned away and hurried towards the bar.

I ordered my drink and then was grabbed around my legs from both sides at once.

"Auntie Jolie!" the twins yelled against my legs.

I dropped down and smiled at the girls. They were wearing matching purple dresses.

"You both look like princesses," I told them and kissed each of their cheeks.

Tamara picked up my wrist, which had their wolf tail hair bracelet on it. "You're wearing our bracelet!"

Both girls smiled wide and I could practically see their tails wagging.

"Yes," I said with a nod. "It is a gift that I will always treasure."

I stood and Sharla whistled. "Martin was right, you look phenomenal tonight."

"You're looking mighty sexy yourself, Sharla." And she was. She had on a tight green off-the-shoulder dress that left little to the imagination.

She hugged me and kissed my cheek.

"Son," the King of the Elves greeted Fox.

Fox bowed. "Father."

"Are you going to formally introduce me?" he asked him while looking at me.

"Jolie, please meet my father, King Katar of the Elves. Father, please meet Jolie," he said.

King Katar picked up my hand and kissed the back of it. "It is a pleasure to formally meet you, Jolie. You are stunning."

I curtsied and bowed my head. "It is an honor to meet you, Your Majesty."

"You should come visit our clan," he offered.

"I would love to," I said and smiled at him.

"We will, soon," Fox agreed.

"You need not wait until her decision has been made," King Katar said. "She may visit as your friend, under my invitation."

Fox's eyes widened, and he nodded.

"Thank you, for the wonderful invitation. I will be sure to take you up on it soon."

He bowed to me and said, "Enjoy your evening."

"Where is she?" I heard Dan ask loudly.

"Father, please calm down. She is here and safe," Deryn grumbled.

I gulped my drink down quickly and pushed through a few people to get to Dan, whose head I could see above everyone else's. "I'm here, King of the Wolves," I called to him.

He spun around and his eyes sparkled with joy. "Jolie," he said and hugged me.

Many people began murmuring at the display of affection between us, and I wondered if it really was so strange for him to act this way to me.

"You and I need to have a serious talk," he told me sternly. "The next time you see an ogre attacking wolf pups, yell for me or the prince, do you understand?"

I put my hands on my hips and glared at him. "I'll tell you the same thing I told the prince. I could not leave my nieces in danger."

"You could have been killed," he reminded me.

"But I wasn't," I reminded him.

"You may not be so lucky next time," he argued.

"I appreciate your concern, but I would rather face down an ogre than see him harm a hair on their heads," I said sternly.

"She's mighty brash when speaking to a king," the mage king said as he came up to us.

I curtsied to him and said, "I would not presume to speak to you or any of the others in such a manner. King Daniel and I have a more personal relationship, which allows for the formality."

"Did she really put herself between an ogre and wolves?" he asked Dan.

"She stood between two wolf pups and an ogre and roared back at the ogre," he said proudly.

"And it scared it away?" mage king asked skeptically.

"No, she was protected by the prince," Dan lied. "She could have died, had her protection not come fast enough."

"True. Are you known for rushing headlong into danger? Is that why my son is constantly in harm's way?" he asked.

"That's a highly inconsiderate thing to say to the woman who ended our war," Nico told his father angrily.

"He's not wrong," I said and met the eyes of the mage king. "He is in harm's way a lot because of me. However, it is not because I rush into danger. I try to avoid danger if at all possible. If you think it's wrong for me to protect children, then…" I trailed off and shrugged.

My mouth was getting the better of me. Perhaps spending so much time with the princes and getting desensitized to them wasn't such a good thing.

The mage king threw back his head and boomed with laughter. He patted Nico on the back and said, "I can see why you like her, son. She reminds me of your mother."

"She does," Nico agreed.

The mage king held out his hand and I set mine in it, expecting him to shake it, but he pulled it up to kiss my knuckles. "It is an honor to meet you, Jolie. I look forward to you visiting my clan soon."

I bowed my head. "Thank you, for the invitation."

He released me and laughed again as he walked away, shaking his head.

"Well, two more kings seem to like you," Fox commented from behind me.

"Two?" Nico asked.

"My father seems enamored with her too," Fox said softly.

"Maybe, I'm just a likeable person," I commented grumpily.

"Jolie," wolf Elder called.

I spun and immediately dropped into a bow, which was difficult in the dress and the reason I had been curtsying instead.

Fox wrapped an arm around my waist to keep me from falling.

"Sorry," I mumbled and straightened myself and my dress.

"Please, come with me," wolf Elder requested with a smirk and amusement gleaming in his eyes.

"May I bring Fox?" I asked softly.

He nodded once in agreement and the three of us moved through the crowd with everyone staring at us. Was it the dress? Was it because of Fox or the Elder? Or was it because I was human? There didn't appear to be many humans, but it was hard to tell between shifters and humans when they were not using their powers. Their stares made my heart pound and my palms sweat. They were all judging me, I knew they were.

Rhys winked at me as we walked by and reached through to bond to brush mine. I smiled as we continued on, the nerves leaving me.

My guards were here for me and that was all that mattered. They would protect me. They didn't care what others said about me.

The crowd finally thinned, and I could see the other two Elders waiting at the front. This time, I curtsied instead of bowing and wolf Elder's lip twitched as he fought a smile.

"Welcome, Jolie," dragon Elder said in greeting.

"Thank you for inviting me," I said. Despite the guys not saying anything, I was sure they had been the ones to invite me.

The crowd had grown quiet and the music had stopped to allow for the Elders to talk.

"Tonight, we sign the long-awaited Peace Treaty between the Four Clans!" wolf Elder announced proudly.

Everyone cheered and then quieted quickly again to hear more of what they had to say.

"Before we sign the treaty, we have to recognize the one who ended the war," dragon Elder announced.

"Jolie, please come up here," elf Elder requested.

Fox squeezed my hand before I walked up to them and curtsied again.

"Jolie, a human with no powers, stumbled into our world and has not hesitated since entering. She returned the stolen artifact, once she learned the item she had been gifted was ours. Then, she protected two wolf pups from an ogre during the day of attacks," dragon Elder informed everyone.

People murmured behind me in shock to each other.

"We owe you much, but are unable to fully repay our debt," wolf Elder told me.

"We have been told that you are already accepted by the Wolf Clan," dragon Elder said.

"She is," Dan replied loudly behind me.

"It has been hundreds of years since a human such as yourself has been born. To repay part of our debt, we offer you this-" elf Elder paused and a teenage boy ran forward with a black wooden box. elf Elder took it and held it out to me.

I took it and wondered if I was supposed to open it now, or just thank them for it and open it later.

"Open it," Fox whispered behind me.

The Elders were smirking at me, amusement lighting all of their eyes now.

I opened it and pulled out a necklace with four bright diamonds in a line down the center. They were at least 2 carats each, and glowed with a strange ethereal light.

"It's too much," I whispered and looked up at them with tears in my eyes.

"Each diamond contains power from each of the kings and the princes," dragon Elder explained to me.

Holy shit! They'd just given me an extreme boost of power, should I need it. If I didn't do something, I would start crying and my makeup would be ruined for the rest of the night.

Rhys took the necklace he had purchased for me off and put the new necklace on for me, brushing his hand across my shoulders after he had finished, sending chills down my spine in a delightful shiver.

"From this night forward, you are welcome at any of the four clans and are named Princess of the Four Clans," wolf Elder announced.

That set everyone off. I thought my legs might give out and was saved by Rhys putting his arm out for me to hold. He took the box from me and held out a beautiful silver crown with branches and cherry blossoms that had pink diamonds in the center of each blossom. Before I could protest, he set it on my head and kissed my cheek.

"Our new princess!" the Elders announced together.

Rhys turned me around and everyone bowed to me, except the princes and kings, who did dip their heads in acknowledgement.

What the fuck had just happened? How? Why? Oh my god.

"Now, to business!" dragon Elder said.

The kings went to the Elders and a wooden table was brought out with a large piece of paper, a quill, and inkwell. The kings each signed the treaty as did the Elders.

Dan held out the quill towards me and motioned at the paper. "We need our savior's signature as well," he told me.

Tonight just kept adding surprises on top of surprises.

I signed my name and everyone cheered.

"Peace has been achieved!" Dan announced and clapped King Katar and the mage king's shoulders.

Everyone cheered and music was turned on again.

"May I have this dance?" Dan asked.

"I couldn't refuse my Alpha," I said with a wide smile and set my hand in his.

"Even my old man is trying to steal her," Deryn whispered jokingly.

"If I were twenty years younger, it wouldn't be a fight," Dan teased.

My face was certainly the color of a tomato at that comment.

Dan swept me out onto the dance floor and surprised me with an elegant waltz.

"You dance very well," I commented.

"All men should learn to waltz," he said adamantly. "It impresses the ladies." He winked at me and I laughed, then twirled under his raised arm.

"You're hogging her," King Katar teased him and twirled me away from Dan.

Dan bowed to me and walked off into the crowd.

"King Katar," I whispered in shock. "You honor me with a dance."

He smirked as he danced gracefully with me. "You don't have to be so formal with me. I'm not as pretentious as some are. You may call me, Katar."

"Katar, I have to admit, your son is growing mighty jealous of our dance," I whispered to him.

As we spun, he saw Fox waiting on the edge of the crowd, and he chuckled.

"He was never good with sharing his toys," he teased. Then he added, "Except with his best friends. That seems to be the case here, as well."

"Katar, I-"

"Don't get upset," he whispered soothingly. "Our kinds are known to have multiple partners."

"What?"

He nodded and pulled me closer so that he didn't have to talk very loud for me to hear him. "Female offspring are rare and so, there are often multiple men for every woman. We also don't normally mate with humans, but you will be an exception."

"You're okay with me possibly mating with Fox?" I asked in a whisper since people were watching us.

"I want my son to mate with someone he loves, and I believe he loves you," he whispered back.

"I love him," I whispered back and glanced at Fox. "Very much."

"As you should...as their queen," he replied and kissed me cheek before letting the Mage King take me into a dance.

"We haven't gotten off to the best start," he said with a smile, thankfully dancing with me during a slow song.

"I'm at fault," I whispered sadly. "I don't have the best control on my temper."

"My name is Johann."

"Jolie," I said with a smile.

"You seem to make my son happy," he commented. "I have not seen him smile as much as I have when you are near him. He is focused on his training and his studies again, something he had been neglecting. He is also much more interested in our politics, things I know I can thank you for. You are a good influence on him."

"I can't take credit for all of that," I mumbled.

"Trust me, it is all because of you."

"You were right about me getting him into danger," I said sadly. "Especially with the curse..."

"Will you take him as a mate?" he asked me suddenly.

"I, uh...I haven't decided yet," I admitted.

He nodded. "You should decide soon. Even with this gesture from the Elders, you are still in danger. Being named mate of the four princes, or even one of them, will greatly increase your safety and make people think twice before hurting you."

"It is strange to me that you kings are all okay with your sons mating with a human, especially a human who will be mated to other princes," I muttered.

"Polygamy is quite common among Other races. Plus, mages and humans aren't so different, right?"

"Right," I agreed.

He kissed the back of my hand and handed me off to the dragon king. My legs were going to be extremely sore tomorrow, from all of the dancing. I wasn't going to complain though. How many females got to say that they danced with the four kings and the four princes?

"Jolie, you look lovely in that dress," he told me.

"Thank you, King-"

"Emrys," he supplied.

"Emrys," I said, hoping I said it correctly.

He smiled, so I thought I had said it right.

"Emrys, how would you feel if I took your son as my mate?" I asked him.

He laughed. "My son has already told me that he will not mate with anyone else, so I suppose it is truly inevitable."

"I love him," I whispered.

He nodded and said, "I know. I can see the love you all share with each other."

"My turn," Fox said and held his hand out.

Emrys kissed my hand before setting it in Fox's. "Visit my clan soon, Jolie. They would love to have you visit."

"I will," I promised. Had I hit my head and this was all a strange hallucination during a coma? That had to be the answer. There was no way that all of this was really happening.

"Hello, Princess," Fox greeted me and guided me through a dance that I didn't know.

"Hello, handsome," I replied.

"Did my father behave himself?" he asked.

"Yes, he was very nice."

"I'm glad. Sometimes he can be a bit...overwhelming," he whispered. I laughed and before I could reply, Rhys stole me away.

"Rhys," I gasped.

His lips were turned up into one of the most handsome smiles I had ever seen on him. "You look amazing," he said and pulled me closer against him. With his lips next to my ear, he whispered,

"I'm going to have you wear that dress when it's my day, just so I can take it off of you."

Our bodies were pressed completely together, not even air could get between us. Our eyes were locked and I swore there were visible sparks between us. His gaze was so intense, so focused on me, like I was the last person on the planet.

Someone cleared their throat behind us, breaking the spell.

"May I?" an older male asked.

"Certainly, Alfred," Rhys said, kissed my knuckles, and then set my hand in Alfred's.

Alfred and I joined the dance and I smiled as he twirled me expertly, matching and exceeding the younger males dancing skills.

"You're quite the dancer," I complimented him.

"You'll often find that the older males have more experience and can provide more enjoyment," he replied with a wink that made me blush.

Another male cut in.

Then another.

And another.

I danced with a whirlwind of males, rarely getting a dance with any of my guards, though they did occasionally sneak in. The next male I danced with was very stiff and kept avoiding my eyes. He had resisted my attempts at conversation, not that I was a great conversationalist by any means.

Rhys slid his fingers along my side as he danced with another female by me. I turned to look for him and felt a sharp pain in my side. Someone screamed and Rhys's gaze, who I finally found, was wide with fear.

"Rot in hell," the male I had been dancing with snarled in my ear.

My body felt cold and numb and it took a lot of strength to look down. In the center of my stomach was a silver dagger, buried to the hilt. Blood dripped down the dagger, creating a pool on the ground at my feet. I swayed and fell onto my back on the ground. That asshole had stabbed me.

More people were screaming and when I blinked, a dragon appeared over me, roaring. I recognized that roar, Rhys.

He was spewing fire, the heat of it warming me a minute as it built in his dragon belly.

"Shit. Shit. Shit," Fox gasped.

He started to heal me, but Katar pushed him to the side. "Stop. We all know that you won't be useful if you heal someone."

Fox stood up and faced away from me, his body glowing softly.

"You with me still, Princess?" Katar asked.

"Yes," I said and hissed as the movement hurt immensely.

"Okay, stay still and I'll heal you," he explained.

"Help…others," I ordered him.

"You'll die if I don't heal you," he informed me.

Tamara and Madison ran beneath Rhys, sliding to a stop next to me with blood coating their fur. Madison shifted and gasped, "Auntie Jolie!"

"You're related to them?" Katar asked.

"Not by blood," Tamara explained.

"Where are your parents?" Katar asked, his hands glowing as he held them over my stomach.

"We don't know," Madison admitted. "That's why we came to Auntie."

"Stay beneath the dragon," Fox ordered them. "He'll protect you."

"Okay," they agreed simultaneously.

A vampire leapt at Katar, but Fox tackled him before he could touch his father. Four more vampires came and Katar had to stop healing me to draw his sword and slice all of their heads off.

Two goblins leapt towards him and Rhys used his tail to smack them away. Once they were gone, he curled his tail around my body, not touching me, but protecting me within his scales.

The female dragon who had stolen me previously, flew into Rhys at an alarming speed, knocking him away from me and into the house fifty yards away.

I tried to watch their fight, but my body wasn't responding to my demands. My chest felt heavy and I struggled to take in deep breaths. Was I dying?

"Jolie!" Fox yelled.

Shit. I didn't want to die. Not yet.

"Jolie!" Deryn yelled.

I stared up at the star-filled night sky and tried to locate Fox's powers within me. If I could heal myself... It seemed impossible, so I went to plan B, use all of their powers. Blinding light from somewhere appeared and I felt like I was weightless. The dagger fell to the ground and I felt my innards and skin healing back together. I took a tentative breath and it didn't hurt any more. *Yes!*

"What the-" someone gasped below me.

I sat up and pressed my hand against my stomach, fully healed. That was going to come in very handy.

Now, I wasn't a liability. I wasn't the damsel in distress that the guards had to protect. I could defend myself. I could heal myself. I was OP as hell!

"Jolie!" Rhys called.

He had shifted back into his man form and ran to me, crushing his mouth to mine.

"Now's not the time for that," I reminded him and pushed him back.

The girls cowered next to my feet in wolf form, staring out at the party, which had been attacked by my father and his army. Thousands of different beings swarmed within the party, attacking the attendees.

Their side was losing, the kings and princes were killing things right and left, tearing down their numbers and protecting their people.

King Johann and the mages used fire and sun powers to obliterate the vampires. My father floated above the chaos in a sphere with a woman who was holding her hands out. She must have been a mage.

"We have to defeat him," I whispered.

"You can't use the powers anymore," Rhys ordered me. "Most will just assume the necklace the kings gave you protected you. If you use them more, or individually, you'll be exposed."

"We can't let them kill people," I urged him.

"Stay behind me and we'll help get rid of these scumbags," Rhys agreed.

The girls followed on my heels, watching our backs and walking backwards. Their hackles were raised and they were snarling and showing their teeth, looking like vicious wolves instead of scared children.

As we moved, Rhys attacked the enemy, helping the weaker beings defeat those who were stronger than them.

"You okay?" Deryn called to me while fighting a large ogre. The ogre slammed a huge club into the ground, but Deryn easily avoided it. The club got stuck and Deryn ran up it and sliced the ogre's head off with a sword.

"I'm fine!" I called back to him. "What happened to the guy who stabbed me?" I asked Rhys.

"I killed him," he said with a growl.

"Did you know him?"

He shook his head. "Never seen him before."

"He was a mage," Nico told me as he walked next to me, his staff glowed nonstop as he sent spell after spell into enemies.

"Any idea why?" Rhys asked.

"He was struggling to provide for his wife. We think someone paid him to do it and the money had too much allure."

"How sad," I whispered. He tried to kill me, but desperate people did desperate things when they were at the end of their rope.

"You're too kind," Nico warned me.

"How bad are things?" I asked. They didn't seem so bad from where I could see, plus my dad looked mad, which meant he had to be losing.

"Tomorrow, we need a massive cuddle puddle," Nico whispered to me.

To them, lying around me in a square, with a hand each on me was a cuddle puddle. We only truly cuddled on our individual days.

"Watch out!" I yelled and ducked, pushing the girls' heads down as I did, avoiding the sword swung at us.

Rhys stopped the blade with his arm, dragon scales covering it to protect him. He turned and punched the attacker, a goblin with green mottled skin. The goblin staggered back and clutched his face, which was bleeding heavily.

"Nico, go help," I ordered him.

He bowed his head and whispered, "Queen."

They had been doing that more lately and I wasn't sure that I liked it. I wasn't a queen. I didn't plan to be one either. Being named a princess was one thing, but queen? Wait, if my dad was the king of vampires, then wasn't I technically the princess of the vampires? Not being a vampire probably played a role in me not being their princess. Not that I wanted to be part of the vampires.

Something slammed into the shield protecting my dad and then dropped to the ground. I realized it was Deryn. He had jumped at him.

Nico and his father stood side by side, sending spells of various sizes and shapes at the shield, which cracked immediately.

The mage with my dad panicked, released the shield and tried to run. Nico froze her, while Deryn and Fox attacked Dad with swords.

He had a sword of his own and was very skilled with it, blocking most of their attacks, despite it being two on one.

"You've lost," Katar told him. "Give up now and we'll spare your life."

"No, we won't," Nico growled and leapt into the fray, setting Dad's shirt on fire and attacking his legs.

The three of them fought seamlessly together, never getting in the others way without even talking. A simple look and they'd attack simultaneously, and then separately. It was breathtaking to watch.

Dad had several cuts on his arms and a nasty gash in his side, which he was holding a hand over. Nico knocked him onto his back and Fox ran him through. I turned, too late to avoid seeing it. My father screamed out, the sound dying in a gargle. When I turned back, his body had vanished. He was dead. My father, my torturer, the king of vampires…gone.

Rhys pulled me into him and gripped my side tightly.

"Why did you kill him?" Katar asked.

"He tortured her," Fox whispered to him. "He tortured her as a child and as a teenager. He tortured her when he stole her from us. I could not let him live."

There were several people laying on the ground, some getting healed and others providing first aid treatment. There were also some who were dead, their bodies stiff and eyes unseeing.

"Girls!" Sharla yelled.

The girls turned and ran to Sharla and Martin who were running in our direction. They had been on the opposite side of the battle from us. I smiled to see the reunited family and felt a deep sadness about my father. He was evil and had never loved me, but he was the only blood family I had left. Mother had died while I was a baby, and my grandmother had died a year ago.

"Let's go home," Deryn whispered. He brushed hair behind my ear and rubbed his thumb down my cheek.

Home. Home was definitely with the four of them.

"Home," I agreed and nodded.

They boxed me in and we took the SUV we had driven to the

meeting in, but Deryn drove since we had left Martin to be with his family. I leaned against Fox in the backseat and couldn't believe that we had defeated Dad and his army. His evil influence was gone from the world. Finally.

No one talked as we drove. No one talked as we took the elevator to Fox's apartment. As soon as the door closed, all four crushed me in a group hug. My head was pressed into Fox's chest with Rhys at my back.

"I've never known fear before," Fox whispered. "I thought I did, but seeing that blade in your stomach-" He couldn't finish his sentence and instead buried his nose against my neck.

"We failed you, again," Deryn mumbled into my left shoulder.

"No, you didn't. Who would have thought someone would do something like that with everyone there?" I asked them. "Plus, I wouldn't have let you stop me from dancing with them."

"I didn't even get to dance with you more than once," Nico grumbled.

"Well, maybe we can go to a club one of these nights," I suggested. I hadn't been to a club in a long time.

"Let's change," Rhys suggested and pulled his blood-soaked jacket off.

All of them stepped away from me to remove their jackets and unbutton their cufflinks and their shirts.

Rhys noticed me staring and smirked. "Are we bothering you?"

"Please, don't stop on my account," I teased and leaned against the living room wall to watch. "I'm quite enjoying the show."

"Food, booze, and cuddles in an hour at Deryn's," Fox requested.

Everyone nodded their agreement and then took turns kissing me before leaving.

Fox locked his door and then was suddenly in front of me. "I need to know you're alright," he said. "I need to get this dress off of you. The sight of the blood on your stomach is making me uneasy."

I slipped the dress off, shivering as the cold air covered me. He slid his hand along my skin, where there wasn't even a scar from the attack.

"I almost lost control of my powers when I saw him stab you," Fox whispered. "I've never lost control."

"It wasn't a picnic for me either," I chuckled.

"Don't joke about this, please," he requested.

Serious Fox was so unfun, but probably right.

"Sorry," I whispered.

His shirt was still on, so I finished unbuttoning it and took it off, leaning back to admire his body. He unbuckled his belt, unbuttoned his pants, and slid them down slowly, giving me a nice view of his backside as he did so.

His strong arms wrapped around me, trapping me to him. "I love you, Jolie. I love you more than anything. I can't stand seeing you hurt. I can't stand knowing I was right there and you almost died. I was powerless to stop it. I don't like being powerless."

His skin was so soft and his muscles were so hard. It was a contrast that I loved exploring with my hands, and my mouth. I kissed my way around his neck and chest. He grew hard against me instantly and moaned as he took my mouth with his.

"Shower," he growled into my mouth. "I need to get this blood off of you."

"You've got blood in your hair," I pointed out.

We kissed the entire way to the bathroom and didn't stop until we started shampooing our hair. It took a few washes to get the blood off of my stomach, but once I did, Fox relaxed and pushed me gently against the bathroom wall.

"You can't die on me, Jolie. I can't lose you."

"You won't lose me," I whispered. "I'm not going anywhere."

"You deserve so much more than I can give you. You deserve the stars and to rule over it all. Martin may have been your first love, but I, and the other three, will be your final loves. I will never take you for granted. I will never stop loving you. I will continue to fall deeper and deeper in love with you as we grow old together."

"You're the greatest thing to happen in my life," I whispered.

He kissed me ferociously, devouring me in a way that was very unlike Fox. Our sexual encounters were normally slow and calm. That night, it was fast and demanding. He whispered promises to love me forever in my ear as he gave me orgasm after orgasm.

"I'm never giving you up," he told me as he gripped my hips and thrust into me as deep and as hard as he could. "You're mine."

"For eternity," I agreed.

"Say it?" he requested.

"I love you, Foxfire."

His body trembled, his eyes fluttered shut, and he exhaled sharply. "God, that is the most amazing thing to hear."

"Say it," I ordered him, moving my hips to match his movements.

He opened his eyes and stared straight into mine. "I love you, my princess. My queen. Jolie. I will love you until this universe is destroyed."

"Foxfire!" I screamed as I orgasmed, my muscles tightening around him and making it that much better.

He grunted and buried his face in my hair as he found his release.

CHAPTER 14

No one brought up the battle after they'd all shared their fear with me and promised to keep me safe in the future. No one brought it up, but it was still evident that it was on their minds with the haunted expressions they got time to time as they looked at me. Try as I might, I couldn't help them get over what had happened. How bad would they have been if I had actually died?

"Your dad messaged me again about visiting," I told Rhys while sitting at the table in his apartment.

"I told him that your visit will wait," he replied as he flipped a pancake in the pan. He was naked, except for the apron that he had tied into a cute bow above his butt.

"Why? Why are you keeping me from meeting your clan?" I asked him angrily. "I met Deryn's and Fox's."

"I'm not keeping you-"

"Are you ashamed to be seen with me by your clan members?" I asked, my anger spiraling out of control. Anger had never been a major issue of mine, but suddenly, I felt like tearing someone's arms off.

He spun to me and said, "That is the dumbest question you've ever asked me."

"You're an inconsiderate jerk," I growled at him. "Do you have a female in your clan that you're trying to keep me from meeting? Maybe your most recent relationship? One you haven't gotten over yet?"

He set his spatula down, turned the stove off, and stalked towards me, his eyes shifted to his dragon's eyes and for a brief moment, I worried he might hurt me. I knew he wouldn't, but the fear was there nonetheless. Stupid human instincts.

"There is only you, Jolie. There's been no other girls for me since I saved you that first day. I am not embarrassed by you. I do not have a secret female I'm—"

"Then why can't I meet them!" I shouted, fists clenched at my sides and my entire body tingling with barely contained fury.

"Because we aren't mated!" he yelled back and then straightened and fumbled over his words. "I-I'm just-"

"Why do we have to be mated?" I asked. "What if I chose to never be mated to you? Would you keep me from the clan? Would you break our bond? Stop being my guard?"

The fury I had felt was gone, leaving me weak and tired.

"You'll be safest as my mate," he replied and reached for me.

I stumbled away from him, tripped over the chair behind me, and fell on my butt on the kitchen floor. He tried to help me up, but I smacked his arms away and stood up on my own.

"I've lost my appetite," I whispered. He hadn't said that he would not break our bond or stop being my guard. Would he really do it if I didn't choose to mate with him?

"Jolie," he whispered softly, fists clenched at his sides.

I stopped at the door, clothes in my hand, and asked, "If I don't become your mate, will you break the bond?"

"Are you planning to only mate with one of us? Or only some of us?" he asked instead of answering.

"No, it's all or nothing," I answered truthfully.

"Then no, I won't break the bond."

"But you would if I chose only one or two of you?" I asked, feeling a pain in my chest that I knew was unnecessary. What was going on with my emotions? Why couldn't I get a handle on them?

"I don't know," he admitted. "I don't know if I could be your guard while you were mated to one of the others and not me."

"You're the only one who feels that way," I told him. "The others said they wouldn't ever leave me, no matter what I decided about my mates."

"They'd consider it too, but wouldn't tell you," he said with certainty.

"Maybe. Or maybe you are finally seeing past the bond and what your true feelings are. Maybe…maybe we aren't meant to be more than friends."

Before he could respond, I ran out of his apartment and up the stairs. I stumbled up the last few steps, but finally made it to my apartment with tears streaming down my face, blinding me.

The door was locked and I hadn't brought my keys with me, so I sat against it, knees pulled to my chest and arms around my legs, and cried.

Why? Why was I so emotionally unstable today? What would I do in Rhys's position? Would I be able to stay if the tables were turned?

Hell, I knew I wouldn't be able to share at all. I wasn't sure how they could all do it as it was.

"Sweetheart," Nico whispered. "What's wrong?"

"Rhys," I sobbed and lifted my head. Nico's eyes were bright with worry, his eyebrows scrunched together. He sat on the floor of the hallway with me, cross-legged.

"What about Rhys?"

"He said-" I didn't want to repeat it. Just remembering the words hurt me again. I threw myself into Nico, who caught me and repositioned me so that I was in his lap sideways, my head on his shoulder and my legs over the side of his.

"It's alright, Jolie. I'm here," he whispered.

"Jolie," Rhys whispered, standing above us. "Let me explain."

"Fuck off, Rhys," Nico threatened him and rocked me in his arms.

"I need to talk to her," Rhys said and moved closer.

"I don't want to talk to you anymore," I sobbed and clutched Nico's shirt.

"Jolie-"

Rhys's body flew down the hallway, slamming into the closed elevator doors. I gasped in shock and looked up at Nico who had his hand outstretched and glowing eyes.

"Don't do this," Rhys begged him and stood up. "Don't start a fight with me over a misunderstanding between her and me."

Deryn walked into the hallway and looked at our tense stand-off. "What's going on?"

"Dickbag said something that hurt Jolie," Nico said.

"I'm trying to talk to her so I can explain what I said. It's a misunderstanding," Rhys told Deryn.

"You said you would break the bond," I accused him.

"What!" Deryn screamed at the same time Nico did.

"I said if you only mated with one of us, or not all of us, that I would *consider* breaking the bond."

Deryn punched Rhys in the jaw, knocking him down to one knee. Deryn's body was partially shifted, fur sprouting from his hands and face. I'd seen this happen only twice before, both times when a werewolf was pissed and barely controlling their shift.

"What the fuck, Rhys?" Nico demanded.

"Don't fucking lie!" Rhys yelled at them. "If she only chose me or Fox, would you stay as her guard? Would you stay and watch them together?"

"It would be difficult," Deryn agreed, thankfully fully human again.

"Exactly!" Rhys yelled and rubbed his jaw. "Fuck, that was a hell of a hit."

"What if she chooses to mate with someone else and not any of us?" Nico asked him, fists sparkling with magical energy ready to be used.

"Nico," I whispered. "Nico, don't hurt him." He didn't respond to me. I gripped his shirt and shook him. "Nico!"

"I don't know," Rhys admitted.

Nico was gone. One second he was beneath me, and the next I was sitting in the hallway alone. He slammed into Rhys, his hands released an electrical energy that made Rhys scream out in pain.

"Stop!" I yelled, but they weren't listening.

"I love her!" Rhys yelled at them, panting on the floor while Deryn and Nico glared down at him. "I can't watch her love anyone, but you three!"

"Our bond isn't to be broken! We swore!" Nico shouted at him.

"I know," Rhys whispered.

Nico looked like he was going to hurt Rhys again, so I screamed at them. My scream was loud and high-pitched, higher than I'd ever screamed before. The glass windows shattered, the lightbulbs shattered, and the pictures and vases exploded. The guys dropped to the ground, covering their heads and looked at me with wide eyes.

"Stop fighting!" I ordered them.

"Jolie," Nico whispered.

"Shut up!" I ordered him. "Shut up and listen to me. There will be times that I fight with you individually. It will happen. But, that doesn't mean you fight with each other. You're brothers. You're best friends. I'm sorry. I overreacted. I've been extremely emotional lately. And no, god dammit, I'm not fucking pregnant. I am sorry, Rhys."

Rhys, Nico, and Deryn stood up slowly, keeping their eyes on me.

"I'm sorry, Jolie. I love you," Rhys whispered.

"I know you do," I said and felt the tears as they dripped down my cheeks.

"Can I come hug you?" Rhys asked.

I nodded, since it was impossible to talk at the moment. What the fuck was wrong with me? Why was I overreacting to everything?

Rhys gently slid his arms around my sides and pulled me against his chest. "I'm sorry."

My tears soaked the shirt he had put on and I gripped his back as I cried.

"It's us," Deryn whispered. "She's feeding off our emotions."

"What do you mean?" Nico asked. "None of us are crying."

"Fox is," he replied with a smirk. "He's watching that movie about the dog and fox who became friends. He always cries when he watches that movie."

"Which one of you was mad earlier?" Rhys asked as he rubbed my back and hugged me.

"Me," Deryn answered. "I was trying to do something and it wasn't working like I wanted it to."

"She looked like she was ready to blow the building up," Rhys informed them.

"How can we stop her from getting hyped up on our feelings?" Nico asked.

"I'll ask my Elder," Deryn said. "Wolves have a pack connection, similar to our warrior bond. I'm sure he will have something to suggest."

"I love you. All of you," I whispered into Rhys's shirt, the words getting muffled by it.

"We love you more than anything," Nico whispered.

"Come on, your breakfast is going to be cold," Rhys said and tugged me down the hallway.

Fox popped his head out of his apartment and looked at us with red eyes. "What's going on?"

"No more sad movies!" Nico ordered him.

"What? Why not?"

"Because Jolie can't handle it right now."

"Why are you keeping me from your clan too?" I asked Nico. "Fox and Deryn are the only ones who have let me go. Rhys said I can't go unless we're mated."

"Ah, that's what started the argument," Deryn guessed.

Rhys nodded.

"I want you to be safe," Rhys reiterated. "After you choose whether to become our mate or not, then I'll take you."

"Why not before?" I asked.

"Because being my mate will ensure that no one tries to challenge you," he explained. "As a mated couple, if one is challenged, it is a challenge for both of them. If you aren't my mate, then anyone can challenge you and I won't be able to help."

"So, if I don't become your mate, then what?" I asked.

"We'll cross that bridge when it comes. First, you have to make a decision. And no, I don't mean right now," he said quickly before I could say anything.

Breakfast was a somber affair, but at least no one was crying or punching each other. I excused myself to sulk in my apartment, curled up on the couch with the blanket wrapped around me.

Too late, I realized that Nico hadn't answered me. These men were slowly driving me insane.

"Jolie," Fox called through the door.

"What?" I replied, my voice muffled by the blanket around my face.

"Can I come in? You're sad and it's hurting me."

Hurting him? Why would my sadness hurt him?

"What do you mean it's hurting you?" I asked and sat up. I still wasn't going to the door to let him in. I needed my privacy.

"We can all feel your pain," he explained. "It's like a sharp stab in the center of our chests."

I had no idea that they felt my pain physically.

"I want to be alone," I told him. "Please. I'll try to stop being sad so it doesn't hurt you."

"Okay," he said with a sigh. "I'm sorry I caused you to be upset earlier."

Fox was always so kind and sweet. Yet, I didn't want to let him in to console me. Why? Sometimes, a girl needs to be alone to thoroughly process her feelings and emotions. And I really needed to process everything.

The guys were all great. They were loving, kind, and protective. They wanted me and me alone.

But, was that really fair? Would it be right of me to stay with them? For me to be with four of them, while they only had one of me?

Knowing that they would feel my death tenfold, did not make me want to agree. No matter what, they would have to deal with my death because they lived longer than I did.

They all wanted to be my mate. I wanted them to be my mates. It should have been a simple answer. Yet, I was hesitant to take that plunge. I felt like I was taking away their futures. I felt like I was ruining their chances of finding mates that would be their equals.

Thinking about giving them up hurt immensely. Picturing my future without them at my side was painful and boring. Even just one of them being gone was inconceivable. I could do it, but I really didn't want to.

Running would do nothing, except put me in danger and cause them to have to rush after me to find me. I wasn't going to do that again. I wouldn't be childish and run away ever again. Though, I wasn't powerless any longer. I could shift into a god damn dragon, after all.

So, that left me with two options. One, break the bond completely. Two, become their mate.

Being their mate sounded like an amazing thing. To know

that we were mated, that there would be no others who could break us up or that they, or I, would cheat would provide huge relief to our stressed lives.

The warning the Elders gave us about the chances of pregnancy increasing certainly worried me. I was not ready for children. Not for at least five years. Or more. Definitely more. Truthfully, I never saw myself having children. Would they want children? That was something I would need to ask them. That might be a deal breaker for some of them.

"Jolie," Deryn called through the door.

"I want to be alone," I replied immediately.

"Please," Nico begged.

I opened my door and was shocked to see all four of them standing in my hallway with pained expressions and half of them with clenched fists.

They were wearing tank tops and sweatpants. All four of them. They were different colors and brands, but they still matched.

"Why are you all wearing the same thing?" I asked, completely caught off guard, since they never wore similar things, except when they wore suits.

"We were training," Rhys answered.

"What do you guys want?" I asked softly, resigned to not being alone today like I wanted. They weren't being manipulative or rude on purpose. I knew that. I just wasn't sure why they were being so insistent.

"We want to talk," Nico said.

"What about?"

"Whatever it is that is causing you so much pain and discomfort," Deryn said with a growl and rubbed the center of his chest with his closed fist.

"Is it really hurting you?" I asked in disbelief.

All four nodded.

"Talking isn't going to change my feelings," I muttered. It might make things worse, actually.

"Is it about mating with us?" Rhys asked softly.

I wanted to lie, to keep their feelings from being hurt and keep them from misunderstanding why it was causing me pain. However, lying was out of the question, since they could see right through my lies. So, I nodded.

"What about mating makes you sad?" Fox asked. I expected him to be upset or sad, but he was only curious. Or at least that's how he appeared. They were pretty good at hiding their emotions.

"It's not mating that is making me sad," I explained. "But the options of what to do if we don't mate."

The tension grew, all of them freezing and clenching their fists at their sides.

"What options?" Deryn asked.

A loud groan escaped my lips, and I spun around, stalking back to the couch where I flopped onto my side, blanket still tightly wrapped around me. "I don't want to talk about this," I mumbled around the blanket which I'd pulled up to my nose.

The guys filed in, Fox coming in last and shutting my door for me. Rhys sat on the floor in front of the couch, Deryn sat on the couch beside my head. Nico sat at my feet, picking my legs up and putting them in his lap, so I didn't have to move at all. Fox sat in front of the couch, beside Rhys and turned to look at me.

"I love you four," I told them softly.

"We love you as well," Fox whispered. "Which is why we want to find the source of your sadness and annihilate it."

I chuckled humorlessly. "You can't."

"Why not?" Rhys asked, tilting his head back so that he could look at me upside down.

"This is my decision," I whispered. "I have to come up with the decision on my own. I have to decide what I'm going to do about you four. About the rest of my life, our lives."

"We don't get any say?" Nico asked. He had begun rubbing my feet at some point, I wasn't certain when, but I was thoroughly enjoying his warm hands kneading my feet.

"You all already told me that you want to be my mate," I replied. "I asked you each about it."

"What options?" Deryn asked me for the second time.

I groaned. Werewolves were not known to give up on something once they had the scent. "Mate with you all. Mate with none of you. If I mate with none of you, then I have to decide if I'm going to stay. If I mate with all of you, then I'm taking away your chance at finding a mate of equal standing. A mate worthy of you." Before any of them could say it, I said, "Yes, I'm worthy. Blah. Blah. Blah."

"If you don't mate with us, you might leave?" Fox asked, his brows furrowed and a perfectly executed pout on his face.

"Yes," I replied, not wanting to hide anything.

"You love us. Why leave if you don't mate with us?" Rhys asked.

He was getting mad again, I could see it in his tense shoulders and the way his eyes were glowing.

"Because I can't see you with other mates," I whispered without looking at him. It was incredibly selfish of me.

"Do you just want to be miserable?" Fox asked. Normally that question would be said with sarcasm or anger, but he was genuinely curious.

"No," I grumbled.

"You want to mate with us, but you are considering leaving? Why?" he asked.

"If I don't want children, are you four going to be fine with that?" I asked instead of answering his question.

That got them all to shut up and think a moment.

"I've always wanted children," Deryn said softly. "You really don't want kids?"

"Not any time soon," I explained. "The Elders said that once you mated, pregnancy was almost a guarantee."

"There are preventative measures we can take," Nico said. "There are spells and herbs on top of human contraceptives that we can use to ensure the increased virality is combated. Not every new mated pair gets pregnant. It just increases the chances."

"How am I supposed to have children with all four of you? How will we even know whose it is?" I sat up and let the blanket fall to my lap. "That's so much drama."

"It doesn't matter whose kid it is, we will all care for it and love it because it is your child," Fox replied instantly.

"And we would know whose it is because of the powers it possessed," Nico said.

"I never wanted more than two kids," I said, leaning my head back against the back of the couch. "I'd have to have at least four for you all."

"No one said you had to have their child," Rhys pointed out.

"Why were you so sad earlier?" Fox asked, probing for more information.

"I was thinking about what my life would be like without you four in it."

They didn't seem to know how to respond to that. We sat in silence for at least three minutes before Rhys got up, grabbed four beers and one cider, and brought them back for all of us to share.

"We aren't going to force you to do anything or decide on anything," Rhys told me, his hand resting on mine on top of the couch. "We just want you to know that we love you. We love you more than anything. We would be devastated to lose the bond we share with you, to lose you."

"Can I put off deciding?" I asked quietly. Maybe if I pushed it off a bit, I would have a revelation and know what decision was the right one for me.

"Yes," Fox answered for the four of them. He turned on a movie, one I told him a few days ago that I wanted to watch because it was supposed to be one of the best comedies of the year.

I sat up, put my legs on either side of Rhys, and ran my fingers through his hair. It was thick, but soft and silky.

"Me next!" Fox said and tried to push Rhys away.

Rhys growled at him and held his spot between my legs.

Deryn lay his head on my left leg. I knew exactly what he was doing, but I still obliged. With my left hand, I ran my fingers through his hair, while still running the fingers of my right hand through Rhys's.

Fox grumbled and leaned his head against my knee.

Suddenly, my stomach became queasy. I leapt up and ran to the bathroom, covering my mouth with both hands. For once, I was glad that the toilet seat was up, or I would have thrown up all over the floor.

Someone pulled my hair back, away from my face, and held it while I continued to empty my stomach. When I was finally done, I stood up on shaky legs, stumbled to the sink, and thoroughly brushed my teeth and tongue.

Nico set his hand on my forehead and immediately frowned. "You're burning up."

"Fever," I agreed and wrapped my arms around myself as the chills set in. My body must have known that I was sick and made me wrap up in the blanket ahead of time.

"Let me heal her," Fox said.

"No," I ordered him. "This isn't a wound. It's an illness. I don't want you weakening yourself just because I have a stomach bug."

"There's a bug in your stomach?" Deryn asked with wide eyes.

Four sets of eyes glued themselves to my stomach.

I chuckled and shook my head. "Have you never been around a sick human before?" I asked them.

All four shook their heads.

"I just need a fever reducer, soup, water, and rest," I explained. "It will go away on its own."

"Do you have those things?" Rhys asked.

"No," I realized sadly. What a terrible adult I was. Normally, everyone kept most of those things on hand. I didn't. "I need to go to the store."

I tried to walk out of the bathroom, but a wave of dizziness hit me and I stumbled and fell into Nico who caught me.

"You're not going anywhere," Nico ordered me. He carried me to the couch, wrapped my blanket back around me, and set me in the corner of the couch.

"I need a big bowl or bucket," I ordered him.

He ran to my kitchen and after several moments of banging cupboards and other items, he returned with a big, red, plastic bowl that I usually used for popcorn.

I took it from him and threw up into it.

Fox French braided my hair from my temples to the back of my head, so my hair wouldn't be in my way when I threw up again.

"Nico, you stay with her. We'll go get her what she needs from the store," Rhys said.

Nico nodded in agreement. He took the bowl to the kitchen, cleaned it, and brought it back.

"Do you need a list?" I asked through chattering teeth.

Nico lit a fire in my fireplace with his magic, and held a flame in his hand near me, helping me stop shaking.

"We'll call you when we get there," Rhys said.

Deryn, Rhys, and Fox left, while Nico sat beside me. He held the bowl in his lap, in case I had another bout of nausea.

"Is this something that could be fatal?" he asked with tense shoulders.

"I'm not going to die. It's just the flu," I answered. "Humans get it all the time."

He exhaled and leaned back on the couch. "That's good to know."

"How did Rhys become the leader of your group?" I asked, since I hadn't thought to ask about it before.

"He was always the take charge one of the group. At first, Deryn and he argued about who was the leader in our games and hunts. They butted heads a lot, but Fox was able to act as mediator and calm them down. He has a real gift for calming tense situations and people's emotions. I don't think it was until we were about twelve years old when Deryn finally gave in and acknowledged Rhys as the leader, deferring to him in situations. We still have our say, he isn't the king of our group or anything. He asks for our advice and doesn't order us around in a way that would be rude. He just tells us the plan, and normally it's a really good plan, so we go along with it."

My phone rang, and when I answered, Rhys's face showed up. I had never done a video call with any of them before.

"How are you?" Rhys asked as they walked.

"I'll live," I said and fought back a chuckle at his relief. How had they never been around any sick humans before? I knew they didn't get sick, but it baffled me that none of them had been around a sick human when so many of us inhabited this city.

"We're at the grocery store," Rhys said and turned the phone around so I could see Deryn and Fox, heading into the entrance.

"What are those for?" Fox asked as he faced the shopping carts.

"You'll need one of those," I told them. "It is to put the items you're buying in, so you don't have carry them around in your arms."

Deryn grabbed one and pushed it a bit before a huge smile split his face. "These would make fun sleds."

Before I could stop him, he jumped into the basket of the cart and Fox pushed him quickly through the automatic doors, which thankfully opened in time.

"You've never been to a grocery store?" I asked.

"We're princes, remember?" Rhys reminded me. "We had professional chefs living with us as kids. Now, we have our food delivered to us or we go out to eat at restaurants."

Fox pushed Deryn so hard and fast, that he slammed into a bin of oranges, knocking four into the cart with Deryn. Deryn picked them up and began juggling them while Fox continued to push him fast down the produce aisle.

"Do you need anything from here?" Rhys asked.

"No, just-"

"Aren't oranges high in Vitamin C?" Deryn asked, still juggling said oranges.

"Yes," I answered him, knowing where this was going.

"Then we will take these," he said.

Knew it.

Rhys walked to the aisle with medicine and I exhaled in relief. If I could get them in and out, we might survive.

"There's a lot of different medicines and variations," Rhys commented as he picked up a cold medicine and then one for indigestion. "Humans need a lot of medicines."

"Yes, we do. You'll want to get a fever reducer. If they have one for flu symptoms, that will work too," I said.

"Do you have any of these others?" Rhys asked, pointing the phone at the long aisle of medicines.

"No, but-"

"Get out of the cart," Rhys ordered Deryn.

"Why?" he pouted.

"I need to put the stuff we are buying in it."

"Fine, I'll go get my own," Deryn said, taking the oranges with him.

Rhys looked at Fox. "Catch and put them in the basket. Oh, and hold Jolie."

Fox took the phone and turned it so I could see him. "Hi, Jolie."

"Hi, Fox."

Fox started catching boxes of medicine as Rhys threw them, one after the other. "Hold on, Jolie." He set the phone in the cart as Rhys increased his speed. Fox caught them, then dropped them into the cart. Soon, the phone was covered by medicine boxes.

"How much are you getting?" I asked. It looked like he was buying the entire aisle.

"What?" Fox's voice called and the boxes covering the phone began to move. Soon, Fox's face shown through. "There you are, Jolie. Hiding."

"I'm not there. You know that, right?"

Fox rolled his eyes.

Sitting up was taking a lot of energy, so I lay on my side, my head on Nico's thigh, and propped the phone up on the coffee table in front of me so they could still see my face.

"I got two of everything, just in case," Rhys told me when he got back on the phone.

"I don't need-"

Rhys had started tugging on one of the medicines that were locked up, but it wouldn't budge.

"Sir, you'll have to show me some ID before-" A woman with bright pink hair started trying to explain to him. He ignored her and snapped the lock off to grab the medicine out. She let out an exasperated sigh. "I need to see your identification, please."

"ID?" he asked. "I don't have any ID."

"You don't carry ID?" I asked him. Everyone I knew carried ID.

"No, everyone knows who I am," he said softly.

Did he realize how egotistical that sounded?

"I have an ID," Fox said. "Deryn! I need my ID."

"Why does Deryn have your ID?" I asked. These guys made zero sense sometimes.

"He carries it for me," he said like that should explain everything. He disappeared and then a few minutes later came back with an ID card from junior high.

"This is your junior high school ID," the clerk said, exasperated.

"So?" Fox asked.

"Why do you have a junior high ID?" I asked him with a groan.

"Look at it," he showed it to me. He looked really good. "It's an amazing picture."

The clerk groaned. "Fine, it's got a year on it, so I know you're over the age required. Just take the medicine and go."

"What's on the next aisle?" Fox asked and practically skipped around.

"This is going to take forever," I muttered to Nico and turned my head to look up at him.

He was focused on the phone, watching the aisles and the merchandise. "What is all that stuff?"

"I think we need to take a field trip together to the grocery store, so I can show you guys how us plebeians live," I said with a chuckle and shake of my head. They were basically, reverse sheltered. I was going to have to show them what it was like to be human.

"Okay, this aisle has baby stuff, so I don't think we need—"

I interrupted Rhys and said, "Get the flavored water that has electrolytes in it. That stuff helps with dehydration and will help me feel a lot better, once I can keep things in my stomach. It's also great for preventing and curing hangovers." I had a lot of experience with the latter use of it.

"Why is your face sideways?" Rhys asked.

"She's lying down," Nico informed him. "Focus and get the stuff she needs. Her fever is pretty high."

"Should we grab one of these thermometers?" Fox asked and held up a thermometer.

"Yes," Nico answered before I could.

Shoppers kept stopping to stare and gossip in the background. I couldn't blame them. This was definitely not your everyday occurrence at the grocery store.

"There's a few different flavors of this water," Rhys said.

"Just get two of each," Fox said and started grabbing bottles. "Oh, there's popsicle of this stuff too. I'll grab some."

"You guys are buying way too much stuff," I told them.

"Next aisle!" Fox announced excitedly and rounded the corner to go to the next one.

"Where's Deryn?" I asked, realizing that he hadn't come back after Rhys kicked him out of the cart.

"Here!" he called as he flew by in the basket of a shopping cart, a roll of wrapping paper in his hand as an oar. Rhys turned the phone so I could watch as he slammed into a display of stacked soda cans, that toppled over. Some of the cans busted open and sprayed soda all over the aisle and Deryn.

"Oh my-"

"I'm alright!" Deryn called and leapt up out of the cart with a shit-eating-grin on his face. "That was awesome."

"You're going to have to pay for all of that," Fox told him.

Deryn shrugged. "Okay." He immediately started stacking the cans into the cart he had vacated.

"You guys are insane," I chuckled.

"Okay, we still need soup, right?" Rhys asked.

"Yes, chicken noodle soup please," I requested.

He looked up at the signs and found the soup aisle, which for some reason had a bunch of clothes on one side of the aisle.

"Why are there clothes in the soup aisle?" Rhys asked me.

"Why would you try to get clothes at the soup store?" Nico asked me.

"I don't know," I said.

"Okay, chicken noodle. Chicken noodle. Chicken…ah! Here it is!" Rhys held up a can of soup to the phone so I could see it.

"Yes, that's the right kind."

"How many do you want?" Fox asked.

"Just a few, I-"

"Get ten," Deryn said. "I want to try some."

"Be right back!" I yelled and ran/stumbled to the bathroom to throw up again.

"I need to learn some healing magic," Nico grumbled behind me.

"You don't need to stay with me," I told him. "I really don't want you guys to see me being so gross."

He rubbed my back and kissed the top of my head. "Vomit doesn't gross us out. We've been in quite a few battles and there's a lot of disgusting things that go on there."

"Okay, but I need you to get out of the bathroom," I said urgently, feeling my guts bubbling.

"Okay, I'll go check on the guys and see if there's anything else we need to get," he said and left.

I locked the door and was glad my bathroom was far enough away from the living room that he wouldn't be able to hear the disgusting sounds my rear was making.

After spraying some air freshener and washing my hands, I stumbled weakly back to the living room. Nico wrapped me up in the blanket and helped me lay down on the couch, setting my head on his thigh so he could drag his fingertips along the side of my face. The movements were incredibly calming.

My phone was still showing the store, but it seemed they were finally at the checkout. Rhys set a carton on the belt and it fell over, liquid ice cream spilling out.

"Why is this melted?" Rhys asked angrily.

"Because a stupid dragon who has a high body temperature was holding it," Deryn scoffed. "I'll get a replacement."

"Cleanup at register three!" the clerk called over the speaker. She was in her late fifties at least, and looked beyond bored and annoyed. The guys tried flirting with her, but she just stared at them with indifference as she scanned the items they were purchasing.

"We'll be home soon, baby," Rhys said and smiled at me. "I'm going to hang up now."

"'kay," I whispered my eyes growing heavy.

Nico turned off my phone and resumed stroking my face. "Is this okay?"

"Mmhm," I mumbled.

"How long will you be sick?" Nico asked.

"One to three days."

"Days!"

I nodded.

"We made it back," Rhys said loudly.

"Shush," Nico ordered him.

"I'm awake," I grumbled.

Opening my eyes, I found piles of bags and soda stacked inside my living room. It had to have cost them hundreds of dollars. Maybe even a thousand.

Rhys brought one of the bags to me. It was bulging with different medicines. "I don't know which is the best to use for the current illness you have," he told me.

I dug through the medicines and took out one for flu symptoms. "This one will work great." Before any of them could offer, I opened it, poured the liquid into the small measuring cup, and then quickly swallowed it.

"Do you want us to heat up some soup?" Deryn asked me, placing his hand against my forehead with a scowl.

"No, I can't eat anything yet. My stomach is still too upset."

Fox opened one of the electrolyte waters and set it on the coffee table in front of me. "Here, this way it's available when you're ready for it."

"Thank you. All of you, seriously, thank you."

The last time I had been taken care of like this was when my grandma had been alive. It was nice to have people who loved and cared about me.

"Open up," Nico ordered me, holding the thermometer. I obeyed, opening my mouth and then closed it when it was beneath my tongue. The thermometer dinged and he looked at the temperature it showed. "Hm," he grumbled, pulled out his phone and searched the internet for something. "It's high, but not life threatening."

All of the guys relaxed, breaths whooshing out of them. I had not realized they were holding their breaths.

"Guys, I'm not going to die. It's a common illness. Do an internet search for it. You'll see," I promised them.

"We'll take shifts," Rhys told everyone. "She needs sleep and there are too many of us here. Nico, you want a break or you want first shift?"

"First shift," he said and resumed stroking my face.

"I love you," I whispered to them as I let my eyelids droop.

The three who were leaving pressed light kisses to my forehead as they went. It was sweet and it filled me with warmth and love.

Three days later, I was finally well. The guys still tried to baby me, but I assured them I was healthy again. After a bit more reassuring, they believed me and the next four days were filled with marathon bouts of sex and hours of cuddling. They'd been terrified they were going to lose me and they all needed skin to skin contact with me in their arms to remind them I was safe. In a weird way, they seemed more scared after my flu, than they had after I'd been stabbed.

I wasn't complaining.

CHAPTER 15

"Why haven't you made a decision?" Emrys, king of the dragons, asked me as we ate lunch at a fancy Italian restaurant a block away from my work. He had invited me suddenly this morning and I didn't want to turn him down.

"Decision about what?" I asked him between bites of my penne Alfredo pasta. It was heavenly, and I wanted to scarf it all down as fast as possible.

"Mating," he replied softly, so those nearby wouldn't hear us.

"I have made a decision, but I haven't told anyone," I admitted to him. I was holding off on telling the guys until it was right. Things just didn't seem right yet.

"Since you haven't told your guards, I'm guessing you won't tell me either," he said with a smirk.

"No, sorry."

"I want you to come visit the dragons," he told me. "I've invited you several times to the den and you have pushed it off time and time again."

"Not because I want to," I told him right away, not caring if I was throwing Rhys under the bus. "Rhys said he doesn't want to take me unless I'm his mate. He said if someone challenges me now, he won't be able to fight with me, but if I'm his mate he will be able to."

He sighed and set his fork down. "He's always been a worrier. I blame his mother. I will have a talk with him. I will ensure that no one can challenge you and you will be safe when you visit. What does it say about us if the wolves can have you over with no problems, but my own son is too afraid of us to have you over?"

"Did I just get him in trouble?" I asked softly and stabbed a piece of pasta.

"No, I figured this was most likely the reason you hadn't visited," Emrys admitted. "Like I said, he's always been a worrier. I will talk to him and then we will have you over. Do you have plans Saturday?"

It was strange to be sitting in a restaurant talking to the King of the Dragons about visiting his clan. My entire life was strange. I had gone from an isolated girl with major daddy issues to the princess of all four clans and queen of the four princes. Who knew one necklace would cause so much change?

"Saturday sounds great," I replied with a smile, which Emrys returned immediately.

"Great," he said. He sat still a moment and said, "My son is right, there's something about you, your presence, it's calming. Sitting with you like this makes me feel much more relaxed than I have felt in at least a decade. Are you sure you're human?"

I chuckled and said, "I'm human, but I'm glad I can offer you some relaxation."

I didn't have much to offer, but I could handle offering a calming presence.

"There's my queen," Rhys said and took a seat next to us after giving me a quick kiss on the cheek.

"I love you," I told him with a smile.

He smiled and said, "I love you, too."

"Dessert!" Fox said as he pulled a chair up to the table. "We need to order dessert."

"Why am I not surprised that you four showed up?" Emrys asked with a smirk.

Deryn grabbed a breadstick and took a big bite before he said, "Because you know that we can't allow our queen to eat with strange men without interrupting."

"Strange men?" Emrys asked. "Is that how you refer to your uncle?"

"Is he trying to steal our queen?" Nico asked, sitting between me and Rhys with a chair he stole from a nearby couple's table without even asking them. Their shocked faces were hilarious.

"I believe, that would be between your queen and I," Emrys teased them with a smirk.

I laughed and enjoyed the banter of the men I loved. This was where I belonged. Wrong or right, this was home. Home is where the heart is, mine just happened to be evenly split amongst the four of them. Something I was perfectly fine with.

"Home," I whispered.

Nico squeezed my hand beneath the table, and the other three winked at me.

Yes, this was home.

THANK YOU FOR READING MY BOOK. IF YOU ENJOYED IT, WON'T YOU PLEASE CONSIDER LEAVING A REVIEW?

ALSO BY CATHERINE BANKS

Song of the Moon (Artemis Lupine, Book One)
Kiss of a Star (Artemis Lupine, Book Two)
Healed by Fire (Artemis Lupine, Book Three)
Taming Darkness (Artemis Lupine, Book Four)
ARTEMIS LUPINE THE COMPLETE SERIES (Books 1-4)

Pirate Princess (Pirate Princess, Book One)
Princess Triumvirate (Pirate Princess, Book Two)

Mercenary (Little Death Bringer, Book One)
Protector (Little Death Bringer, Book Two)

Royally Entangled (Her Royal Harem, Book One)
Royally Exposed (Her Royal Harem, Book Two)

True Faces (Ciara Steele Novella Series, Book One)
Barbaric Tendencies (Ciara Steele Novella Series, Book Two)

Demonic Contract (Dragon Kissed Trilogy, Book One)

Anja's Secret (Anja of Plisnar, Book One)
Daughter of Lions
Centaur's Prize
Dragon's Blood

The Last Werewolf

Last Ama Princess

Bitten, Beaten, & Loved

Lady Serra and the Draconian

Alys of Asgard

Printed in Great Britain
by Amazon